The End of Longing

Ian Reid is a widely published author of literary and histori-cal non-fiction. His poetry has earned him the Antipodes prize in the USA. Originally from New Zealand he now lives in Perth where he is Winthrop Professor at The University of Western Australia and Emeritus Professor at Curtin University.

Best wishes, Susie —

Ian Reid

The End of Longing

Ian Reid

UWA PUBLISHING

First published in 2011 by
UWA Publishing
Crawley, Western Australia 6009
www.uwap.uwa.edu.au

UWAP is an imprint of UWA Publishing
a division of The University of Western Australia

THE UNIVERSITY OF
WESTERN AUSTRALIA
Achieve International Excellence

National Library of Australia Cataloguing-in-Publication data:

Reid, Ian,
The end of longing / Ian Reid.
ISBN: 9781742582740 (pbk.)
A823.4

Australian Government

This project has been assisted by the Australian
Government through the Australia Council, its arts
funding and advisory body.

Typeset in Sabon by J&M Typesetting
Printed by Griffin Press

Cover photograph: Claude Monet (1840–1926). *Garden at Sainte-Adresse*.
1867 (detail). Oil on canvas, 38 ⅝ x 51 ⅛ in. (98.1 x 129.9 cm). Purchase, special
contributions and funds given or bequeathed by friends of the Museum, 1967
(67.241). The Metropolitan Museum of Art, New York, NY, U.S.A.

Photo Credit: Image copyright © The Metropolitan Museum of Art / Art
Resource, NY

To the custodians of family stories.

Prelude

He could hear nothing. Light snow continued to fall, slowly turning pallid the rows of upright stones and wooden markers. Powder thickened on the paths, and on the clothes of the shivering boy. As he stared at the small mound in front of him, near the boundary wall, its raw covering of newly dug soil began to fade under the blanket of whiteness.

With each breath, the cold was piercing his chest. His feet and fingers ached. He shuffled along the paths towards the gate, hardly glancing at the graves on either side. An empty glass vase glinted at him. He smashed it against the nearest stone. Picking up a jagged piece, he stabbed his hand repeatedly and stood trembling as bright blood dripped. Upon the solitude, upon the blank desertion, crimson splashes printed his pain.

Part I

Dunedin, 1892—97

One

Not knowing what had really happened: that was the worst of it. But other things mingled with their craving to discover the truth. There was the frustrating difficulty of having to depend on fragmentary information from a medley of second-hand sources that seemed incomplete and sometimes inconsistent – the letters, newspaper articles, reported rumours. Being so distant from the many places she had travelled through was a further hindrance, protracting all enquiries and making the Phillips brothers feel powerless. There was a tinge of guilt, too. Perhaps they could have done more. But it all came back to that lack of certainty about what to believe, about Hammond's actions and motives, and even about Frances herself. How well did they know their own sister?

* * *

As soon as Edward saw the first report he took a carriage up to Half Way Bush. His temple throbbed in unison with the thud of hooves on the wet clay road. It was a miserably wet evening, and when they reached the house he told the driver to wait. The snuffling horse twitched its flank, sending up small sprays of misty discontentment.

It must have been the maid's night off: Frederick himself opened the door, Mary just behind him in the passageway wiping her hands on an apron and peering to see who had come unannounced.

'Ted! This is a surprise. Why the frown? Everything all right?'

Shaking his head, he drew out a folded newspaper from under his damp coat and slapped it peevishly against his palm.

'Have you looked at today's *Times*?'

'Why, no, I...'

'Listen to this!'

Edward turned to a small item and his voice quavered as he read aloud to them. After he finished they sat in a long silence, broken only when Mary put her hands to her face and started to weep.

They decided that Edward would write to Melbourne seeking further information, but some days passed before he could bring himself to do so. Frances had been headstrong and foolish and now his warnings were turning out to be well founded. Yes, he was anxious, of course – but also angry with her, angry at such wilfulness. She had made her bed.

But shared blood stirred him. Penning a short enquiry, he sealed it with a sigh and walked through chilling drizzle to the post office.

No. 2 London Street
Dunedin
New Zealand
28 September 1892

The Superintendent of Police
Melbourne
Sir,
I herewith enclose a cutting from the *Otago Daily Times* of 22 September 1892. It is a portion of the 'American Letter' to the *ODT*, in which the

correspondent states that the chief of the Melbourne police is making enquiries concerning 'a certain Rev. William Hammond.' The Rev. Hammond, or Dr Hammond as he is known in Dunedin, is wedded to my sister; and, as I have not heard from her for some considerable time, you will quite understand how deeply it concerns me to know whether the statement contained in this paper is true or not. I shall therefore take it as a great favour if you will be kind enough to inform me whether the Melbourne police are indeed looking for Dr Hammond, and if so, provide some enlightenment concerning the charge against him.

Yours respectfully

Edward A. Phillips

PIOUS FRAUDS

I venture to suggest the desirability of thoroughly examining the past record of any itinerant evangelists or prohibition lecturers from this country who may happen to honour you with their presence. There are numbers of foolish people in every community perfectly willing to support any fraud who may claim to be either of the above, and to denounce any man who has the good sense to ask for credentials. The discovery, unfortunately, is generally made after the scoundrels have disappeared. A certain Rev. William Hammond is at present being inquired after by the chief of the Melbourne police. The latter has written to the authorities at Boston desiring some information as to this reverend

doctor. He is described by the papers as a
Baptist minister, bigamist, embezzler, thief,
and general all-round rascal. He was once
a minister at Franklin Falls, N.H., then at
New Haven, Conn., and later at Boston. He
is alleged to have claimed a new wife in
every town he settled in, and sought female
companionship for his vacation trips. The
last three years he has been missed from
this country, during which period he has
been anxiously sought by the police, who
are disposed to think his present location is
Japan. I am under the impression the name
is familiar to me, but I mention the matter
here and now to emphasise the fact that the
fellow is but one of many others of the same
kidney, and who, having duped and lied and
tricked in this country until the place is too
hot for them, invariably gravitate toward the
far south lands.

The Melbourne police never responded, but a few weeks
later a letter came to Frederick and Mary from Frances herself,
describing an apparently idyllic life in an inland region of British
Columbia. Another Canadian letter followed not long afterwards from the west coast. She seemed contented, and made no
mention of any difficulty or unease; so, when writing back, her
Dunedin relatives could think of no prudent way to refer to the
alarming report about her husband, and it went unmentioned.
Perhaps, they told themselves reassuringly, the 'pious fraud'
was not in fact her husband. There might well be some

confusion – a case of mistaken identity. William Hammond was surely a common name, after all.

* * *

Frederick and Mary often spoke to each other of Frances, and made particularly solicitous mention of her welfare when they knelt together by their bedside at the end of each evening.

'Lord, we ask Thee to watch over our dear sister Frances as she journeys through the wilderness of this world. Keep her, we beseech Thee, from all harm. Bring her and her little ones safely home to us at last...'

Safely home. Frederick had no doubt that Dunedin was indeed his sister's proper home, and that she would return to it when she tired of all this restless travelling. She belonged here, though she didn't seem to know it yet. Coming home meant recognising the importance of solid familiar things. For Frederick, homeliness was most happily present in the furniture he had shaped so painstakingly from rimu heartwood with its fine streaky grain. Few things gave him as much pleasure as rubbing his fingertips over one of his own well-finished chairs, tables or cupboard doors. It had become increasingly difficult to make a decent living as a cabinet-maker, but that was the only work he knew. These were not comfortable times. Several people owed him money, including some from his own congregation. Downright disheartening, it was, to find that his Christian brethren often put themselves first and took advantage of his patience. Having two young daughters now and hoping for more children, he and Mary would need to live more frugally.

Church matters claimed his earnest attention as an office-bearer of the Tabernacle in Great King Street, and the growth of new places of worship in surrounding districts had brought additional calls on his time. Mornington, North East Valley, Burnside, and other sister congregations further south in Kaitangata and Mataura – wonderful to see them all carrying the Lord's work into fresh fields; but they looked to senior brethren such as himself for practical support. Recently the North East Valley Sunday School teachers had sought his guidance in creating a Boys' Bible Band in order to attract the local lads. While Frederick laid no claim to musicianship, his hymn singing was hearty and he knew how to link it to the drum and fife that could make young pulses race.

But not everything in the life of his church was moving to a cheerful rhythm. The Tabernacle elders had resolved, after soul-searching debate, to refuse any affiliate recognition to the divergent group that had begun to meet separately in the City Hall. Schismatic tensions troubled Frederick deeply. The Christian faith should bring believers together, not drive them apart. Were they not all pilgrims on the same road, travelling towards the same ultimate destination?

* * *

On a Friday afternoon, Edward was at his most irritable. Trying to teach the basic rules of Latin syntax – let alone the nuances of that noble language – to scruffy New Zealand schoolboys was an irksome task. Not for the first time, he thought his choice of career had been unwise. He could have done better for himself than this.

'*Qui trans mare currunt,*' he repeated impatiently. '*Currunt, currunt* – can none of you translate the verb? Jackson? Smither?' He whacked his desk with the textbook. 'Think of English derivatives like "current"...'

'Does it mean "flow", sir? Flowing through the sea?'

'No, Jackson, no. The literal sense is "run", but linking it here with the preposition we might say "traverse" or simply "cross". So this Horatian aphorism, "*Coelum non animum mutant qui trans mare currunt*": how is it to be rendered, then?'

'They who cross the sea change their sky but not their soul.'

'A satisfactory approximation, hardly elegant. But do you grasp the meaning, lads? What point is Horace making here about travellers?'

He let the silence hang in the stifling air of their little classroom. A blowfly zigzagged across the room, blundered into a coil of flypaper and stuck there in a buzzing frenzy. The smell of blood drifting up the hill from the slaughterhouses was even more pungent than usual. Wiping his pallid brow, Edward twiddled the chain of his fob watch.

'No inspiration, anyone? Well, I'll ask you the same question on Monday, so turn your attention to it in the meantime. Class dismissed.'

That evening he found the passage he was looking for. He would read Emerson's words to his dim-witted class at the beginning of the next Latin lesson. Perhaps he should also copy them out and send them to his sister, the wilful wayfarer.

Travelling is a fool's paradise. Our first journeys discover to us the indifference of places. At home I dream that at Naples, at Rome, I can be intoxicated with beauty and lose my sadness. I pack my trunk, embrace my friends, embark on the sea and at last wake up in Naples, and there beside me is the stern fact, the sad self, unrelenting, identical, that I fled from.

Two

Letters continued to arrive from Frances intermittently, written from a bewildering succession of different places. It seemed it was the doctor, as Frances called him, who decided more or less at random when to leave a place and where to go next.

'Canada now! How does she cope with all this moving?' Mary looked up from the letter and Frederick raised his hands in a gesture of worried puzzlement. 'Sometimes,' she went on, 'we're given the impression they're settling down comfortably, then it turns out they've been off on their travels again, wandering here and there. It seems aimless.'

Later from Alaska came the heart-rending news of the little girl's sudden death from cholera. When Mary read Frances's account of it she clutched her own two daughters and carried them out into the fresh air, as if contagion could reach them from the page. Grieving and perplexity deepened when they learned just six months later that the infant boy, too, had passed away – in Guatemala. *Guatemala?* The very name was utterly barbarous. Why ever go to such a strange-sounding place?

A few months after that, with the sickening force of a sudden blow to the belly, a letter arrived for Frederick from a church acquaintance in Melbourne.

1021 Drummond St
N. Carlton
21 November 1894

Dear Bro. Phillips,
It is with very deep regret that I send you this extract
from a letter that came to Bro. Houchins from
Bro. Randall in Jamaica. Its content will distress
you greatly but I feel a duty to impart the sad news
concerning your sister.

'A brother Dr William Hammond arrived in
Kingston three weeks ago, with his wife. She was sick
on their arrival. He sought us out and I found him
very pleasant and genial. Mrs H. rapidly grew worse
and her case proved beyond human help. She died
Aug 30. Bro. H. remained for a week, opening and
repacking relics and curios, and then left for London
via New York. I think it is probable he will return
here in a few months. I told Bro. Ramsey about Bro.
H., and he remembered that when in Kentucky he had
heard some strange reports about him from someone
who had returned from Australia. The thing appeared
to me so incredible that I thought it best to write to
you and ask if there was anything amiss with Bro. H.
He showed me his letter of recommendation from the
Dunedin church and that appeared very satisfactory. I
would like to know the truth.'

I am still working away with the N. Carlton
church, where several of us remember affectionately
your sojourn with us some years ago. I heard Sister
Hislop speak last night on women's suffrage. She did
splendidly.
Yours truly,
A. M. Bryden

For days, Frederick and Mary circled numbly through the same fruitless questionings, the same disconsolate thoughts, the same feeble attempts to coax each other into accepting the calamity resignedly as God's will.

'There's nothing we could have done to prevent this, Fred. No cause to blame ourselves. It's a terrible thing that's happened, but the Lord gives and the Lord takes away. As for putting her money and safety in Hammond's hands, she was so stubborn about following that path. "Broad is the way that leadeth to destruction." Hardly the first young woman to let her affections and her fortune be snared by a plausible devil.'

'But every one of us was taken in! We should have seen what he was really like. We were *all* – all of us who worship together here – blind to Hammond's real character. He must have rejoiced at our gullibility. He charmed us, Mary. Charmed us, to our shame. True, he made some of the brethren a little uncomfortable at times, yet we all thought he seemed so very gifted, so dedicated to the Lord's work. Such a powerful preacher! It was only when he later insisted on the sale of our family property that we began to doubt his motives.'

'There may be more to this than just deception,' said Mary, dabbing at puffy eyes with a handkerchief. 'How far does the man's wickedness extend? What if he's not only a swindling impostor? We know his previous wife died suddenly – and now dear Frances has gone, too. And those two little babes, Fred. Can any man be so cruelly callous, so utterly evil, as to have...?' She left it unspoken. 'It's a dreadful thought.'

He sucked in a noisy breath and shook his head slowly, trying to dismiss the ugly possibility. 'Someone may be a smooth-tongued fraudster, even a bigamist, without being a murderer. We must get more information.'

Although Frederick had always been less comfortable with a pen in his hand than with a chisel or plane, on a Christmas

Eve overcast with grief, Mary helped him to compose a letter to Randall pleading for details. Could Frances have been poisoned? Was there a certificate showing cause of death? Was there any further information about Hammond's whereabouts? There were also things on his heart that he could not write about. The sheer fact of her death, stark and sudden, was hard enough to bear but what made it so much more painful was the way the terrible news had reached them at such a remove: through a distant acquaintance, Bryden, relaying a notification sent to Houchins, who was only a name to them, by a complete stranger, Randall, writing from a far distant island they had not even known Frances was intending to visit. It was no fault of anyone in this chain of messages, but it all made Frances seem even more utterly lost. Eyes closed, Frederick tried to picture the place where she had died, but it was too remote and vague in his mind. He wouldn't have been quite sure where to find Jamaica on a map.

Reading about the end of his sister's life like this, weeks after the event, made her seem hardly more than a name in some book or newspaper. She had been snatched away without any leave-taking, and he knew so little about the circumstances. He ran his fingers through his hair. Surely Randall would be able to tell him more.

But the reply from Jamaica added little. No symptoms of poisoning, reported Randall. It seemed the trouble had been brought on by miscarriage – whether natural or otherwise. She was on affectionate terms with her husband, who appeared considerably affected by her death and who himself gave the certificate of cause: 'Uterine Inflammation'. He had left soon afterwards. No word from him since. Mrs Hammond was interred in a quiet corner of the church's own little burial ground.

Frederick handed Randall's letter to Mary and bowed his head. A solitary unmarked grave in some shabby yard on the other side of the world! Her remains lying there for months before her Dunedin family knew she was no longer alive. How wretchedly different from the way her friend Isabella Morrison had been farewelled at First Church, a solemn funeral that surely must have consoled her husband and daughters, surrounded as they were by so many people paying their respects. No such ceremony to mark Frances's abrupt departure from this life.

Months passed without dislodging the heavy lumber of grief that toppled against Frederick. Mary alone shared the measure of his feelings. Although friends spoke to him of Frances from time to time, her death could not press on their lives as it did on his. Even Edward, now surprisingly married, did not care to talk much about his lost sister, whom his wife had never known.

As the end of that year approached, Frederick wrote again to Randall, yearning for greater certainty. But the response was cheerless. There had still been no news of Hammond.

* * *

'Flypaper! Or even wallpaper! He could have used them.'

Mary looked up quizzically as her husband gestured towards a page of the *Times*.

'That's how anyone can get a supply of arsenic without having to buy it openly. It says here you just soak those papers and extract it.'

He showed her the article he had been reading, 'Notorious Poisoners'. 'It's what was done in that Maybrick case. Look!'

Mary shook her head. 'But the letter said there was no evidence of any poisoning.'

'Perhaps they missed the signs. Arsenic could fit with the things we've been told. It produces severe abdominal pain, so I suppose it could bring on a miscarriage, too.'

'That's just conjecture, Fred. We can't know what really happened. And besides, we can never alter it.'

But she knew he would continue to do everything he could to uncover the facts. He felt a debt to Frances. There had always been, Mary knew, a bond of loyal affection between Fred and his young sister. Losing her was intensely painful, and not knowing the full story made healing impossible for him.

Three

News of the deaths of Frances and her children had spread far beyond family and church circles. People remembered the sensational item two years earlier in the local newspaper, warning that her husband was a 'pious fraud' with a dark past. Scenting now the possibility that this bold deceiver might turn out to be a vicious murderer, journalists from every paper in Otago and some further afield were trying to find out more about the mysterious William Hammond. Several had visited Frederick or written to him, asking about Frances and her travels. Some mentioned having alerted correspondents in the United States to the story.

Two days after Randall's last letter reached him from Jamaica, Frederick read in *The Evening Star* a piece that he knew was forthcoming. He had provided some of the material himself to an eager young reporter, but other parts were new to him, apparently drawn from American sources.

Under the heading 'A Noted Bigamist', the long article described the felonious exploits of one William Hammond, 'who styled himself a physician and minister of the gospel' but had committed 'almost every crime in the calendar'. Oddly, he was said to be 'aged about 40 years' – younger than Frederick thought him to be. The rest of the report mixed familiar details with novel information about notable episodes in his 'career of crime'.

'Listen to this, Mary,' said Frederick, and read a portion aloud:

> 'In 1886 Hammond was made pastor of
> the Freewill Baptist Church in Franklin
> Falls N.H. During this time he married Mrs
> Brockway, the widow of a wealthy physician.
> He subsequently swindled his wife out of
> 3,000 dollars, and the people of the town out
> of several thousands more. Later he travelled
> through Canada and then disappeared. He
> was next heard of at Eureka Cal., where he
> officiated as a minister, married one of his
> flock, and upon her sudden death collected
> the life insurance before embarking on a tour
> of the world…

'What an arrant rogue!' He read on for a while and then exclaimed, 'But they've got some of it wrong. It says here, look, that one of the children was still alive when Frances died. For all we know, some details about the years before he came into our lives may also be incorrect. Journalists rely too much on hearsay, and then add their own mistakes to what they glean from different sources.'

He tossed the newspaper on to the table. Mary picked it up and turned the pages slowly.

'A whole succession of wives!' she said, shaking her head.

'And a whole succession of congregations!' Frederick added. 'To say nothing of his many roles as a bogus physician.'

Other reports reached them. A clipping from the Oamaru newspaper, the *Mail*, characterised Hammond as 'a man of plausible character and a ready tongue' who initially made a positive impression during his time in Dunedin; but it hadn't taken long, the report claimed, for astute local Christian folk to detect a problem. The fraudster had overplayed his hand, so that 'the lack of credentials and the man's assurance and bombast had aroused suspicions'. Since Frances's death, 'the police have been hot-foot upon Hammond's tracks'.

'But it seems he covers his tracks so shrewdly most of the time,' Mary said, 'that any suspicions are nearly always going to be belated. Despite what it says here in the paper, the truth is that nearly everyone fell under his spell while he was with us as our evangelist.'

A little later, Archie Bryden wrote again from Melbourne with two enclosures. One had come to him, he said, from a missionary colleague in Honolulu: a hand-written copy of a newspaper item published in the *Hawaiian Gazette* some years before, itself quoting at length from a much earlier police newsletter that pre-dated Hammond's time in Australia and New Zealand. It described him as 'an oily tongued son of Sheol who is kept astir by the disclosures of his evil deeds', and referred to the success of two senior Boston Police Inspectors in thwarting his 'scheme to appropriate to himself his wife's property' in Franklin Falls. There were also, said the newspaper, 'records of crookedness' left by this 'outrageous liar and licentious scamp' in New York, Indiana and Pennsylvania. Wherever he went, he 'soon got very solid with the good people' in that location, staying there until 'facts regarding his past record came out', whereupon he 'skipped away'.

The second enclosure with Bryden's letter was a recent clipping from the *San Francisco Examiner*. Titled 'Another Degenerate', it told of the recent arrest in New Orleans of Dr William Hammond, who was 'charged with nearly every penal offense in the code'. This disgraceful rogue now had a senior sleuth on his trail:

Chief Inspector J. M. Coulter of the Boston
police has taken much care in searching Dr
Hammond's past. He says the prisoner has
rare native ability and a liberal education.
According to Inspector Coulter, Dr Hammond
was born in Montreal in 1841. He married
early, but his wife died young and he entered
the priesthood. Then in 1855 he came to the
United States and, Mr Coulter says, settled
in Yreka, Cal., as pastor of a Baptist church,
married a member of his congregation and
insured her life. He is said to have secured
policies subsequently on the lives of different
wives in other places. One of them, Mrs
Brockway, widow of a wealthy physician at
Franklin Falls, N.H., was taken suddenly ill,
but recovered. Hammond, it is charged, had
$12,000 of her money in his possession, but
returned it on the agreement that he was not
to be prosecuted.

From 1890 to 1894 Mr Coulter is
unable to trace Hammond's movements, but
the scoundrel is believed to have pursued his
various professions on three continents and
had six real or ostensible wives in ten years.
His many adventures will not bear publication
for general distribution.

* * *

To Mary it seemed that the Phillips family now resembled a
hapless old half-empty house: nothing like the real home where
she and Fred and their daughters were living snugly but an

imaginary place, a cramped habitation of shadows and whispers, in which the painful memory of Frances was shut away for months at a time in some gloomy back room, curtains drawn, air stale, furniture draped with dusty sheets, its atmosphere like that of a funereal vault. And then Fred would open the door again and rummage around in the dark, searching for what was not to be found there, trying to make sense of the inconsistent reports, trying to locate some truth.

A few evenings later, as Mary sat knitting a scarf, her husband shuffled through the news clippings.

'What age do you think Hammond is?'

'Hard to tell,' replied Mary. 'Well, he'd be quite a few years older than our Frances – perhaps fifteen older? So mid-forties, I suppose.'

'That's what one of the other reports said, but this one gives his birth year as 1841. Older than he looks, if that's right. Old enough to be her father!'

'That may be part of his attraction.'

Frederick nodded reflectively. 'You're probably right. She always felt our father's absence very keenly. Only a toddler when he died, you know. Can't have remembered much about him, but for a long while she kept asking where he'd gone. Used to distress our mother, that question.' He paused. 'The lack of a grown man in the family, well it affected me too, of course, and Ted, but in a different way. For Frances it would have…perhaps…'

His voice trailed off as the partial insight receded into incomprehension. He turned back to the clippings, frowning as he looked from one report to another.

'Some of this, anyway, must be untrue,' he told her. 'The details just don't fit together. According to this latest article, he would have been only fourteen years old when he moved from Canada to the United States – having already been married and widowed, with time spent as a priest! At fourteen!'

'But my dear, isn't that just a misprinted date? The rest sounds all too likely.'

'No, no, there are other inconsistencies when you put some of the reports side by side. Look at this one, for instance: it says he was a pastor in Yreka, California, spelt with a Y – but that other one says *Eureka*. Improbable he lived in both places.'

'Perhaps Yreka and Eureka are the same place?'

'No, I asked Ted to look at a gazetteer in the Athenaeum library. He confirms they're two quite different towns. But you see my point? Some things we've read about Hammond are probably borrowed from earlier accounts, not verified in the first place, and then a few bits get changed because the journalist is careless, or wants to embroider a story. Here's an example: *The Evening Star* reports that he swindled a woman in Franklin Falls out of three thousand dollars, but this piece in *The Examiner* from San Francisco says he still had twelve thousand dollars of her money left when he was apprehended. And surely there are touches of sheer invention, too – remember that fanciful anecdote about sending Frances a book with a marriage proposal in symbolic form? Let me find it. Wait. Here it is:

'While in Dunedin this impostor made the acquaintance of a local girl, and he subsequently wrote to her announcing the death of his wife, and sending her a book containing some "silver" leaves, an old-fashioned relic of folklore, which she rightly construed into a proposition of marriage. The unfortunate girl married the sharper in Victoria, and he then returned to New Zealand to secure his share of the spoil, the girl being joint possessor with her brothers of considerable property in Dunedin.

'Where on earth did they get that folklore nonsense from? A gift symbolising an offer of marriage? It simply can't be right. We'd have known about it. She was never untruthful, and if Hammond had written to her before she went to Melbourne I don't believe she would have kept the matter secret from us.'

Mary put her hand gently on his arm. 'But Fred, what does it matter now? It's all too certain that Hammond was a criminal, a confidence man, and that Frances was caught up haplessly in his cruel deceptions. And that she and her infants are dead. Beside those stark facts, nothing else has much importance, does it?'

Four

But the report from San Francisco with its mention of Hammond's pursuit by the Boston police prompted Frederick to resume his enquiries, wanting to know more in exchange for relating yet again what he already knew. 'The account given in *The Examiner* of 5 January 1896,' he wrote to Chief Inspector Coulter, 'says you have no record of him between 1890 and 1894. I can tell you pretty well all his movements during that time...'

With a pile of letters from Frances beside him, checking dates and placenames as he wrote, Frederick went on to trace in detail as much as he could of her meandering travels during that long period, and of the three deaths. Providing the Boston officers with this extra knowledge should help them to track Hammond down.

It was a long while before a reply came. Signed not by Coulter but by someone who appeared to be his successor, it was the first typewritten letter that Frederick had ever seen, a fact that made it seem even more impersonally curt. 'Your letter of 22nd ult. has been received,' it stated. 'The last we have heard of Wm Hammond is the fact you relate in your letter, that he was arrested in New Orleans. We have never heard what disposition was made of the case but it appears he is not in custody there now. If you wish to know what was done with him I should advise you to communicate with D. S. Gaster, Supt of Police, New Orleans, La.'

Frederick no longer had much confidence in the ability of any police or detective agency to keep up with such a clever criminal. It was one thing to be able to uphold law and order within a local area, where people were known and their behaviour could be readily observed. It was quite another to trace the sudden movements of someone who never stayed long enough in one place for his plausibility to wear thin, and who could so easily switch the direction of his travels whenever he wanted to throw pursuers off the scent. Evidently Hammond had not even bothered to change his name as he slipped from one place to another. Somehow he must have managed to get off with a light sentence in New Orleans and was on the loose. There seemed little likelihood now that he would be caught again.

But it was hard to accept that the whole truth about Frances's death would never be known. Wearily, almost in a kind of trance, Frederick took up his pen again and addressed an enquiry to Superintendent Gaster.

* * *

Mary would look back on 1897 as a muddle of sombre commemoration, dwindling hope and sad surrender. She saw these things not only within her family and among Frances's former friends but in public life as well. It was the year when her brother-in-law Edward, on the third anniversary of his wedding, first showed the wilting symptoms of Bright's disease. It was also the year when dignitaries from every corner of the Empire, including New Zealand's premier, travelled to London for Queen Victoria's Diamond Jubilee, knowing the occasion to be less celebratory than elegiac: her period of inconsolable mourning for Prince Albert had now lasted thirty-six years and her own life was plainly approaching its end. And 1897 was the year when, according to local gossip, William Larnach's third wife defiled their extravagantly monumental mansion, built two decades before, by beginning a licentious liaison there with the son of his first marriage, though it would still be some months before her husband killed himself with a pistol in Parliament House, Wellington, once the scandalous rumours reached him. Larnach's great stone edifice towering up on a bony ridge of the Otago peninsula would seem more and more like a mausoleum or a cenotaph.

Early in the same year Mary encountered David Morrison – not having seen him since Isabella's funeral – in the Northern Cemetery, where he had replaced his late wife's temporary grave marker with a large granite stone from Scotland, carrying plaintive lines from Tennyson's *In Memoriam*. Mary fell into conversation with him and he told her about people Isabella and Frances used to know: young Grace Hutton's wordless melancholy had become so severe, David said, that her husband made the painful decision to have her committed to the Seacliff Asylum, while Stuart Donaldson (Mary remembered his name, the lawyer who once proposed to Frances) had married an impecunious widow with two young children and a speech impediment.

And it was in 1897 that Mary's own dispirited husband finally abandoned hope of ascertaining the full facts about his sister's death, after every reply from American police officers confirmed only that William Hammond was well known to be a versatile and incorrigible criminal but that his trail had gone as cold as a corpse.

Frederick sat with elbows on the table and fingertips pressed against his temples. Mary slipped a bookmark into the Bible from which she had been silently reading. Putting an arm around him, she voiced what she knew to be in his own thoughts.

'Fred, dear, it will soon be three years since her death. We'll never find out what happened. We must set this burden of despondency aside, for our daughters' sake.'

'If only Hammond could be found and brought to justice...'

'We're unlikely to have that satisfaction. But he'll have to answer for all his sins on the day of reckoning.' She picked up the well-thumbed Bible again, found her place at the end of Ecclesiastes, and read aloud: '"For God shall bring every work into judgment, with every secret thing, whether it be good, or whether it be evil."'

Frederick was only half-listening. Lips parted, lower jaw slack, he seemed to be staring at nothing. Mary could hear a slight wheeze in his breathing. Those pouches of tiredness under his eyes made him look older than his years.

The photograph in his hand, stamped 'Inspector's Office, Boston, Mass.', was not recent: the Hammond they knew in Dunedin had less hair on the top of his head. But the features were unmistakable, especially the broad brow and compelling gaze. Frederick turned over the photo, and scanned the inscription once more:

> *Rev. William Hammond*
> *'Confidence Man'*
> *40 yrs 5ft 11' 160 lbs*
> *Light hair*
> *Blue eyes*
> *Light comp*
> *Belongs in Franklin Falls N.H.*
> *Arrested Boston Mass. on*
> *1 April 1886 by Inspector*
> *Richardson for larceny of*
> *money in Franklin Falls N.H.*

He stared for a long while at the impassive face, trying not to be overcome by revulsion, trying to glimpse a soul behind the eyes. Frederick would always feel, under his wounds of sorrow, a baffled curiosity. Troubling questions still perched in his mind like ghostly birds. Exactly what part had Hammond played in Frances's death? The babes, too, his own flesh and blood: had he somehow contributed to their suffering? And whatever had happened to their young Japanese servant girl, Ada, mentioned in Frances's earlier letters but not in the reports from Jamaica, so presumably no longer with them when they arrived there: was she another victim?

The character of the man himself was a persistent enigma. Who was he and how could so many people – including someone as sharp-witted as Frances – be so easily duped?

She gazed at Frederick from her photograph on the mantel-piece. In her eyes he imagined he could see the exquisite clarity of her mind, and there was that familiar hint of a shy smile at the corner of her mouth. Though not what most people would call beautiful, she had a pleasant face that expressed intelligence. He had seen how men looked at her appreciatively, if sometimes with slight uneasiness. Only her steadfast commitment to nurse their mother through that long illness had prevented her from being surrounded by plenty of suitors in her earlier years, though most men failed to engage her interest anyway. She had a way of lifting her head slightly as if she wanted to look beyond those around her and focus on some distant point.

He wondered what she had found over the horizon, in all that restless wandering with someone who, it now turned out, was not what he purported to be. Had she seen through him before the end?

Part 2

La Chute and Owen Sound, 1852–63

Five

Mr Meikle drew in one of his deep long breaths as the children held theirs expectantly, watching his broad shoulders lift and his huge hands come together in a slow theatrical clasp. He closed his eyes, raised his whiskered chin, and began to recite:

> Dust as we are, the immortal spirit grows
> Like harmony in music...

Even the youngest in the classroom had often thrilled to this weekly performance from their spellbinding teacher. Hearing such passages again was a Friday afternoon highlight for all of them, though most would have found it hard to say exactly what some of the sonorous lines were describing. To remember whole long stretches of verse and declaim them without hesitation: that was wondrous enough in itself, whether some parts seemed obscure or not. But for Will, the oldest among them, every word reverberated.

> And, as I rose upon the stroke, my boat
> Went heaving through the water like a swan
> When, from behind that craggy steep till then
> The horizon's bound, a huge peak, black and huge,
> As if with voluntary power instinct

Upreared its head. I struck and struck again,
And growing still in stature the grim shape
Towered up between me and the stars, and still,
For so it seemed, with purpose of its own
And measured motion like a living thing,
Strode after me.

Everything felt by the boy thumped through Will's own veins in
surges of joy and dread. Will would listen intently, teeth clamped
on a thumbnail, scalp atingle, as his counterpart crept stealth-
ily around the hillsides at night, climbed windswept cliffs, or
peered through the mist while crouching scout-like high above
a fork in the road, watching for the horse that would take him
home. 'Scout-like': the word dangled and flickered. And he never
tired of the skating episode, with its echoes of children shouting
and the noise of steel on polished ice rebounding from the hills
and leafless trees, with shadowy banks spinning past into the
distance, their shapes becoming indistinct, 'feebler and feebler...
till all was tranquil as a dreamless sleep'. Eyes screwed shut, he
could almost imagine it as a scene on their own big lake not far
north of La Chute, near the top curve of the river's big S-bend.
Will had seen this expanse of water frozen right over in the
winter months, and now he saw it again with his inward eye as
he listened to Mr Meikle's recitation.

Though the teacher's manner always appeared formal and
stern to those in his charge, he took a kindly interest in the
lanky Hammond boy, whose brooding intelligence, uncommonly
acute from the moment he started his schooling, had darkened
since his father's horrific accident. Until then he had seemed a
candid and contented child, seldom merry but always sociable,
and quietly protective towards his younger brothers. All three of
the Hammond boys had the same fair colouring and bright blue

eyes as their father, Hamish, but everyone agreed Will was the handsomest lad and the most quick-witted.

George and Stewart followed their big brother wherever he went. On long steamy summer days, once their chores on the farm were finished, the trio would walk together into the woods to look for berries or birds' eggs. Once there, they would half-scare each other with imaginary sightings of lumbering bears, ravening wolves or bloodthirsty Algonquin savages. Other creatures, not frightening but pertinacious, really did want to pierce their flesh, and when the sucking of the fierce black flies became intolerable the boys would run back homeward through the stump-littered fields where, in years gone by, the men who came up from Vermont had felled acre upon acre of maple and beech for potash-making and paper-milling before the Scottish farming folk took over the abandoned areas and began to work the land.

The Hammonds' own farm, like most of the others around La Chute, was small and raw. With the short growing season, the harsh winters, and the uneven stony terrain that resisted plough and hoe, only unremitting toil could make their tenement productive. Hamish would often come in with an aching back after a day spent trying to uproot massive stumps with thick wooden poles, and Jeannie would rub oily liniment into his shoulders while he slumped forward with his head and arms resting on the back of a reversed chair near the fire, and the boys listened to their parents' weary conversation about all the tasks that lay ahead.

Will admired his mother's steadfastness as much as his father's strength. He liked the calm unshakeable way she applied herself to every bit of household work. He watched her hands, always moving, always doing something, but gracefully, even if just to stir a pot or darn a sock or peel a vegetable. In his eyes she had the quality of a tall forest tree that could sway with the winds but remain securely rooted. Her slow half-smiles, puckering one cheek more than the other, brought warmth to his heart even on the most bitterly cold days when the swollen purple chilblains on his fingers cracked and bled.

Keeping up her husband's spirits was a constant need. There was much to discourage him. Neither wheat nor corn would thrive and the Hammonds relied on turnips, potatoes and swedes. Meal after meal consisted mainly of fried mash cakes. The meagre surplus crops would be taken by jolting cart to St Andrews over the rough roads. Their neighbours, the Christies, had a horse that other families around those parts could some-times hire, but Hamish wanted one of his own. 'It isn't just having to pay him for the use of his beast,' he said to Jeannie. 'It's a matter of family pride, too. I don't like to have to go asking Charlie Christie to use something that's his. I don't like the tone in his voice when we talk about it. He's a mean-spirited man.'

So when the next Harvest Fair took place in St Andrews, Hamish had eyes only for the animal market that was part of the big event. A man from Grenville had brought along a rugged young black horse for sale, thick-built, sixteen hands. Hamish looked it up and down, walked around it and patted its twitching flank.

As he bent forward to inspect the hooves the horse gave a vicious kick, hitting him full in the face. With an anguished cry he fell back, blood pouring from his shattered nose, mouth and eye socket. Will ran to his father and was horrified to see the body convulsing. He stood helplessly until the shudders ceased and an onlooker covered the crumpled corpse with a sheet of tarpaulin.

* * *

After the funeral service in the grim stone church, several people came up to Will, put a hand on his shoulder and murmured words of commiseration before turning away. As he walked slowly home beside his silent mother, with George and Stewart snivelling and blubbering behind them, it seemed that part of his own life had closed down, and nothing would ever be the same again.

For a few weeks Jeannie tried to work the farm, with Will staying away from school most days to labour beside her; but it was a hopeless project. He knew they could not keep going for long, and was unsurprised when Mr Christie knocked on the door of their shanty one evening. He was an ungainly thickset man – 'Burly Charlie', people called him behind his back – with bruise-coloured cheeks framed by big red lugs.

His mother made the visitor a cup of tea, waving the boys off to bed. Will lay there in the candlelight, shivering under the thin blanket and listening to the voices.

'You just can't expect to manage on your own, Mrs Hammond, with the lads so young. It's too much.'

'But Hamish laboured so hard to make our family independent. Leaving this place now would be disloyal to him – and where on earth would we go?'

Will could hear his mother's suppressed sob.

'Well now, Mrs Hammond, don't upset yourself. My suggestion is that you stay here, and let me take complete charge of this farm – join it with my own, keep it in good shape, cart the crops to market. Tilling, planting, harvesting – I can manage all that. Naturally I'd have to keep whatever its produce will sell for. But you'd still have a roof over your head and food on your table in return for the work you'd put in with hoe and shovel. The lads can help a bit. Young Will is as thin as a yard of pumpwater right now, but within a year or two he's going to be strong enough to take on a full measure of duties around the place.'

The conversation faded into a drizzle of words as the boy slid into sleep.

Six

He smouldered with grief. In his mind, day and night, hung the image of his father's wrecked, bleeding face and inert body. To have been so full of life, and then to perish like that in a moment – it was horrible to remember, a brutal thing, and he could not be rid of it. Nor could he subdue the sharp pang he felt at his mother's attempts to hide how she continued to suffer. He could do little to assuage the bewilderment that made his brothers look so forlorn and turned wee Stewart into a stutterer. And he was powerless to protest at Christie's snatching of their land, at the way their neighbour had made himself their master, walking across the fields into the Hammond house as if it had always belonged to him.

Each icy night as he lay under his coarse blanket waiting for sleep, hands clenched, Will felt the weight of those afflictions like a great boulder on his chest, as if every breath had become a struggle. But he could have continued to bear all of that, could have coped in his silently resolute way ('The poor youngster seems as stoical as Job,' thought Meikle, watching him in the classroom) had he not discovered a terrible thing.

He had been sent home from school at the end of a morning because he was feverish. 'Get yourself to bed, laddie,' said Meikle. 'I don't like the sound of that cough, and your face is flushed. No, I won't let you take George and Stewart with you; they need their writing lesson this afternoon. I'll see they get home safely. Off you go now, while there's still a bit of warmth left in the air. Your mother will get you some vinegar and sugar in hot water. You need plenty of rest.'

So he dragged himself home, full of aches and tremors, his hands tucked under his armpits.

As he came up the path he could hear his mother's voice crying out, pleading: 'Please don't...not again. Let me be. Stop! No...no! Please...'

He pushed open the door of the cabin. The cries were coming from her bedroom, mingled with other noises – something being slammed against wood, a chair knocked over, a man's voice grunting and muttering. Will tiptoed towards her room and looked in. His mother, struggling and weeping, was pinned to the bed, her skirt thrown back around her waist. The man was kneeling on one of her legs, forcing the other one back with his hand, when he turned and caught sight of Will.

'Away!' yelled Christie, his purple face contorted, flecks of spittle flying from his mouth. 'Get out, you bloody little snooper! Get out!'

Will bolted and took shivering refuge in the little woodshed behind the cabin until he heard Christie leave.

* * *

His mother never spoke to him about that shameful afternoon. Her eyes, now red-rimmed and rheumy most of the time, said enough.

Several months passed. Will tried to lose himself in the poetry that Mr Meikle recited, and in the book-length story that was being read chapter by chapter to the hushed class: *The Deerslayer*. But often a stirring phrase or incident would bring him suddenly back to his own situation. When Deerslayer deftly caught the tomahawk that the Panther hurled at him, and flung it straight back so hard that it split the fierce Huron's skull, Will felt a surge of vengeful hatred towards Christie and imagined the satisfaction of felling him with a single blow.

As soon as Jeannie's pregnancy became obvious, the news spread quickly around the district. On the rare occasions when the pressure of daily toil eased enough to allow her a few hours away from the farm, she found that hardly anyone wanted to greet her. At the chapel she was shunned. As she approached a group of women who had been her friends for years, they turned away coldly.

After repeated slights and rebuffs, Jeannie stayed at home, even on Sundays. She sent her increasingly silent and worried eldest son to fetch supplies and carry any necessary messages.

As Will was marshalling his brothers for the long walk home from school at the end of a morose grey afternoon, Mr Meikle took him aside and put a hand on his shoulder.

'Will, please tell your mother that I'd like to come to your house this evening for a brief talk. I'll be there about seven o'clock. I'm just mentioning it now so she won't be alarmed when there's a knock at the door.'

Meikle arrived punctually. Jeannie sent the boys to their room for discretion's sake, but through the thin walls Will could hear everything their visitor said in that formal elocutionary manner of his.

'Mrs Hammond,' he began, 'I want to express my concern, Mrs Meikle's too, for you and your young lads – and to make a suggestion.

'Let me be direct. It's quite apparent you're in a troublesome plight. I say this without any hint of blame, believe me. Indeed it makes me indignant to hear that you're being ostracised by many people. They should be ashamed of themselves. Not long ago you suffered a terrible misfortune in the loss of your husband, a very fine man, and I venture to surmise that what has evidently happened since then was not initiated by you. I neither know nor wish to know who's responsible for your condition, but it seems obvious you're receiving little or no material support.

'I wouldn't presume, Mrs Hammond, to speak to you in these terms about so personal a matter if it weren't for the fact that the wellbeing of your sons is particularly important to me. They've spent so much of their lives in my classroom. Fine boys they are too, all three of them. Although my role is by no means equivalent to that of a parent, I do feel keenly, in the present circumstances, something of a guardian's duty.'

Will heard his mother murmur an indistinct response.

'Now I hope this won't strike you as impertinent, but Mrs Meikle and I, well, we've been discussing what might be done. We think your situation here in La Chute can only become more and more difficult for you all with another mouth to feed. There's not, alas, a very neighbourly spirit hereabouts, for all the pretence of piety. I wouldn't anticipate much in the way of practical help. These are narrow people, most of them. Hard-hearted. In such a place, facing such distress, what's to become of Will, George, little Stewart and the baby? And you, Mrs Hammond? I've heard you and the boys have no blood relations anywhere in this country.

'And so I come to a suggestion. I have a brother-in-law – a shipping merchant and a widower – who lives in Owen Sound. Jerome has a comfortable house, not as small as most, and makes a fair living. Business matters often take him away and I think he'd be glad of a housekeeper to look after the place while he's absent and to do the cooking and other domestic work when he's present. I'm sure there would be room enough for the Hammond family under his roof. With your agreement I could enquire on your behalf about a position with him.'

There was a pause, broken by the sound of sobbing.

'Forgive me,' said Meikle. 'I've added to your pain when I meant to alleviate it.'

'No...'

Will strained to hear his mother's muffled words.

'No,' she said. 'No. Not at all. It's your kindness that makes me weep. Your understanding words. I've felt so much alone, and it's a comfort, truly, to know that you and Mrs Meikle have been thinking so charitably about our family's problems.

'But I know nothing at all about Owen Sound – where it is, what it's like. How could it be a better place for us? Life here has become very hard, but at least we're still living on the land that dear Hamish tried so hard to turn into our home.'

'Owen Sound could give you a fresh start. It would be an opportunity to meet people who need only know that you were recently widowed – let them suppose that you were with child before Mr Hammond's sudden death. As for the land you occupy here, the sad truth is that Christie has made himself the actual owner in all but name. He's not a generous man, and he'll squeeze every drop of dignity from your veins. To walk away from that now would merely be to recognise the reality of his power over you.

'But think, at any rate, of what the move to another place would mean for your children. Already at school I've overheard coarse comments directed at them. They'll have a rugged future if they remain in La Chute. Will is an exceptionally capable young-ster, but I've seen the hurt in his face and he'll suffocate here.

'I'm not surprised you don't know about Owen Sound. It's a small town, and until recently it was called Sydenham. It's located on the southern side of Georgian Bay – a port for the Great Lakes traders. It may hold a reputation for being rowdy but there's plenty of vigour in the place.'

Seven

Less than a month later they were living in Jerome Davin's house near the mouth of the Sydenham River.

The journey there had been long and miserable, each day colder and slower than the one before. During the last stage, from Barrie to Owen Sound, their small supply of stale potato cakes and hard cheese ran short, and the water in their cask had a sour smell. The horse – Meikle's horse, which he had insisted they take, and his cart too, explaining that Davin had promised to reimburse him – trudged on wretchedly with its head down. All three boys had sore throats, and spasms of coughing made their heads ache. Bad weather had turned the crude roads into furrows of mud that sucked at the wheels and axles of their cart and often brought them to a halt. Unprotected against the wind and rain, they thought they would never arrive. Their mother said little, but looked worried and pale. Will could see that she clutched at her belly as the jolting went on, mile after dreary mile.

Davin made the travellers loudly welcome and seated them at once in front of his glowing fireplace, where they soon began to smile as their clothes dried out and numbness left their limbs. He was a large man, florid and paunchy, full of sociable noise and given to sudden gesticulation. Whenever he spoke to Will he accompanied his words with a friendly thwack on the boy's shoulder.

For nearly a week, heavy falls of snow kept them all inside the house, attending to little chores during the daylight hours and huddling around the hearthstone during the evening. The Hammonds began to grow accustomed to Davin's rugged heartiness. Happy to have an audience, he sang some silly shanties, played sentimental tunes on a tiny mouth organ and recounted tales of fierce Ojibway people who used to live by the shores of the bay. When he talked of the islands he knew out there beyond the Sound, the eyes of the children widened.

'Giant's Tomb Island, now there's a fearsome place, lads. Why? Ah, too terrible to tell you at your age. But it's not given that name for nothing.'

And he winked at their mother as she looked up, amused, from her knitting.

There were family stories, too. He was Mrs Meikle's only brother, he told them. As children they had come out from Ireland with their parents, settling in Gore with other Irish folk.

'And a hard time we had of it,' he said, sucking on his pipe and staring into the fire. 'Cruel winters. Not much food. Even with potatoes the soil was stingy: just one crop a year, not the three our folk had always expected in the past. And then we lost our da to a fever, while we were still young. So I know how hard it has been lately for you...'

As the story went on, Will was puzzled by Jerome Davin's frequent mention of some 'father' who had continued to look after the family.

'But you said your father died.'

'He did, my boy. I'm talking now about Father Kelly. Our priest.'

'What's a priest?'

Davin chuckled, smacking his hand against his leg and rocking in his chair.

'A special kind of minister,' Jeannie explained.

'But better educated!' laughed Davin, clapping Will on the shoulder. 'No offence meant, Mrs Hammond, to people of your own persuasion,' he added jovially, with a crackle of phlegm. 'Still, the fact is that around these parts there are some very clever men who belong to our Roman tradition. Proud of their history here, they are, and rightly so I must say. D'you know, the Jesuit mission began its work on the eastern side of the big lake long before the English came and named it Georgian Bay. It was two centuries ago that those French Catholics came, no less – imagine that! The wildness of the place back then! Some of them were martyred, oh yes, martyred. No easy death for them. Think of it, lads. But their fellow priests persevered. Spread the faith and brought knowledge to the heathen. Great teachers, those Jesuits. And their work goes on in Owen Sound today. Well, enough of that. But in my view you boys could do worse than gain your education from the Catholic school. When the worst of winter is past, you'll need to get into one of the classrooms.'

* * *

The weather became dry and mild for a few days, but thick ice continued to block the head of the Sound. It could be a month or more yet until the thaw began, and longer than that before Davin and other traders could set out in their boats to carry lumber to the northern parts of the lake and bring back loads of early spring supplies.

Davin took the Hammond boys out walking around the town, his enthusiasm feeding on their admiration.

'D'you know, lads, more than a thousand souls now live in Owen Sound,' he announced, as if claiming personal responsibility.

He introduced them with particular pride to Boyd's Wharf, where most of the boats were wintering in big sheds and men in heavy coats and thick gloves stood around with arms folded, eyes half-closed, puffing on their pipes. He showed the boys how most of the Sydenham River had silted up. He pointed out other sights including the newly opened Corbet's foundry, the office of their latest newspaper, *The Times*, the grand county court-house with its limestone facings, the narrow rutted road twisting towards Rankin's Mill Dam, two schools, four churches, five taverns, '...and just a single Temperance Hall! What does that tell you, lads?'

The largest of the tavern buildings had a balcony above the street, and some brightly dressed women were standing at its rail, calling out to a group of men below.

'What are they doing?' George wanted to know. 'What's this place?'

'Never you mind, laddie. You'll find out when you're older. Not a place for the likes of you or me. A magnet for badness. Ill repute.'

On market day he took them to the town square to see what the farmers had brought in. It was not the season for produce but there was plenty of wood for sale – oddments of building timber, short lumpy logs to split for heating. The new post office was the market square's other attraction, and Davin found a letter from La Chute waiting for him there. Opening it on the spot, he read aloud to the boys some greetings and good wishes for their wellbeing from the Meikles.

As two weeks turned into three, Will started to feel that he could be happy in this town. Spring would soon be coming to Owen Sound, and the prospect of warmer weather signalled an opportunity to explore the wharf, the far side of the river, and other spots that promised adventure. When school re-opened there would be new friends, perhaps. He liked Mr Davin, who was already treating the Hammonds as kindly as if they were his own kinfolk, not servants. Will felt comfortable in the house, with its solid walls and big kitchen, and had begun to think of it as home. His mother seemed less anxious, too. She was taking her household tasks slowly now that her belly had grown so large, but her shoulders no longer sagged with sadness and worry. That morning she had given Will some smiles while he helped her to scrub and rinse the laundry in the big tub and later to hang it on the clothes hoist where it dripped on the kitchen floor and filled the house with damp smells.

'Well done, son. You're a good helper. Take a rest from this now. Your brothers would be glad to hear one of your adventure stories.'

It was a sleety day, and whenever the weather kept them all inside George and Stewart liked nothing better than to listen to Will's improvised tales of danger and daring. He needed little encouragement. There was a gratifying sense of power in being able to hold their attention so tightly, and another kind of pleasure as well: freeing his mind from all that was constrained in his present situation and entering a world where everything that happened was entirely within his control.

Whatever names he devised for his heroes and villains, Will felt them to be his agents. Through them, scout-like, he could explore the frozen wilderness, pilot big boats up and down Georgian Bay, ward off ferocious savages, deal masterfully with all sorts of perilous trials, surmount every tribulation. And when things became too troubling for the protagonist, or too tiresome, Will would abruptly move him on to a new place, a new set of opportunities and challenges.

By the fireside after dinner there were fragments of other stories that Davin read aloud to them from the newspaper, holding the smelly sputtering candle so close to it that they expected to see the printed page burst into flame. The boys hung on his words, often asking him to explain this or that reference in a news report, or plying him with other questions that drifted into their minds.

47

'Who is Mr O'Ryan?' asked George one evening, in a lull between newspaper items.

Davin looked puzzled.

'O'Ryan? Don't know anyone of that name.'

'But I heard the postmaster tell you yesterday that O'Ryan is rising earlier.'

Davin burst into raucous laughter, slapping his hand on his thigh, and it was a full minute before his guffaws subsided.

'Well now,' he said at last, wiping his eyes. 'Yes, indeed. I do remember the fellow. He's a famous hunter, a giant of a man. An impressive sight. I'll tell you what, boys, if the weather stays clear, I promise you'll see him this very evening.'

An hour after sunset he took them out into the street and pointed to the darkening sky, low in the east.

'There he is, George, there he is! The constellation of Orion the Hunter.'

The boys peered uncertainly through the indigo twilight.

'A constellation is a group of stars, you know. Those three in a row, straight over that roof, they form Orion's belt. And see that shiny star down there, the blue-white one? That's his foot. Can't pick it out? Stand behind me, then, and let your eye follow the line of my sign-posting finger. Got it, Stewart? Good. Now a bit higher, look – that one with a reddish colour? It marks his shoulder. And see his big club down to the side there. And the very bright star, lower left – that's his faithful dog, Sirius. Follows him everywhere. Or leads him everywhere – I'm not sure which.'

Will imagined Orion to be a stealthy figure, like Deerslayer, moving unerringly along tracks that others could hardly detect. He himself, he decided, would also become that kind of skilful hunter, scouting his own way through the world and leaving hardly a trace.

Eight

For years afterwards, in febrile nightmares, he would hear the terrible long wail that brought him running in from the snow-covered yard to where she lay in a sprawl at the foot of the stairs, her face white and twisted in pain.

Knowing that Jerome Davin was down at the wharf, too far away to be fetched in a hurry, Will left George to hold their mother's clenched hand while he raced to find a doctor. He stumbled along the slushy streets to the post office, where someone directed him to Doc Green's house at the other end of the town. Green was not there. A neighbour suggested Will look for him at one of the taverns. It was more than half an hour before he could be found and prised away from his rum.

When at last Will led the crapulous physician into Davin's house, it was too late. Jeannie Hammond lay in the same spot, unconscious now. Beside her sat George, all sniffs and sobs and hiccups. Blood had already soaked through Jeannie's skirt and spread around her ankles. They moved her to a bed, but that night she stopped breathing. The baby had never taken a breath.

The next morning, distress separated the mourners. Davin, hardly able to speak, could only pat each boy repeatedly on the shoulder as he whispered to himself, 'God Almighty, this is too cruel.' George took up a silent station at the window, staring out into the grey street and trying to suppress a small spasmodic whimpering noise. Stewart knelt on a chair at the kitchen bench, drawing, erasing and redrawing shapes of houses and people on a squeaky slate that Davin had found for him. Will sat hunched morosely on a fireside stool, jabbing with a long poker at the incandescent lumps of wood and scowling at the memory of every pernicious mischance and misdeed that had poisoned his life since that day at the St Andrews fair. He thought of his father's grim death, of Christie's annexation of their farm and assault on their mother, of the miserable exodus from La Chute to Owen Sound, and of this climactic disaster that had wrenched from them the only adult member of the family. Christie was to blame for her death: his violence had made her pregnant, and the pregnancy had killed her.

Anger and fear tightened Will's throat. What would now become of him and his brothers? They knew no-one here except this man in whose house they could no longer be sure of having a secure place.

As if hearing the boy's fretful thoughts, Davin came over to the hearth and stood beside him, clearing his throat noisily. 'It's going to be a hard row to hoe, young Will,' he said. 'A very hard row. You'll just have to square your shoulders for what lies ahead.' Although the tone was gruff, Will knew the words carried sympathy. 'But don't go worrying now about the necessities of life. I can't be your parent, of course. I can't cook meals for you, or anything like that. All the same I'll make sure you lads are taken care of. I'll arrange for someone to feed you and look after your education.'

* * *

'Someone' turned out to be a series of minders and mentors.

One of them was the tall, shy, serious-minded priest and schoolmaster, Father John Cushin. He presided over a cramped little log-clad classroom built at the rear of his church by Jesuits who had come to Owen Sound from the nearby mission of Sainte-Marie Among the Hurons. Though Father Cushin hid as much as he could behind his thick eyebrows and formal manner, he was patient and even gentle with any child who showed an interest in the codified form of knowledge he himself professed.

In Father Cushin's orderly instructional routine there was none of the vitality that had made them so responsive to James Meikle's teaching and poetry recitations back in La Chute. Where Meikle had opened a window towards imagination and self-invention, Cushin offered them an orderly world, strictly framed by classifications, hierarchies and procedures. Will took from it what he could. He studied structures of argument and techniques of persuasion, learned to speak fluently and forcefully, wrote essays that astonished Cushin with their command of style. Geography became a passion and Will committed to memory a great range of information about foreign places and strange cultural customs, gleaned from a gazetteer in the Mechanics' Institute library. He consumed avidly every idea, fact and book that came his way, but it was always the heuristic power of language that attracted his keenest attention. Through words, he was beginning to see, you could shape yourself and others. Most of those who had influence in the world – as teachers, political leaders, men of religion or medicine – were people whose speech could grip you like a strong hand and draw you towards them. To become a person of substance, Will understood, you had to know how to act like one and talk like one.

Jerome Davin saw the boys from time to time but in the summer months his work often took him away from the town for long periods. Although cheerful in his role as their unofficial guardian, he seemed to be acting from a spirit of decency rather than from anything more personal, let alone paternal. His tone in conversation with them was usually jocular, yet cautious, as if he felt unsure how to relate to them, and particularly how to respond to Will's intensity. For his protector's kindness and hearty good intentions Will felt grateful; but Davin was not, in his eyes, to emulate. He was weak. He lacked steely resolve. Will wanted to be different: to anneal his own mind, harden its edge, so that he would become impervious to hurt and unrelenting in the pursuit of control over others.

* * *

The Hammond boys were housed nearby, in Widow Shaw's shanty. Jerome Davin paid her for their board and lodging. She was a compulsive chatterer who would conduct endless conversations without expecting responses from anyone she was addressing.

'You're getting to be a strapping lad, Will,' she said one afternoon as he came in from his new job at the newspaper office, 'and a wee bit more handsome than is good for you. My word! Those blue eyes of yours are likely to get you into trouble if you're not careful...'

After years of hearing his landlady's prattle, Will knew she needed no interlocutor. Almost all her remarks constituted a self-sustaining commentary on the world at large, and Will seldom paid much regard to any of it. This time, however, something hooked his attention.

'I dare say if any of those young girls who were your little classmates a few years ago in La Chute could see you now, they'd be smitten with admiration!'

Will remembered them well. There were just five girls in Meikle's class of fifteen children at the time when the Hammonds' departure reduced the total to a dozen. Eldest in the gaggle of girls, and nearly Will's age, was Sally Christie. Will had disliked her air of smugness, reflecting the Christie family's status as the most prosperous in the local farming community. By now she must be approaching her seventeenth birthday, and he supposed she would be helping out on her family's large farm, which had absorbed what used to be his own family's acreage. The memory of Charlie Christie's rapacious acquisition of the Hammond land reminded him of how the brute had forced himself on Jeannie. Tightening his fist, Will fell into a moody silence.

The next morning brought thick snow swirling across the lake into Owen Sound. The town was quiet apart from the whoosh of wind. Will trudged to the little cemetery, as he had done every Sunday since his mother's death. He re-wrapped the scarf across his mouth to stop his frozen exhalation making it into a rigid icy mask. Pulling off his left glove, he stared at his scarred palm, its white weals witnessing to the angry grief that had assailed him when he stood beside her newly covered grave on that other snowy morning a few years earlier.

Stabbing himself with a broken vase seemed now the act of a different person. The anger was still in him, but time had hardened it into a cold metallic instrument, something he could use against others. Standing there among the grave markers, adjusting his scarf and gloves, he thought again about La Chute and about Widow Shaw's remark, and a plan began to form.

Nine

When the spring thaw began, Will left Owen Sound and made his way eastward. His brothers were nearly old enough to fend for themselves, and while they remained at school Jerome Davin would look after their welfare. Will had decided to seek farm work where he could find it around the lakes of southern Ontario and Quebec. He would save every penny he could, and then make his way to La Chute and see what opportunities a shrewd youth could seize – opportunities for self-advancement, yes, and perhaps something more: requital.

A taciturn farmer making his long journey home with supplies agreed to take Will most of the way to Barrie. Although the road surface was not much better than when the Hammonds had travelled over it in the opposite direction several years before, he hardly noticed the discomfort this time. As their cart trundled and jolted out of town and away from the bay, big chunks of clicking ice blocked the culverts and ditches. From the road they could see a broad grey spate coursing above the riverbank. The snow season was over but the wind gusts were chilling and as Will looked back along the valley he saw the smoke from hundreds of chimneys swirling towards them from the settlement.

He spent the next eighteen months in and around Barrie just the way he had hoped. There was plenty of casual employment available on farms in the district – repairing fences and barns, felling trees, clearing stumps, doing odd jobs here and there. At seventeen he now enjoyed the physical exertion and the pleasant tiredness in his broadening shoulders. But the pay was meagre and his other work was proving more profitable: under a pseudonym he wrote occasional articles for several newspapers, including the *Owen Sound Times*. Much of it was adapted without acknowledgement from Dr Coffin's *Botanic Guide to Health*, bought second-hand at the Owen Sound market. There was an amusing satisfaction in sitting down in the evenings to compose these little essays that purported to give expert advice on natural cures for various ailments. Will embroidered his remarks with invented quotations from imaginary authorities on medical topics and a scattering of pious reflections about spiritual wellbeing. Some editors paid him in shillings, some in dollars, but whatever the coinage he was glad to see his savings and self-reliance grow.

He might have stayed longer in Barrie if it had not been for his encounter with Mrs Campbell. He struck up conversation with her at the Summer Agricultural Fair where they were both admiring a bowl of succulent-looking blueberries. She was a handsome woman, and he noticed the way she tilted her head and ran her tongue over her bottom lip. They exchanged pleasantries. He introduced himself, she seemed happy to talk, and from the way she looked him in the eye he could tell at once that she was responsive to charm. She mentioned that her husband, an insurance man, was away for a few days in Midland on business. Will bought her a glass of cider at the refreshment tent and learned that she lived near the centre of the town, in an imposing two-storey house that he had often walked past on his way to the newspaper office.

When he called there unannounced the following afternoon she showed no surprise and made him welcome. Over cups of tea, he told her in detail about the writing he was doing for newspapers and she suggested he consider giving public lectures around the district.

'Your youthfulness would be no impediment,' she said. 'You speak uncommonly well. There's something very compelling about your voice – a certain magnetism – and you have a great gift of fluency. These days everybody wants to hear about natural medicine. The uses of herbal tinctures, especially. You'd soon attract audiences, and earn good money.'

Will's thoughts moved quickly.

'It's flattering that you think so, Mrs Campbell, and the idea does have some appeal, I must admit. But I lack the resources to venture into anything of that kind. To rent public rooms, to advertise...'

'Perhaps I could lend you enough to get you started. Come back tomorrow at about three o'clock.'

When he arrived the next afternoon she opened the door herself, explaining that it was the maid's day off. By the time he left the house two hours later, he had in his pocket a substantial amount of money, and in his kit of experience a gratifying carnal initiation. It had all happened effortlessly. She had an ache in her neck and shoulder, she said. He suggested gentle kneading of the muscles around the area of discomfort and, at her invitation, demonstrated what was necessary. This required some loosening of her bodice; and before long they continued the treatment more vigorously in her chamber.

He set out for Kingston early the next morning. Having taken what there was to give, he could not expect further generosity from Mrs Campbell, and Barrie would soon become a hazardous place to remain.

* * *

Finding no suitable work in Kingston, he moved further east a few weeks later, picking up casual jobs where he could but never lingering long. Rolling stone, he thought to himself. One of the things he used to enjoy about his schooling in La Chute was the little ritual of The Day's Proverb. After they had recited in unison the previous day's piece of folk wisdom, Mr Meikle would present them with a new proverb to memorise. Most were fairly plain in their meaning: 'Fine words butter no parsnips' or 'A stitch in time saves nine'. The one that had seemed ambiguous to William despite his teacher's explanatory words was 'A rolling stone gathers no moss'. According to James Meikle, this maxim signified that a shiftless person who kept moving on from place to place would never accumulate any material assets. 'But sir,' said William, puzzled, 'why must it mean that? I wouldn't want to have moss growing on me. Better to roll along smoothly, not letting anything cling. Like a shiny river pebble.'

And now that's what I'm doing, he thought. When he reached St Andrews, just seven miles from La Chute, it was an easy matter to make casual enquiries about the Christie family. He learned that Burly Charlie had been struck down by an apoplexy, leaving him unable to speak or write; that his wife had died in childbirth a few years earlier; and that their large farm was now being managed and worked by the children – Sally and her younger brothers – with some intermittent help from their uncle, a tailor at St Eustache who had no liking for life on the land.

To Will, the situation seemed perfectly propitious, and he wasted no time. Within a week he was working on the Christie farm. Sally seemed pleased to see him again and grateful that he offered his labour during the summer season without wages. Food and shelter would be recompense enough for the time being, he told her. She was a plain-faced earnest young woman, anxious about the responsibility of managing the farm and keeping house. Her three brothers were too young and slow-witted to make decisions. Her father had become a constant burden, spending each day huddled under a blanket in a rocking chair, glaring speechlessly. Will was sure the old man knew who this newcomer was. He seemed to understand what was said in his hearing, and one afternoon when they were alone together in the house Will squatted in front of the hunched figure.

'There was a time, you despicable reprobate, when you thought you had complete power over the Hammond family,' he said. 'You violated my mother, and she'd be alive if it weren't for you. You snatched everything you could from us. Soon it'll be my turn to seize something back.'

The old man's eyes bulged and his tongue lolled at the side of his dribbling mouth.

Three months later Will and Sally were married by Rev. Thomas Henry in the new brick Presbyterian church near the corner of Main Street and Francis Street, just along from the old East End School where James Meikle, now deceased, used to enchant them with his sonorous recitations from Wordsworth's *Prelude*.

La Chute was growing steadily as the district's farmers became more prosperous. Small ancillary businesses had begun to establish themselves and the town now boasted a saddler, a blacksmith, three shoemakers, Dudderidge's carriage- and sleigh-making warehouse, Lane's general store, Raitt's tailoring shop, and Fish's three mills – a grist mill, a sawmill and one for carding and fulling. Education was also expanding. Five years after its founding, the La Chute Academy now had over 200 students, half of them over sixteen years of age, and the Mechanics' Institute boasted nearly 300 members and a thousand books.

Yet in Will's eyes the town was much too small, too restrictive, to hold him. He had no intention of staying long, though Sally would have been surprised to know this. 'The earth is all before me...' – he could hear Meikle's voice. But meanwhile he was married to a tiresomely dull woman whose bovine devotion annoyed him. Her body, solidly passive, soon ceased to give him any pleasure and her conversation had always been trite. Except as a means of access to the Christie property, she would never have attracted his interest.

Much to Will's irritation, she was reluctant to comply with his insistence that they sell her portion of the farm to her brothers or her uncle.

'Why?' she responded with a puzzled frown. 'I belong here. And this is your home, too.'

'But we don't want to be drudges, do we? The money can allow us to leave behind the monotony of life on the land,' said Will. 'Break away from this unremitting toil. Travel abroad. Go into business.'

'I thought you liked it here.'

'La Chute is such a narrow-minded place,' he said with a twitch of exasperation.

She shook her head, pursed her thin mouth, and would not be budged. But it was only a matter of days later that budging became unnecessary when a sudden illness gripped Sally Christie and carried her off. She became delirious and convulsive, showing signs of scarlet fever or a similar poisoning of the blood, and the emetic that Will insisted on administering brought no improvement.

Not long after her burial, Will went to see the town's only lawyer. Peter Priddle was a narrow-shouldered, scraggy-necked runt of a man, bent with age, who had a disconcerting way of sucking noisily on his sputtering pipe, which he seldom removed from his mouth for long enough to utter more than a half-sentence at a time. This fitful style of speech was punctuated now and then by puffs of pungent smoke and a faint fizzing sound as spittle encountered hot fragments of tobacco.

Will wanted to know how to expedite the sale of what he had assumed to be his share of the farm, but as he grasped the implications of what Priddle was explaining in this piecemeal way his impatience turned to deep dismay. The expectations he had brought with him into the lawyer's office had no legal basis at all. Burly Charlie, though unable to speak or act, was still deemed the owner of the whole farm; and when he eventually died it would pass to the eldest son.

'Impartible inheritance, you see...assets preserved for later transmission...not a situation where demise can enrich a widower.' Having delivered this information bit by bit, Priddle slowly inspected his hissing pipe. When it was clear there was nothing more to be said, Will left the office abruptly, and a few days later left La Chute forever.

Part 3

Dunedin, 1889–90

Ten

The nights were long and sometimes frightening. Images recurred, looming indistinctly as if through a thick fog. Frances pictured herself in a kind of den, with a wilderness all around, and then a dark shape appeared that became a man clothed in rags, standing in front of his house, a hand stretched towards her as he cried out in distress, 'What shall I do?'

Now that she spent so much time alone, there was no-one who could share the retrieval of her dreams. It had been for years a little narrative ritual over protracted breakfasts: she could nearly always recall in detail the oneiric swirls that eddied through her sleep, and her mother, even at her most infirm, had always wanted her to talk about them.

These days, with Edward leaving early to prepare his classes, breakfast was a brief routine and the hours that followed it were usually quiet and companionless. The social ritual of making calls on acquaintances never appealed to Frances and she had let it atrophy. Occasionally one of the solicitous church stalwarts would visit her. On Tuesdays the washerwoman came; Alice the maid needed help occasionally with the cleaning of carpets or curtains, or other tasks; and there were the usual summer routines that Frances liked to supervise in the kitchen – the making of raspberry and gooseberry jams, redcurrant jelly, blackcurrant vinegar. But much of her time was spent communing moodily with her solitude: painting in watercolours, reading poetry, walking as far as the port and back, or just listening to silence. Like a sleepwalker she drifted from one room to another, lifting up something here and something else there, staring at every object in turn, and putting each one back in its place with an absent-minded solicitude. She would pause in front of mirrors, not to preen but simply to soften the sense of vacancy and funereal stillness that pervaded the house. Just recognising her own image was somehow less forlorn than seeing no human shape all day. In her reflected face, behind the steady gaze of the grey-blue eyes, she glimpsed a kind of puzzlement, as if she felt uncertain what kind of self inhabited this body of hers. At the thought that she would soon turn thirty, loneliness began to tighten its grip, and the prospect of empty years among echoes felt unbearable.

* * *

That evening she sat by the hearth and tried to recall in detail the eight-month period of Hammond's ministry among them, from the impact of his first sermon up to her mother's sombre funeral service that he conducted just before leaving to return overseas.

She herself, at the beginning, had not known what to think of him. How strange that inaugural address had seemed! – and many others that followed it, too, Sunday by Sunday, throughout his sojourn in Dunedin. She could recall vividly his deep mesmerising voice, and the firm clasp of his hand as he stood at the Tabernacle door after the service to talk with each member of the congregation when they emerged. He had a way of enclosing her pressed hand by placing his left palm firmly against her wrist while continuing to hold her fingers with his right. Had her glove disguised the way her hand trembled faintly at his touch?

He was quite unlike the predictable evangelists who had preached to them previously. Their sermons always followed a familiar pattern, affirming routinely the simple fundamentals that this congregation cherished: the primacy of personal faith, the rejection of ecclesiastical hierarchies, the insistence that the only true sacraments were the immersion of adult believers and the breaking of bread together. But Dr Hammond's sermons were often startling, with a prophet's dramatic eloquence. On that first Sunday he seized their attention: there was a grave power in the way he rose to stand tall at the pulpit, squared his broad shoulders, drew in his breath slowly as he swept the rows of worshippers with a steady gaze, and then began after a long taut silence to speak with words that seemed to burn into their souls. That intense and resonant voice of his, first quiet, then rising suddenly to fill the building, suffused every element of the unexpected stories that he told and the unusual biblical imagery that he threaded through his discourse.

Frances remembered clearly how he began his first sermon with Paul's statement to the Hebrews that without shedding of blood there is no remission. A well-known text, but he went on to link it in surprising ways with several Old Testament passages, and with a tone of such lacerated emotion that it was almost as if the edges of his own sentences began to bleed into the dusty air of their church. He recounted the story of Cain and Abel so dramatically that the fratricidal act seemed less terrible than the father's anguished accusation: 'The voice of thy brother's blood crieth unto me from the ground.' He turned to solemn words from Leviticus about the efficacy of carnal blood in making an atonement for the soul; to a pronouncement in the book of Numbers about the cleansing of the land through bloodshed; and to a frightening prophecy from Ezekiel: 'I will prepare thee unto blood, and blood shall pursue thee'. He evoked the fearful ancient Hebrew ritual through which two innocent beasts were chosen for sacrificial purposes: one to be symbolically laden with the sins of the community and set loose into the wilderness, the other to be slain.

Then suddenly, somehow, he had wrenched their thoughts from those biblical images to the stark reality of the death trade thriving in and around their own young city as he described the slaughterhouse nearby, the gore that ran in the gutters of the gruesome factory where quivering animals were hacked into meat and packed into frozen cargo for the long sea journey to English markets. Making no concession to squeamishness, he forced his flock not only to see and feel all that violent suffering but also to recognise how the very existence of human society required it.

'Bloodshed,' he cried, stretching forth his hands as if they were as crimson as a butcher's block, 'is the necessary basis of our communal life. Though we may dread it, yet we depend upon it for our food, for the regulation of our physical health, for the maintenance of law and order.' Human beings, he declared, were created as carnivorous killers, and must accept their God-given nature. In compelling detail he drew on his own medical knowledge of the use of bloodletting and leeches as a means of reducing excess circulation, slowing the pulse, and ridding the body of impurities. He spoke, too, of the collective reliance of all people on the effusion of human blood through judicial punishment. And from there, just as suddenly, he swung the hearts of his listeners back to the redemptive oblation of the slaughtered Lamb of God, and drew his passionate sermon towards a close by appealing vociferously to that central tenet of their belief, enjoining them all to 'affirm, with the Scriptures, that the cleansing blood of Christ, as the expression, synonym, and consummation of his sacrifice and propitiation, is our hope and only hope.'

Frances could recall how Dr Hammond's oratory had transfixed her, and no doubt many others also in the pews that day: how it seemed to cast a troubling spell on them; how, as if he knew exactly what they felt, he concluded by talking about the greatest spell of all, the *gospel* of salvation, rendering eternal life through sacrificial death.

Her sense of the doctor's strangeness didn't completely subside with familiarity, even after he and his wife moved into the same street in Roslyn, almost opposite the Phillips home, and became frequent visitors. Her invalid mother soon placed her trust in Dr Hammond as both spiritual adviser and personal physician. He would call at the house frequently to take her pulse, discuss her symptoms, provide scriptural consolation, administer medication when necessary. On most of these occasions Frances was present and he often drew her into conversation. Their exchanges of words always left her faintly perturbed, though she could never quite decide why. Every detail of every encounter seemed imprinted on her mind, and she found herself repeating silently afterwards the things they had said to each other. Then it became her habit to imagine, as if rehearsing a play for which the script was still being improvised, the things that might be spoken at their next meeting, and the next again.

He had a serious manner, neither distant nor presumptuous. The embodiment of gravity, he seldom smiled at Frances, yet often asked her opinion and always listened closely to whatever she said. An apparent constraint in many of these conversations was his wife, who usually accompanied him on his visits, saying little but watching everything sidelong. Frances was puzzled: the Hammonds seemed to her an ill-assorted couple. The doctor was such a fine figure of a man, and highly intelligent, while Mrs Hammond was small, stooped and sallow, by no means youthful, with a persistent catarrhal problem and nothing interesting to say.

Although they were reticent about their past lives, some particulars emerged as the months went by. He had grown up near Montreal, Canada, he said, and in his early years the only life he knew was subsistence farming. She was from a southern region of the United States. Before answering the church's call to Dunedin they had been a short while in Melbourne, having travelled there by way of Malta, where there was some kind of commercial connection. His hostility towards the Roman Church, an attitude expressed in smouldering denunciations from the pulpit, had its origin, he told them, in his own experience as a young seminarian, quickly disillusioned. No person of integrity, he maintained, could undergo training for the Roman priesthood without soon discovering that it was a self-serving and corrupt religion with no firm biblical foundation. This is why he was drawn to the simple devotional practices that centred on the priesthood of all believers.

While these and other glimpses of his colourful past made him even more interesting in Frances's eyes, they never amounted to a full narrative. There were fragments, elliptical references, odd gaps. She would have liked to press for further detail but didn't wish to appear inquisitive.

As Mrs Phillips declined towards her final days, Dr Hammond was on hand to give comfort. Having so long nursed and coddled her increasingly querulous mother, Frances felt grateful for the calm manner in which the doctor took over some of the tasks of support.

At the funeral service, he spoke in a more subdued tone than she had heard him use before, softly elegiac. It was that quality in his voice, more than the bereavement itself, that moved Frances to tears as she sat in the cemetery chapel. To the familiar biblical phrases of consolation he added words that she could not recall having heard before. They had the rhythms of poetry, both disturbing and soothing, and he seemed to draw them from a distant place in his memory:

Dust as we are, the immortal spirit grows
Like harmony in music. There is a dark
Inscrutable workmanship that reconciles
Discordant elements, makes them cling together
In one society.

And then, hardly a week later, the Hammonds startled everyone
by announcing that they were to leave New Zealand. There were
business matters in Florida, the doctor said, that required urgent
attention – something concerning orange groves. And besides,
he believed that it was now time for another man to take up the
preaching role with God's faithful in Dunedin. Suddenly, he and
his wife departed.

Frances was doubly at a loss. The domestic role tacitly
assigned to her years before had evaporated; and she could
no longer talk with the man who had begun to enlarge her
imagination.

Eleven

Three months after the funeral, in an effort to lift herself out of her doldrum spirits and claustral habits, Frances enrolled in drawing and painting classes held in a lecture room at the university. The *Otago Daily Times* had been expostulating that such splendid buildings were seldom accessible to members of the general public. In response, the governing authorities announced that special Saturday classes would be arranged in conjunction with certain amateur groups and societies. Frances seized this opportunity eagerly.

From childhood days she had always loved having a pencil or paintbrush in her hand. There was not only the quiet satisfaction of recreating on paper what she saw around her, but also the stranger pleasure of imagining shapes inwardly, drawn sometimes from the murk of dreams, sometimes from just closing her eyes and pressing her fingertips against the lids to produce patterns of light and dark. Having spent countless hours alone with her sketchbook as a young girl, in recent years she had turned her hand to watercolours to relieve the tedium of caring for her mother. While the artistry of Alfred Walsh – the most brilliant of Dunedin's young painters – was beyond her talents, she felt she knew exactly how such a person looked at the world, and she shared Walsh's fascination with the dappling and dimpling of surfaces, always streaked with shadows.

At the first class she sat next to a somewhat older woman with pale skin and golden hair, who wore a stylish light green dress. Frances herself, with the elapse of the full mourning period, had recently discarded her black crepe covering and chosen a costume of dark grey wool, but was conscious that it looked severe beside the fine tailored garment worn by the elegant person on her left.

They introduced themselves to each other and walked together out of the building to linger talking in the quadrangle. Frances soon found that Isabella Morrison was refreshingly forthright in her opinions: about the scantiness of serious cultural activity in Dunedin, about their earnest art teacher's affectations, about the university's quaintly decorative architectural style, and much besides. She made Frances laugh for the first time in years.

A week later they extended their after-class walk into a more leisurely ramble. The mid-October weather still had a wintry bleakness; but despite a biting wind and the need to lift their skirt hems above the muddy puddles, they strolled together for more than half an hour, talking animatedly about the constraints that made social life so disagreeable for a young woman in this colony.

'Not that I can be regarded any longer as a young woman!' said Isabella, with an exaggerated show of chagrin. 'Nor am I as isolated as you seem to be. My husband does include me in his circle whenever he can, but it's just a little irksome, I confess, that my social standing often feels somewhat secondary. Derivative. Your choices about where to go and whom to see may be restricted, but at least they're entirely your own.'

By the time the short sequence of art classes finished, Frances had come to regard Isabella as a close friend and con-fidante. Their common interests, they discovered, went beyond painting. Isabella was the more self-assured, expressing without hesitation opinions that Frances had scarcely begun to formulate but found agreeable. Both women keenly followed newspaper accounts of current political debates, were not loath to discuss what the government ought to be doing to lift the colony out of its incipient economic depression, and found much to agree with in Miss Marriott's contentious Athenaeum lecture on women's suffrage. Both resented the disapproval expressed by acquaintances and family members who thought these interests 'unfeminine'. To Frances, previously accustomed to criticism from Edward for her 'decided opinions' and 'headstrong' ways, it was liberating to discover in Isabella a person who shared so many of her own attitudes.

Frances recognised a mind like her own but with fewer inhibitions, reflecting a more extensive education as a young woman in Edinburgh and a more secure family background. Before marrying and migrating to New Zealand, she had belonged (she told Frances) to a lively circle that included several writers associated with *Blackwood's Magazine*. Her husband had studied literature and rhetoric at Edinburgh University under the renowned Professor Masson before deciding to become an architect. Frances was awed by the mention of such august connections. Always hungry for knowledge, she had been encouraged in her youthful learning by a bookish family friend, earnest old Dr Angus Gordon, but though her reading was far from narrow she felt keenly the incompleteness of her formal education.

This sense of lack gave an anxious edge to the prospect of dinner-party conversation when Isabella and her husband invited her into their home. For all her scornful remarks about the tongue-tied men in her church circles, shyness would tend to hush her voice on the rare occasions when she was in the company of those who appeared to be not only eloquent but also worldly-wise.

She had previously admired as a passer-by the imposing villa in Graham Street with its ornate verandah, broad set of steps rising to the front door, and the square turret enclosing an additional room at the third-floor level. Now she saw that a large staircase dominated the interior of the house, and the dining room was exuberantly furnished.

Several other guests had already arrived, all appearing to be much more at ease than Frances felt. She regarded David Morrison with particular deference: though not physically imposing, he spoke with such fluency that she was all the more conscious how hesitant her own little contributions to the table talk must seem. Yet the company was pleasant, and the tone genial. As the evening progressed she began to respond more confidently to the warmth that others expressed.

She had remained quiet during a long discussion of the disgrace recently suffered by Robert Lawson, the colony's most esteemed architect until the part collapse of his grand Seacliff Asylum construction, and the subsequent public enquiry that held him chiefly responsible. It was a terrible misfortune, said David Morrison, that this should happen to a man who had done so much to make their young city a place where civilised people could feel at home – a man whose achievements included the splendours of First Church, the superlative design for the Boys' High School, and the astonishing mansion created for Mr Larnach.

'Larnach's back from Melbourne, I hear,' said Stuart Donaldson, a tall thin man with wide ginger whiskers and baggy eyes, who looked like a circus clown but was said to be a person of substance in the legal fraternity. 'It seems his business venture there ran into some kind of trouble. Someone told me he's already considering a return to parliamentary life. No doubt wants something to engage his mind. Must be a lonely fellow in that huge edifice. What is it now since his second wife died, a couple of years?'

'Wasn't there some question about the way she died?' someone asked.

'Toxaemia, I heard.'

There was more about Larnach, but Frances did not attend to it. The idea of a poisoned bloodstream troubled her imagination. That the fluid of life itself could become deadly: it was a sickening thought. Would such an infection be palpable, she wondered, as it coursed through one's body? Would the veins themselves feel fiery, or icy? A familiar line of verse came into her mind: 'blood that freezes, blood that burns'. She shuddered.

The talk turned to local journalism, and then to literary matters. New Zealand, averred Isabella, was in need of its own poet laureate.

'Surely this remarkable landscape deserves to be celebrated in song and story. And not only where we live but the way we live, too – all the fresh contours of society here at the edge of the old world's map. It's half a century since British settlement began, and our adopted country still remains, in a sense, undiscovered! We need someone to turn into memorable words what it means to be here. Don't you think? What it means to belong distinctively to this place. It will happen soon, I've no doubt. Perhaps the person is already born who can make our new little domicile leap through the page.'

Frances listened intently but looked down at her folded hands and let the conversation flow past her – until one of Donaldson's opinionated pronouncements stirred her to take issue with him.

'Every writer of merit,' he pontificated, caressing a moustache that seemed sculpted to support his pendulous nose, 'takes his own society as his main subject matter. Exotic settings tend to produce trivial literature.'

'If that's indeed so, Mr Donaldson,' Frances responded quietly, 'how does one explain the enduring success of Robert Browning's compositions? Surely he's one of the finest English poets, yet his writings often transport the reader elsewhere – to an Italian or Spanish past, far from his homeland and from his own day.'

Isabella clapped her hands. 'You must concede that Frances is right about that, Mr Donaldson. She knows Browning's poems very well. I've heard her recite whole passages from memory.'

Donaldson seemed to take this as a personal challenge. His nostrils flared. 'Then you must be familiar, Miss Phillips, with his "Home Thoughts, From Abroad", which I dare say will support my view. "Oh to be in England!" – wouldn't you admit those sentiments as plain evidence for the case I was making? The poet's excursions into distant times and places could never weaken his ties to the nation that shaped him.'

Frances hesitated before replying, her eyes still fixed on her dinner plate. 'It seems to me more complicated than that. There are, I believe, different kinds of "home thoughts"…different – What should one call them? – different points of attachment for one's sense of longing. Or belonging.'

She glanced up. Donaldson had stopped smirking and now appeared to be genuinely interested. The way everyone was looking at her seemed to imply that they all wanted to hear more.

'Well, the hearth, the place where…where we happen to be nurtured, isn't our only dwelling, is it?' she went on slowly. 'Even those of us who've always lived here in Dunedin tend to regard the British Isles as, in a certain respect, our true home-land – don't we? We look back to its traditions as having cradled us, nourished us. But then we also look ahead to an ultimate domicile: "Man goeth to his long home", as the scriptures put it.'

The attentive silence continued. 'So perhaps,' Frances suggested, 'all human wandering, physical or imaginary I mean, is impelled by some…by an inkling that no single abode can wholly accommodate our spirit. The explorer, the traveller, the poet – they're all seeking, I think, an elusive habitation…' Her voice trailed off.

'..."whose margin fades forever and forever as we move",' added Isabella, explaining with a half-apologetic smile: 'Browning for Frances, Tennyson for me.'

Twelve

In the following days Frances found her thoughts returning to the dinner-table discussion and her own part in it. She had surprised herself when she began to speak about the ambiguous meanings of home and travel. And yet, once expressed, those thoughts seemed important to her, giving definite form to a conviction previously inchoate and barely even recognised. She knew then that one day she would need to leave Dunedin behind. There was a wider, stranger world where she would search for a home of another kind, even a series of homes, which might provide more complex satisfactions than this one where she had chanced to be born.

Material samples of the world beyond her circle and her city were soon afterwards on display in the centre of Dunedin itself. Frances went with Isabella and David to the crowded opening of the South Seas Exhibition. Its grand pavilion in Clarence Street, capped by a Moorish dome nearly 100 feet high and sheathed in lead, had an imposing air of solidity, belying its ingenious method of prefabricated construction. For many visitors the exhibition was mainly a place of wonderful entertainment. They thronged the concert hall, refreshment bar, art gallery and fun fair.

There was so much to see that some people went day after day to goggle at the astonishingly diverse range of displays:

geological and mineralogical collections, metallurgical apparatus, sparkling glassware and elegant pottery, boldly designed household furniture, textile fabrics, new fashions in boots and shoes, surgical and pharmaceutical appliances, splendidly manufactured musical instruments, ingenious photographic productions, printing machines, armaments...The modern world had come to Dunedin, wearing its glittering panoply and brandishing its trophies.

To Frances and her companions the industrial exhibits were of greatest interest. They marvelled over new technical achievements, especially the telephone and phonograph. The inventions and commercial innovations conjured up an international network of rapid economic developments, portending such clamorous change and such a dizzy velocity that the high-speed railway rattling above them seemed an appropriate symbol for it all.

'And yet,' said David, 'there's something artificial about this spectacle of industrial progress, don't you agree? Too triumphant. Almost illusory. Our colony is deeply anxious now about its financial future. The prosperous glow of earlier times has long since faded.'

'David, you sound like a politician,' said his wife. 'Or a newspaper editor.'

'Perhaps so, m'dear. But I think it will take more than this exhibition, for all its flourishes, to restore the sense of opportunity, expansiveness, call it what you like, that once permeated our commerce and industry.'

They knew he was right. On their walks through the town after their art classes, Frances and Isabella had seen families being evicted from cottages and urchins begging on street corners. In recent newspaper reports and general gossip a recurrent theme was the spread of financial hardship facing individuals without employment and businesses without capital. The heady years of the golden economy, when bankers and builders prospered mightily, when trade burgeoned and tramways bustled, had suddenly gone. Dunedin had lost its momentum. Frances felt surer with each passing month that she wanted to leave before her city's mood of dejection crept into her bones.

That conviction strengthened in the aftermath of a calamitous Saturday picnic.

* * *

Isabella had suggested that Frances join her and two friends from the Otago Art Society on a sketching party excursion to Waitati village and Blueskin Bay. Her husband, she explained, would escort the little group in their wagonette, leaving early enough to allow the ladies to spend a few leisurely hours around Blueskin, where they would try to emulate some of the late George O'Brien's meticulous pencil drawing and watercolour scenes in that area. Isabella was an enthusiastic admirer of O'Brien's landscapes and townscapes – 'So finely detailed,' she remarked, 'that it hardly seems possible they could come from the podgy hand of such a corpulent man' – and his recent death had only intensified her aspiration to produce pictures comparable in their delicacy.

The trip to Blueskin was cheerful enough. The previous day's fierce storm had gone as quickly as it came, and they set out in good time, blithe at the prospect of a clear sky and mild breezes that were already drying the roads. Frances found the wagonette's bench seats surprisingly comfortable and her companions perfectly pleasant. Both Isabella's friends were married women. Young Grace Hutton, full of impressionable vivacity, responded excitedly to everything they saw along the way. Constance Mouatt, somewhat older and more reserved, had little to say at first but proved to be well informed about the area. She, it turned out, was the only one who knew how their destination had acquired its colourful sobriquet.

'My neighbour told me on good authority,' said Constance, 'that the earliest pakeha settlers in the district had frequent dealings with a senior Maori man whose face was covered with blue tattoos. They regarded it as his domain – Blueskin's bay.'

As they jolted along with patches of thick bush on their left and glimpses of the sea on their right, there was much to catch an artist's eye. For Isabella, with her love of pencilled precision, the most salient aspect of it all was the way everything seemed to form itself into patterned outlines, whether threadlike or thickly edged. She exclaimed at the tracery of branches, the strong shaft-lines and ledges of rock, the skeins of kelp strung along the shore, and twice she insisted that David bring the pair of horses to a standstill so she could sketch the contours of this or that feature. For Frances the scenery had a different kind of visual impact. What impressed her especially was the colourful jostle of slabs and streaks: layered variants of green, grey or bleaker black, distinct shadings of light and darkness, pressed against each other in a quilted motley. She wanted to reach for a paintbox, not a pencil.

They made good time to Waitati. In a sheltered nook beside a stream that flowed towards the tidal mudflats, they spread out their picnic lunch and took their ease. Later, while David stayed behind to attend to the horses, the ladies walked down to the shore nearby. Grace and Isabella sat to watch a young Maori family slowly gathering cockles, and made quick little pencil studies as the children knelt and dug. Frances strolled with Constance further along the water's edge towards some indistinct dark shapes, like lumps of seaweed, scattered at one end of the bay.

'Wrecked birds!' Frances cried out as they approached. 'More than half a dozen of them, carnage washed up after yesterday's storm. Mutton birds, aren't they?'

'Yes. Sooty shearwaters. Bigger than I'd thought. The span of the spread wings on that one over there must be at least a yard from tip to tip.'

'Rather dull, that dark muddy colour, isn't it, compared with the plumage of some of the other birds we see around the coast?'

'But look more closely,' said Constance. Turning over the nearest carcass with a stick, she pointed to the silvery white feathers on the underside of the wings. 'If we had time for water-colour painting, I'd like to try to capture that splash of milkiness. And the beautiful curve of its beak. But to a lot of people the mutton bird is just a good source of meat. The Maori call it *titi*. In late summer they plunder the underground nests where the fledglings are, and sometimes seize the parent birds, too, when they come in with food at night. Brutal slaughter.'

'No more brutal, I suppose, than what we do to sheep and cattle,' said Frances, remembering Dr Hammond's first sermon.

Returning to their carriage, the party journeyed on past the estuary, a couple of miles further up the narrow winding coastal road in the direction of Seacliff, before turning across towards the steepening slopes of the Kilmog.

'It's another strange name, Kilmog,' said Grace as they looked up at those dark ridges. 'Borrowed from some Scottish place, is it?'

'One might think so,' said Constance. 'Like Kilmarnock. But no – in fact it's from a Maori word, I'm told. It refers to those tall solid manuka trees.'

'Splendid!' cried Isabella, with the clapping gesture that often accompanied her effusions. 'Those are the very trees I particularly want to sketch! I'm keen to capture the way the light seems to sink into that manuka foliage. Kilmog! Kilmog! Wonderful word, wonderful tree.'

The small side road taking them up the hillside was narrow and rutted, hardly more than a bridle path. The horses snorted in protest and the passengers murmured nervously, tilting one way and then the other.

'Not much further!' David called out, as they headed for an area where the track bent around a craggy outcrop and appeared to level out into a patch of shade. It looked to be a suitable spot for their purposes, a comfortable vantage point where they could spend an hour drawing. But before they reached it one of the horses, stumbling on the rough shingle surface, fell. The wagonette tipped suddenly sideways, crashed on its side, and hurled them all out down the stony slope.

Frances felt a sharp jab in her shoulder, and pain spread quickly into her neck. Reaching up instinctively to touch it seemed only to aggravate the ache, so she tried carefully to ease herself into a sitting position. Isabella and Constance, sprawled near her, were picking themselves up, and though dazed did not appear to be badly hurt. Further down the hillside was a plangent moaning and Frances could see Grace lying head down, her skirt half torn away and both legs twisted.

It took a long while for David and Isabella to carry Grace, barely conscious but crying out piteously, back up to the shady area. Frances, with her throbbing shoulder, could give them no help; nor could Constance, incapacitated by shock. A jag of bone jutted from one of Grace's bent legs, and her face was covered in blood still oozing from deep gashes in her forehead and cheekbones. Isabella knelt beside her, made an improvised pillow under her head and talked to her quietly. Unharnessing the calmer of the two horses, David led it down the rough track, assuring the women that as soon as he reached the safer coastal road he would ride hard to Waitati and seek a medical man.

Long hours later, as darkness began to close in, he returned with help. Grace, inconsolable in her distress, was carried down on a rough stretcher to the road. A pair of buggies waited to take them all to a house at the rear of the Waitati store for the night. No proper medical attention would be available until the following day. After a slow return journey to Dunedin, the doctor who examined Frances said that recovering the full movement in her shoulder would require rest and a comfrey poultice: she had cracked her collarbone, and there was also deep bruising. Still, she had come off lightly. Grace, she learned, would be confined to bed for months, might always have difficulty walking, and would carry disfiguring scars on her face.

Thirteen

Frances spent much of the Sunday and Monday in bed. On Tuesday afternoon, as she sat reading with her arm in a sling, she heard the knocker, and then a man's voice. Alice came into the sitting room to bring a card from the unexpected caller: Mr Stuart Donaldson was at the front door, and wished to know whether it would be convenient for Miss Phillips to receive him.

'Show him in, Alice.'

The ginger giraffe, she thought with a smile, remembering how his long neck with its wobbly Adam's apple seemed too scraggy for his collar, and how comical he looked with his carroty whiskers and the unruly wisps of hair above his large ears.

'Miss Phillips,' he said, entering with a stiff bow, 'pardon me for arriving without notice, but I heard only this morning about your party's alarming accident, and wanted to convey my sympathy to you in person without delay.'

'Very kind of you, Mr Donaldson,' she replied, gesturing to a chair, 'but – as you can see – there's really nothing much the matter with me. Nothing that rest won't remedy. I was fortunate. Just a sore neck and shoulder, uncomfortable but quite bearable. It's poor Mrs Hutton who deserves your sympathy. She's in a bad way, I fear.'

'Yes indeed, David Morrison reported that she continues to suffer terribly. The doctors have had trouble setting the bones, and they suspect the wound on one leg may be turning septic. But Mrs Hutton isn't known to me personally, whereas you are. Having thought often of our spirited conversation a few weeks ago at the Morrisons' dinner table, and then hearing just now that you yourself had come to harm, I felt impelled to visit you as soon as I could. I hope this is not presumptuous.'

'I wouldn't say presumptuous. A little surprising, I confess, because our acquaintance has been slight. But I do thank you for your concern.'

There was an awkward pause. Donaldson was stretching his arms forward in an odd way, so that the knobs of wrist bone strained outwards against his thickly freckled skin. He seemed to want to say something else, and she wondered what was on his mind. Why had he come?

'I see Browning's poetry remains in favour with you,' he said, pointing to the book she still held in her hand.

'Certainly. I was re-reading "My Last Duchess" when you came to the door. A most compelling portrait of a very sinister character – the poem's speaker, I mean. Do you know it?'

'I have read the poem, yes, but not recently.'

Nor with much interest or insight, evidently, thought Frances, as he made no further comment. There was another silence.

'Shall I ask Alice to make us a pot of tea?'

'No, no thank you. I…There was…There is a particular thing I want to mention, Miss Phillips.' He cleared his throat, crossed his legs, uncrossed them, glanced quickly at her and then inspected the carpet.

'Please speak freely,' said Frances, puzzled.

Donaldson began to stare intently at his hand, as if it might hold the text of what he needed to divulge.

'My dear Miss Phillips, since we met I've thought often about our conversation that evening. Your words made a deep impression on me. When I heard about your accident I felt a kind of sickness at the news that you'd been hurt. It made me realise at once that my...well, in short, that I've developed a strong affection for you. I hope that, when you've recovered, I may be granted the opportunity to have more of your company – to spend, in fact, a good deal of time with you...'

'Mr Donaldson,' Frances broke in, 'this is beginning to sound like a serious declaration. We've met on only one occasion.'

'Nevertheless, you would allow us, perhaps, to become better acquainted – when you're well enough to venture forth again? I thought we might enjoy a stroll together through the Botanic Gardens?'

Frances could not imagine enjoying any conversation any-where with this ungainly fellow. 'I must be frank, Mr Donaldson,' she said after a brief hesitation. 'Your words have startled me. On our previous meeting I didn't sense any special congeniality of temperaments. It would be false of me to encourage your sentiments.'

His patchy cheeks paled and then flushed.

'I'm sorry to hear it,' he responded stiffly, 'and sorry, too, if what I've said has been too forward, and not to your liking. I won't linger, but please take time to reconsider my invitation. I do have a respectable professional situation and a very substantial income.'

That note of haughtiness irritated her, but she held back the impulse to respond.

After he left, a sense of indignation filled her. Did he really imagine that she would regard greater material comfort and enhanced social status as alluring enough to cancel out personal indifference? Did he suppose that, because of her age, she would clutch at the chance of a marriage offer, no matter how uncom-panionable she might think him? Donaldson's visit had made one thing clear: while loneliness might be a dismal prospect, a mismatch was something she would never contemplate.

* * *

'But why Melbourne?' Frederick asked. 'If you must leave us for a while, need you go so far? Have you thought instead of Christchurch, or Nelson? We know good folk in both places, and it would be much easier for you to return here if the grass turned out not to be greener.'

'Of all people, Fred,' she said reproachfully, 'you should understand what draws me to Melbourne. It's not so very long since you went there yourself! And you came back with tales of what a vigorous, go-ahead place it is. I want to see a larger world than Dunedin, just as you did – and in the whole of the southern hemisphere there's nowhere that's growing with more speed and vigour than Melbourne.'

'But what exactly will you do there, and how long do you intend to stay?'

'No firm plans or timetables. If Melbourne disappoints, perhaps I may wish to go on elsewhere. I've enough funds in the bank to make further travel possible without fear of penury.'

'I trust,' said Frederick, contriving a droll expression to show he spoke in jest, 'that you have no ambition to rush around the world in eighty days!'

'I have no stomach for that kind of heroic solo effort. Though I'll confess that if I meet someone as energetic as Verne's Mr Fogg I may find the idea of such an expedition in his company quite irresistible.'

She did not mention that the serious injury to young Grace Hutton had somehow reinforced her determination to travel. She thought it had to do with the way their accident had dramatised the sheer fragility of one's wellbeing. A possible response to that heightened awareness might have been to reduce every risk, to live with safety as one's watchword. But for Frances the opposite impulse had emerged: she wanted to seize the day, to increase the scope of her experience, to go in search of her future.

There were other considerations too. At first her friendship with Isabella had seemed a good reason for staying: not only was there the pleasure of frequent contact, but through this lively woman she also had access to a much more stimulating circle than her church group. Yet Frances now saw that the self-confidence on which the lives of Isabella and David Morrison pivoted had much to do with the fact that they already knew well a world elsewhere, enabling them to inhabit Dunedin with an ease that combined grace with a sense of irony.

There was something further in the way Isabella spoke to her husband and daughters, or about them. At such moments her voice carried a loving timbre that made Frances feel peripheral to their family situation. Isabella's blood and David's ran together in the children's veins. For Frances there was no such current of intimacy, and she did not believe she could ever find it by remaining on the bleak edge of the southern ocean.

Nor could she draw any comparable emotional sustenance from the things that linked her to her brothers. With Edward she might perhaps have shared some literary and intellectual interests if he had been less aloof, less schoolmasterly. That peculiarly unpliant manner of his kept her at a distance. When he stepped stiffly along a path, shoulders lifted, his limbs seemed somehow to lack ordinary suppleness, as if jointed and jerked by string: duty's marionette. Fred, on the other hand, had always been warm towards her but they had little in common. He was comfortable, as she could never be, within the small enclosure of the local congregation, enjoying his position as Sunday School superintendent and the little churchy tasks that came his way. His recent marriage to Mary affirmed his contentment with this parochial sphere. For Frances it was intolerably restrictive, and she was intent now on leaving it.

Yet when she thought of flight it was not unshadowed. There was some apprehension, even an element of foreboding. One night she saw in a dream a multitude of dark heavy shapes gliding in from the sea as the last of the light faded away behind the hills. Landing all around her, they shuffled and staggered and stumbled their way through the scrubby rain-soaked bushes towards their burrows. She saw men with clubs leap up suddenly to grab the clumsiest of the young mutton birds and smash their skulls in a flurry of feathers and splintered bone. She could not hear, or remember, any sound from the birds that fell or the birds that flew away, but it seemed that the sea was groaning. Then the men threw the bodies into sacks, and left, and the blackness deepened. Near where she stood, the wet earth had been scraped and trampled into a sticky mire: 'the mud,' a voice whispered, 'kneaded up with blood'.

Part 4

Burlington, Plattsburgh,
Dannemora, 1864–72

Fourteen

When Will crossed the border into Vermont, the Civil War was within a year of its end. He had taken little interest in this confusion of quarrels; but though he had no inkling of danger at the time, the protracted warfare was already beginning to cast a long cold shadow across his path.

He had left La Chute with no plan beyond a general intention to sample some affordable pleasures in the nearest American states. The money in his purse would not last long, and if congenial opportunities for augmenting it came his way he would take them.

It was on a whim that he decided to travel south to Burlington. He remembered how the farmers of La Chute used to talk ruminatively about the early days when men came to their part of Quebec from the Champlain Valley region to manufacture potash. More recent reports told him that Burlington was now New England's largest lumber port, and he was keen to compare it with the log-laden wharves of Owen Sound, to see what benefits prosperity had brought to this town, and to keep an eye open for possible benefits of his own.

This was Will's first rail journey, and the speed of it astonished him. The train that he boarded in Montreal took him racketing to St Albans, then briskly on down the eastern shore of Lake Champlain to Burlington. As he moved along the forest-fringed track, bright October foliage dazzled him with its splendour. But the admirable scenery was not his main reason for coming this way; what he wanted most to see was the town.

It did not disappoint: a restless, bustling, clamorous, hasty place, abuzz with urgent commercial vigour. He spent much of his first week strolling along the streets, past the humming general stores, raucous grog shops and shabby shanties, past the lakeside factories, around the busy docks and the railroad station, where amazing quantities of lumber were being noisily hauled, stacked, loaded and unloaded.

And yet it was not the town alone that impressed itself on his attention. It was also the contrast: for softening all this hubbub were the peaceful surroundings of the township – the high hillside with its winding avenues, cool currents of air, and the homes of prosperous families scattered among the russet trees; the forest purlieu; the calm waters of the lake, and miles beyond the lake's far side the distant misted double ranges of the Adirondacks.

He took an idle boat trip down towards Fort Ticonderoga and was surprised by the changes of vista. The broadest part of Lake Champlain lay between Burlington and Plattsburgh. In its southern reaches it became narrower, more sinuous, with little river-like twists and turns. Returning to Burlington, he could see how the lake curved inward to form an elegant bay where it met the least elegant parts of the town.

Back at his hotel Will struck up conversation with a pale, morose man of about his own age, Thomas Brindle, who could talk of little else but how the war had maimed his body and his future. His shoulder had been shattered in the Battle of Chancellorsville, and kept him in constant pain. His right arm now dangling uselessly, he was not fit for the farming jobs he had known before enlisting.

'What good am I now to anyone?' Brindle asked dispirit-edly. 'What can a one-arm man hope for, eh? What chance a cripple got, marryin' and raisin' a family? Ain't nothin' ahead for me. Nothin'! Nothin'!'

Though Will could find no words to alleviate Brindle's misery of spirit, he did manage to provide some nocturnal relief of his pain. Obtaining supplies from the Burlington druggist, he prepared a liniment that combined a few grains of morphia and some alcohol, mixed with a little gum camphor and oil of cloves.

'I slep' sound firs' time in months!' Brindle told him the next morning. 'You're a magician, Dr Hammond.'

Will liked the sound of 'Dr Hammond', and saw no reason to disclaim the title. He had casually mentioned having written regular newspaper columns on medical botany, and if Tom Brindle interpreted this to mean that he was a qualified physi-cian, it would be pedantic to correct the assumption.

Then Brindle produced an appealing idea.

'With your skills, bein' a medical man,' he said, 'you oughta go across th' lake to th' Barracks. Plattsburgh Barracks. It's jus' a mil'tary hospital now. What I hear, they need someone like you. Plentya men there mangled by this tarnal war. Every kind of injury and illness. Army pays doctors well, but there ain't enough of them to care for th' sick soldiers sent back here – mos' are down south with th' regiments.'

Will wrote to the Surgeon at Plattsburgh Barracks to offer his services, and received a prompt and positive reply. Within a few days he boarded the two-masted schooner *Excelsior*, a fine long shapely vessel, which took him swiftly across into the sheltered space of Cumberland Bay. Disembarking near the mouth of the Saranac River as a light misty rain began to fall, he walked the muddy mile to the Barracks.

* * *

Within a week of his arrival Will could see trouble looming. The first sign of danger was that his supervisor, James Abernethy the Surgeon, turned out to be the sourest kind of drunkard. Will had always regarded fondness for strong drink as an indication of weak character, and in his eyes even a genial tippler like Jerome Davin forfeited respect. But Abernethy's moods were never genial. By noon there was usually a smell of whiskey on his breath and a grating harshness in his voice. In the afternoons he grew sullen and by evening he would sink into spiteful belligerence.

He insisted that Will play whist with him regularly after dinner, making up a foursome with Mrs Abernethy and the hospital matron, Nellie Dixon. During these sessions the tone of conversation, dominated by the sottish surgeon, was invariably unpleasant. Abernethy sneered at the younger man's teetotalism, mocked his mellifluous voice, laughed mirthlessly each time he dealt the pack.

Whist failed to engage Will's interest. He soon tired of the pastime and in particular his playing partner, the uncomely Nellie Dixon, who would grin at him in an over-familiar, ingratiating manner. Time and again it was necessary to remind her which suit was trumps. Indeed, she seemed hardly to heed the fall of the cards: he himself was the all too obvious object of her fawning attention. He told himself that she was not to blame for her lumpish thickset body, bulbous eyes and noisy breathing, but he felt oppressed nonetheless by the way she seem to soak up most of the air in the room.

Sitting directly opposite her at the small table as hour followed hour, evening after evening, he could not avoid meeting her eye much more often than was comfortable. If he looked instead to either side, there was Abernethy's large mottled nose with its fleshy flanges, or the meekly lowered head of Mrs Abernethy.

Daylight hours were generally more tolerable, though the

role of hospital steward proved to be no sinecure. His duties went well beyond attending to the sick. Being responsible also for the commissary storehouse and for procuring various supplies, he needed to deal with the local sutler, but quickly learnt not to count on him. It was difficult to obtain even fresh victuals, let alone an adequate supply of chemical drugs, herbal remedies and medical equipment. A half-acre hospital garden not far outside the grounds had plenty of fertile soil, but by the time Will took up his post the growing season was well past and he had to be economical with the store of dried plants harvested before his arrival. There was a further problem: the money available to him for hospital provisions was miserably insufficient, and although he pointed this out to Abernethy the financial situation did not improve.

Plattsburgh, he knew, was the place where more than a thousand recruits from Adirondack counties had been mustered into service as the New York 118th Volunteer Infantry Regiment. Now the main function of the Barracks was to minister to those men who, less than three years after enlisting so eagerly, had become mere particles in the pathetic debris of warfare. The wounds incurred by some of them were distressing to see: there were maimed limbs and lividly scarred heads. Will could hardly bear to look at one youth his own age, slumped in a corner of the ward. At twenty-four he had lost not only a leg but also half his face: metal had gouged its cruel path through jaw, cheek and eye-socket. Other men, wasted by diseases of the lungs or bowels, looked equally wretched. Injecting muriate of morphia was often the only thing he could do for many of them.

The limestone barracks buildings stood on a sandy plain a hundred yards from the lake. The commodious second-floor rooms, initially designed as dormitory quarters for enlisted men, served to accommodate the most seriously ill, who could be warmed by coal stoves while enjoying some light and ventilation from the window. Abernethy seldom had contact with the patients in his charge, and made it clear that he expected his steward to spend several hours each day monitoring their condition and keeping notes. As Will moved from bedside to bedside, he found his lack of medical training less of a hindrance than he had thought it might be. What most of the men needed was a warming conversation. This young hospital steward seemed to them a good listener and a sympathetic talker, someone who knew what to say, and how and when to say it. Words could sometimes ease the pain more effectively than any drugs.

But in the evenings it was different. There seemed to be a hostile edge to anything Abernethy addressed to him, and although Will tried not to let this trouble him it could hardly be ignored.

After putting up with weeks of provocation, Will spoke back. 'It appears, sir, that my manner displeases you in some way. Yet you continue to require my company at the card table. If you'd care to explain what you find unsatisfactory, perhaps I could make an effort to amend it.'

'Come now, Hammond, you're altogether too touchy! Anyone from Canada must expect to be met with suspicion and raillery around these parts, especially after the St Albans incident.'

'I have no idea what you're referring to.'

Abernethy snorted with scorn. 'No idea? No idea! Never heard of the northernmost action of this war? Never heard of it? The infamous raid on St Albans banks last October? They were recruited in Canada, you know. Disguised Confederate agents, robbed three of our banks and fled back across the border into Montreal. Cold-blooded killers – shot two townspeople during the robbery and tried to burn the whole place down!'

'Yes, I do recall now having heard something about the episode. I didn't take much notice of it.'

'A disgraceful action that *your* people aided and abetted. So don't act surprised when Lakeside folk show some rancour towards Canadians. We don't trust them. The bad blood goes back much earlier, too. You do know about the Battle of Plattsburgh Bay?'

'I confess I don't.'

'Well, we haven't forgotten, and we make sure the story stays alive. It was the turning point in our second War of Independence – 1814. Vermont and New York were under threat. But your Canadian provinces had taken the British side and sent thousands of troops from Montreal. Our brave men made a stand at Plattsburgh. We were outnumbered but we outfoxed you. Our modest ships were nimble enough in the bay to catch yours by surprise, killing the commander and forcing a quick surrender. Your infantry ran back to Canada, the renegade curs.'

Will started to protest that none of this had anything to do with him, but Abernethy waved a dismissive hand. 'Nothing more to be said,' he snapped, turning back to the cards in his hand.

One snowy evening a week later, as the weary ritual of whist came to an end, Nellie Dixon asked Will to walk her to her quarters in the next building.

'I wouldn't wish to trouble you, Dr Hammond,' she said coyly, 'except that the path is so slippery on a night like this and my ankle is a little sore from a stumble today. If I could just lean on your arm as far as my door...'

'Of course, Miss Dixon.'

As they reached her rooms, she drew closer to him and murmured lewdly that on such a cold night her bed could warm them both. Seizing his hand as she spoke, she placed it on her saggy breast.

Repelled as much by her effrontery as by her fetid breath, Will pulled sharply back and strode away without a word.

* * *

The next afternoon he was summoned by the commanding officer and informed of two grave accusations. He had brutally ravished the hospital matron, according to her own tearful testimony; and he had been embezzling army funds, a matter reported in a formal statement by Surgeon Abernethy.

Within a fortnight Will had been summarily tried on both charges. His protestations unheard, he was declared guilty, despite the lack of material evidence, and sentenced to six years of hard labour.

Fifteen

To the eyes of an increasingly sardonic observer like Will Hammond, Clinton Prison had become a travesty of the era's passion for profitability. Although mid-century North America was yet to feel the full surge of commercial and industrial growth, dominant voices in the country's north-eastern corner were already beginning to gauge public benefit in monetary terms. The longer Prisoner 5342 Hammond spent in the state penal system, the more it seemed to parody the venal values of the civilian economy that contained it.

Seventeen miles west of Plattsburgh, the village of Dannemora existed solely because of its prison, and the prison existed solely because of an optimistic estimate of the area's capacity to mine iron ore. Its purpose was to manufacture nails for the state, engaging its whole inmate population in this task. But things did not go smoothly and by the time Will arrived the expectation of financial success had become the butt of ridicule. The mining operations faced several unforeseen practical problems. Will soon found that the best source of information about these and all other prison matters was the chaplain – who for most of the time was in fact the only person with whom he could converse on any subject. Prisoners spent nights in separate cells and, though working in groups during the daytime, they were strictly forbidden to speak to one another. The chaplain, an affable Presbyterian minister who rejoiced in the name of Francis Bloodgood Hall and divided his time between Dannemora and Plattsburgh, had three duties: to conduct worship services every second or third Sabbath, to provide counsel to prisoners in their cells, and to supervise the use of the library. The cell visits and book-lending arrangements provided Will with the opportunity for conversation, which he cultivated assiduously.

Glad of the occasional company of someone intelligent and articulate, Rev. Hall ('Call me Frank') showed no reluctance to talk about the difficult situation in which Clinton Prison found itself. There were two essential requirements, he explained, to keep the bloomery furnace working steadily so that it could produce enough forgeable sponge iron for the rolling mill and nail factory. Those requirements were plenty of ore and plenty of power; but neither was actually plentiful.

'The ore supply has been a big disappointment,' said the chaplain. 'Within the tract allocated for prison use – more than 200 acres in all, and our part within the security walls only a tenth of it – the ore turns out to be more meagre than early reports promised. This is forcing the state to pay heavy rent to private interests for the privilege of working adjacent lands.

'And the energy source here has been just as troublesome,' he added, warming to his theme. 'That's because they got the location wrong. They should have sited the operations close to a river that could be dammed. The Saranac is five miles away – much too far. For other bloomeries around this region, a short sluiceway from a dam to a forge building will provide a good head of water to drive a waterwheel. But the furnace here must rely on steam power, and that's meant consuming a vast quantity of nearby woodlands for charcoal. It's taking longer and longer for the wagons to bring the felled timber here and the horses are quite as exhausted as the men.

'Then there have been other setbacks. Why, in the space of

the last couple of years, fires have destroyed a coal stockpile, a barn, a store, and eleven head of cattle. Already the authorities here are trying to develop other industries for contract labour. You've seen the footwear factory at the western end, near the tram rail? Twenty-five or thirty prisoners labour in that building now. But there's no profit in boots and shoes. This place is simply too remote to belong to a commercial system. All the state's major cities and towns are a great way off. Distance makes it as expensive for Clinton Prison to market what it produces as to bring in food and other supplies. It will come to this sooner or later, mark you: all the capital stock here will have to be put out for auction.'

Being young and strong, Will was set to work fetching charcoal in sacks from the storage bins and shovelling it into the fireboxes of the bloomery forges, day after day for most of his first year. It was a miserable grind, exhausting, hot, repetitive and filthy. But the physical discomfort galled him less than the apparent pointlessness of his toil. The buildings, the machines, the timber-felling, the cartage, the supervision, the conscripted labour – all this just to create *nails*! Yes, he could see that the country needed nails to hold together its expansive construction industry, its endlessly ramifying railroad tracks, but did it need the cumbersome apparatus of a prison to fill those innumerable cases of iron spikes?

As his time in Dannemora wore on, the sheer hardship gradually began to vex him. The bed in his cell was hard and sometimes damp. The food was always poor, the dirty clothing chafed his skin, and the water for washing was strictly rationed. For most of each year the cold bit into his flesh as soon as the day's labour ceased. Summer lasted but a few weeks, and the brief warmth it provided brought another kind of misery: the stench from excrement buckets in the corners of cells became nauseating to men and inviting to flies. Then, in the long winters, when the overnight temperature often dropped below freezing, sickness was common, with several cases of consumption.

As time dragged on, Will's simmering anger at the injustice of his imprisonment congealed into a resolution to avenge himself – but cleverly, calculatedly. Among his fellow prisoners there were plenty of cautionary examples of foolish impetuosity. In the next cell William Willis, a man whose name seemed a mocking derision of his own, had just begun a life sentence for murdering his sweetheart with a harness knife. 'I spent my savings on her,' Willis kept shouting into the corridor at night, defying the rule of silence, 'all my savings! – and then she went off with a dandy. Went off! Just went *off*! But I caught up with her. Caught *right up*!'

Most of the prisoners ranged from the imbecilic to the vicious, and would have been hardly capable, Will guessed, of expressing rational thoughts in civil terms. The most seriously threatening among them was a brawny ruffian known simply as Piggot, whose whole demeanour seemed to convey a pugnacious challenge to anyone in his sight. From time to time, whatever task he was engaged in, Piggot would suddenly let out a snarling guttural noise, like the yawl of a wild animal. The whisper was that the war had made him crazy and he had shot his own brother at Salem Heights. Everyone tried to give him as wide a berth as possible.

When Will was ordered to haul coal on a trolley from the coal house to the engine room he found that his fellow hauler was the formidable Piggot, who glared and grunted as they toiled together. One afternoon the supervising guard was called away urgently to the nearby southern gate where a supply wagon had broken its axle, blocking the entrance to the inner part of the prison.

'You keep that tarnal trolley moving, you two!' he called over his shoulder as he walked away. 'I'll be back here very shortly, so don't think of anything foolish.'

As soon as the guard was out of earshot, Piggot seized his chance and turned towards Will with a hostile grunt.

'I know about your part in the St Albans raid,' he rasped, thick fingers flexing and unflexing.

'My part? I had no part in it, none at all. You're mistaken.'

'Don't try to deny it, you filthy son of a bitch! I've heard what you did. Word spread here from Plattsburgh. The Barracks. You're a Canadian, you bastard. You were part of the damned gang that planned it.'

Suddenly Piggot lunged at him, thick arms swinging. Though taller, and well built, Will was taken by surprise and could not fend off the flurry of blows. Piggot's big slab of a fist caught him hard under the eye and he staggered back, gripping his hulking assailant's sleeve so that they fell heavily together. Will lay underneath with Piggot's elbow in his face as half a dozen guards came running. They whacked at the two men with their truncheons, pulling them away from each other. Will's eye had begun to swell and his lip was bleeding.

Both men were deemed to share the blame for fighting. Shackled, Will was led off to a foul-smelling dungeon cell and immured there alone for two days without food or light, his arms strapped at shoulder level, his toes just touching the floor, and his clothes soaked by jets of chilling water from a hose. A deep sense of grievance gnawed at him.

Sixteen

In all of Clinton the only one with whom Will could sense any affinity was the chaplain, and for much of his first year of imprisonment he would often talk to Frank Hall about his wrongful conviction. Listening to Will's repeated and vehement protestations, Hall, a fair-minded man, began to form the view that there might indeed have been some kind of miscarriage of justice. Back in Plattsburgh he made discreet enquiries, and while one source suspected that the cunning Abernethy had siphoned government money for his own purposes while throwing the blame on Hammond, no evidence emerged. As for the barracks matron, Nellie Dixon, there were rumours that Hammond was not the first man she had accused of forcing himself upon her – but even if so, it wasn't enough to prove him innocent. All in all there was no solid basis for seeking to have his case reviewed, and Hall conveyed this regretfully to the prisoner. Though Will took the dispiriting news with a semblance of equanimity, his mood was furious. But none of his silent anger flowed towards Hall, whose sincerity and good intentions could not be doubted.

The Reverend Francis Bloodgood Hall was earnestly proud of his middle name, which came from his mother's family; and Will thought it an amusingly fitting epithet for such a well-bred worthy. Bloodgood: there was an almost allegorical ring to it, as if he had stepped from the pages of Bunyan. Will liked this

affable man, liked talking with him, and liked such odd man-
nerisms as his habit of fingering his throat while he spoke, as if
to guide the passage of air into the shifting shapes of his words.'

Through the chaplain a prisoner could have access at certain times to the small library, in which almost all the books
and pamphlets were on pious topics. As few of the Clinton men
were literate and even fewer studiously inclined, Will was almost
alone in taking advantage of this privilege. After a few months
he asked Frank Hall for a particular favour.

'I wonder, sir, whether you'd be so kind as to try to obtain
for my use in the library a certain literary work – a long poem?'

'I don't see why not, if it's from the hand of a respectable
writer, morally improving.'

'It is indeed: William Wordsworth's autobiographical poem,
The Prelude. Very large work, published some years ago as a
single volume. Used to be on my teacher's desk in the little classroom I sat in as a boy. Perhaps it's still procurable, and there'd
be much pleasure for me – instructive pleasure – in being able to
hold it in my hand.'

'Well, I'm not familiar with that particular composition,
but from what I do know of Wordsworth's poetry and reputation
I presume it would be suitable reading, yes. The sentiments of
the "Immortality Ode" are very fine. I'll enquire about having a
copy of *The Prelude* sent to me from a bookseller acquaintance
in New York.'

When at last the book arrived, Frank Hall allowed Will
to keep it in his cell. He read it with a kind of hunger, falling
ravenously on the imagery of physical liberty in its opening lines.
Some of the phrases continued to stir under his breath like a
muted incantation: 'free, / Free as a bird to settle where I will...'
Meikle's compelling voice sounded in his ears as it had done
years before.

Turning the pages slowly, Will became absorbed in the

story's leisurely yet intense unfolding, in how it conveyed the momentum of a mind in search of something – ultimately, of itself. Much of it, he recognised, had the shape of an uncertain journey, a journey that gathered several different kinds of movement, and his own enforced immobility made him feel these differences with a painful acuteness. He saw that the poet-traveller described himself ambiguously near the outset – 'Keen as a truant or a fugitive / But as a pilgrim resolute'; and that towards the end of the long wayfaring narrative he was still irresolute, equivocal about the meaning of it all, looking back on a tale 'of lapse and hesitating choice, / And backward wanderings among thorny ways.'

* * *

As a general rule, prisoners at Dannemora were not permitted to send or receive letters directly, but the chaplain could act as postman on behalf of the few who attended his worship services. Will wrote to his brothers, letting them know about his plight and seeking news of their own circumstances. A reply came eventually from George, who reported having been kept busy in regular work for nearly a year, carting supplies from the Owen Sound wharf to surrounding farms; but he added that he was worried about young Stewart, who had fallen victim to the influence of a Jesuit priest. George had chanced to witness them in an indecent act. And this was the same priest, said George, who sternly admonished boys at the school to keep their minds and bodies pure.

A whited sepulchre, thought Will. He knew to be wary of churchmen, yet they had power. In his own situation, he was dependent on the chaplain if he wanted to surmount the rule of silence. Only through the filter of religiosity, and only by special arrangement, were prisoners' voices permitted to be audible. A weekly session with the chaplain in their cells, ostensibly for the purpose of prayer and penitential meditation, was one possibility. The conversations soon moved to other topics.

'I witnessed enough suffering in the sick ward at Plattsburgh Barracks,' said Will, 'to convince me that battlefields reduce men to a brutish condition. Anyone who inflicts such terrible pain is as much degraded as the one who incurs the injury. Wanton violence of that kind disgusts me. Nothing can justify it.'

'War is cruel, certainly,' Frank Hall agreed. 'I've seen it at close quarters in the Chancellorsville campaign. There were things I'll never forget. Maimed young bodies. Unspeakably horrific wounds, and the stink from scorched flesh.'

'So how hard was it, then, to hold on to your faith in divine providence?'

'Oh, never shaken. Never. What I experienced during that time made me feel all the more keenly how necessary it is to put our trust in an all-seeing God. If there were not a loftier vista than ours, a luminous perspective that has its divine source far above our shambles, then human life would be a pitiful thing indeed. I recall one chilly night. I was sleepless and left my tent to walk up to a hilltop overlooking the waters of the Rappahannock. An unclouded sky. Everything lay still and calm in the moonlight. There was a light mist beginning to rise from the river, and it mingled with wisps of smoke drifting along from a rebel encampment on the other side. For the few minutes that I stood watching that silvery scene, I felt I'd glimpsed something larger than time, something that surmounted our little world of folly and suffering.'

Will smiled. 'Transcendence,' he said. 'Transcendence. Your anecdote echoes lines written by someone who had a visionary revelation very much like yours.'

Reaching under his pillow, he pulled out *The Prelude*, soon found the passage he was looking for, and read it aloud:

'The Moon hung naked in a firmament
Of azure without cloud, and at my feet
Rested a silent sea of hoary mist...
There I beheld the emblem of a mind
That feeds upon infinity, that broods
Over the dark abyss, intent to hear
Its voices issuing forth to silent light
In one continuous stream; a mind sustained
By recognitions of transcendent power...'

'Hammond, you're an astonishing fellow! A prisoner who can immerse himself in such fine poetry, and can talk of subtle things. You don't belong here, man! You have special talents. You should be using them out there in society, as a doctor or a teacher.'

'I'm not here by choice. Nor through any just process.'

'I know, I know. I'll try again. I'll see what I can do.'

Seventeen

Towards the end of Will's third year of incarceration, Hall brought two companions along to attend one of the chapel services: his wife Fanny and another Plattsburgh parishioner, Miss Amelia Temple. They returned a couple of months later, and again after a similar interval. On these occasions a prisoner could, under the watchful eye of guards, mingle with the visitors for a few minutes at the end of the service. Will sought out particularly Miss Temple, a slight bespectacled woman with a shy lisp and a wistfully wavering smile, who seemed delighted to find in this place such a well-spoken man, not only mannerly but also appreciative of the fact that she and Mrs Hall took the trouble to make the uncomfortable journey from Plattsburgh to join the prisoners in worship. Her usual reticence dissolved and she soon began to describe to him the slow jolting progress of the double buggy that had brought them to Dannemora. After listening patiently, Will asked whether Miss Temple would kindly alleviate his 'terrible isolation' and keep his mind 'fixed on spiritual matters' by writing letters of encouragement to him from time to time.

* * *

C/- Peristrome Presbyterian Church
Plattsburgh
18 November 1866

Mr William Hammond, Prisoner 5342
Clinton Prison
Dannemora, NY
Dear Mr Hammond,
Mrs Hall and I were very pleased indeed to meet
you after the recent prison chapel service and to
hear about your efforts to maintain your study of
the scriptures and other devout habits despite your
present circumstances. It is particularly encouraging
for the work of our Prisoners' Aid Society to find
that some men at the Dannemora institution, such
as yourself, are already persuaded that the Lord can
sustain them through their time of trouble and lead
them in the paths of righteousness.

Any soul may stumble from time to time; but
His forgiveness, if sincerely sought, will lift the
sinner up again. May the Saviour's Word be a lamp
unto your feet.

I trust that, with the guidance of Rev. Hall, you
will continue steadfast in your faith and penitence
so that when your sentence has expired you can re-
enter society with a cleansed spirit.
Your sister in Christ,
Amelia Temple

Correspondence with Miss Temple continued throughout the
remainder of Will's time in prison. It was easy for him to
attune his language to her formal solemn tone, and to express
enthusiasm for causes that she espoused, such as the Temperance
Union.

Despite their predictability, he liked to read the neatly penned pages that she wrote to him. Each letter, with its demure twitches, was a small bird flitting into his cell – somewhat drab, like a house finch, but welcomed as an envoy from an unconfined world.

* * *

Apart from Miss Temple's letters and Wordsworth's poems, Will had little to distract him from the discomfort and tedium of prison life. Few of the library books engaged his interest, and by the fourth year conversations with the chaplain had become repetitive. During the day there was little respite from heavy physical effort. His chores changed from time to time, and the months he spent in a woodcutting squad, swinging an axe in the fresh air, lifted his spirits – until one of the guards began to taunt him because of his fair hair and blue eyes. Will knew better than to show any reaction, let alone retort; he had seen men flogged mercilessly for 'impudence' and made to work faster and harder than anyone could bear for long. He had seen men maim themselves to avoid the endless cycle of toil and exhaustion, deliberately cutting off their own fingers with an axe, or slicing through their heel tendon. Some found in music a simpler way to lighten their load and circumvent the ban on speaking to one another. Groups sang popular ditties as they worked. These could help a man forget his aching arms and back for a while, forget the dark red blisters.

A trio of blacks sang as they laboured alongside Will, felling timber. The words drooped plaintively and the tempo stretched out to fit the measured movements of arms and feet:

I'm just a p-o-o-o-r wayfaring stranger
A-travelling through (ooh-ooh) this world of woe;
And there's no sickness, no toil or danger

In that bright world to which I go...
I want to sing salvation's story
In concert with (ah yes) the blood-washed band;
I want to wear the crown of glory
When I get home to Beulah land...

* * *

Will found in the library something that gave shape to his plans
for life after prison. It was a new publication, commended to him
enthusiastically by Frank Hall: *The Abominations of Modern
Society*, a series of sermons by the famous New York preacher
Thomas Talmage.

'I knew Tom when we both served as Union chaplains
during the war,' Hall told him. 'Thomas De Witt Talmage, now
a Doctor of Divinity. After the conflict ended, Tom began to
draw huge numbers as a preacher in New York City, and became
pastor about three years ago to the Central Presbyterian Church
in Brooklyn, where they erected for him a large building known
as the Tabernacle. A couple of months ago it was burned down,
and even though they're constructing another designed to hold
no less than five thousand persons, it's said that this may be
unable to contain the crowds. When he preaches, so I'm told, the
streets around are thronged with people for hours beforehand,
and carriages can't pass.'

The opening pages caught Will's attention at once and he
read on, engrossed, admiring the theatrical appeal of Talmage's
rhetoric and imagining its impact on those pleasurably shocked
audiences. From the pulpit, declaimed by a gifted orator who
knew well how to wring passion from every little inflexion of
voice and gesture, his words would have thrilled the hearts of all
who heard them.

The book's first chapter, or sermon, was called 'The Curtain

Lifted', and its Gothic extravagance made Will smile even as he acknowledged how enticing it was:

> I open to you a door, through which you see – what? Pictures and fountains, and mirrors and flowers? No: it is a lazar-house of disease. The walls drip, drip, drip, with the damps of sepulchres. The victims, strewn over the floor, writhe and twist among each other in contortions indescribable, holding up their ulcerous wounds, tearing their matted hair, weeping tears of blood; some hooting with revengeful cry; some howling with a maniac's fear; some chattering with idiot's stare; some calling upon God; some calling upon fiends; wasting away; thrusting each other back; mocking each other's pains; tearing open each other's ulcers; dropping with the ichor of death! The wider I open the door, the ghastlier the scene. Worse the horrors. More desperate recoils. Deeper curses. More blood. I can no longer endure the vision, and I shut the door, and cover my eyes, and turn my back, and cry, 'God, pity them.' ...
>
> However pleasant the block of houses in which you dwell, the wretchedness, the temptation, and the outrage of municipal crime will put its hand on your door-knob, and dash its awful surge against the marble of your doorsteps, as the stormy sea drives on a rocky beach.

Will put the book aside and stared into his future. I could do something like this, he thought. I have a strong voice, a ready tongue. I have the knack of holding a crowd's attention. The Jesuits taught me well the twin languages of hope and fear that can clutch hearts and make feelings vibrate. It's a skill I can use for my own purposes. Not on a big stage like Talmage – little congregations here and there will be easy to impress.

He thought bitterly of how the churchgoers in La Chute had turned their backs on his mother in her distress. He would not hesitate to prey on their counterparts elsewhere. 'To me belongeth vengeance and recompense; their foot shall slide in due time.'

Yes, he knew there were also many decent, good-natured Christian men and women, like the Halls and Amelia Temple. But their lives were comfortable. For them there had been no struggle to be virtuous. Was it to Frank Hall's own credit that he was earnestly sincere, a paragon of 'good works'? Not at all, in Will's opinion. He knew that this minister had independent means and never needed to work for a living. Lacking that kind of birth-luck, Will resolved to *acquire* the means of independence for himself, by his own wit and determination.

The Prisoners' Aid Society in Plattsburgh, if he played his cards carefully, could be very useful to him. He would need money after his release to set him on his way, and Amelia Temple seemed a likely helper. His letters to her were patiently laying a foundation for that assistance.

* * *

More than a year before Will was due to be liberated, the chaplain made a submission on his behalf to the warden.

'Prisoner 5342 Hammond,' he wrote, 'has shown himself to be a reformed character, and a firm adherent to the Christian faith. Remission of the remainder of his term here would enable this exceptionally intelligent, talented man to contribute in a positive way to society. I vouch for him, and urge that a special dispensation be granted for his early release.'

* * *

His first day as a free man was spent in stinging wind and rain as he trudged and stumbled the long miles from the prison gates to Plattsburgh. Hall, riding beside him, was cheerful and chatty, but Will remained withdrawn. Grateful though he felt for the minister's intervention to gain his freedom, this could not staunch a resurgent sense of rancour towards those whose false testimony had sent him to Clinton – rancour not just towards James Abernethy and Nellie Dixon as individuals but also more generally towards the kind of people they seemed to represent: those with power to damage others and profit from their vulnerability.

He opened his hand and stared at the jagged scar. It would always remind him of what others had done to him and his mother; and whenever he looked at it, his determination to seek recompense rose up again. He had settled the score with Burly Charlie; Abernethy, he knew, had recently drunk himself to death; Nellie Dixon had left Plattsburgh. They were no longer the particular objects of his smouldering resentment. He would suck the juice from whatever fruit he could pick.

Part 5

Melbourne, 1890

Eighteen

Throughout the voyage she cowered in her damp cabin, feeling utterly wretched and alone. It was not only the violent sickness in her stomach and the inescapable bone-chilling cold; a sudden uncertainty about the meaning of this journey was also making her ill. The gusting westerly had ripped away her sense of purpose. What if Melbourne was going to be, after all, no more than a change of scene? Was it some kind of imaginable goal, the end of a pilgrimage? Or if not a final destination, would it perhaps represent a wayfaring stage in a larger, less definite quest for...*what*?

* * *

Clamour everywhere around her, flurries of wind and traffic, mud underfoot, throngs of hurrying people – the roads and footpaths of the city were all bustle, pungent smells and rowdy haste. Frances gripped Miss Shacklock's elbow tightly as they waited at the corner for a space to clear between the carriages so that they could cross safely. Further up Bourke Street there was a sudden commotion as a horse slipped and fell on the wet cobbles, bringing down its hansom cab with a fearful crash. The wretched animal threshed around convulsively, kicking and twisting its neck from side to side, its desperate cries mingling with the shouts of bystanders.

Frances could not bear to look or linger. The accident was a sickening reminder of what happened near Blueskin Bay; and besides, the crowded streets oppressed her, the weather had turned sour, and Ethel Shacklock was not the most congenial of associates. Frances insisted that they retrace their steps to the tramway line and travel back to Carlton. Later, in the drab seclusion of her little room, she took a sheet of paper and began to write.

Composing the first letter took only a few minutes. There was little she could report to Mary and Fred except church matters: she told them what she had heard about the emergence of young congregations in Malvern, Brunswick, Richmond and Fitzroy; and about the growing Sunday School numbers at the local Temperance Hall. She mentioned church folk who, having befriended Fred during his time in Melbourne, wished to be remembered to him – Samuel Wilkins, the Vercoes, the Burbidges, and a few others. She allowed herself only a brief remark on Miss Shacklock's lodging-house: 'It has the smell of pious thrift.' Even that mild gibe, she thought, would seem impolite in their eyes, and so she did not elaborate. Fred and Mary were good people but it would puzzle them to know many of the things that engaged her mind. So with a few perfunctory words about good health and bad weather, and an affectionate formula, she brought the message to a close.

In her other letter Frances felt able to write from the heart. She yearned for Isabella's companionship, but there was consolation in being able to share unguarded thoughts with her on paper. She could describe Miss Shacklock's firm policy of preserving a demeanour of relentless cheerfulness and letting no-one admit to any other feeling. Living in the Shacklock house, Frances told Isabella, was like being confined in a cage with a chirpy little canary, but one that lacked any colourful plumage or tuneful variation. Her landlady's favourite maxim, repeated emphatically on all possible occasions, was 'We must never succumb to discouragement!' This meant admonishing the frail and needy, when distributing food and garments to them on behalf of the Ladies' Endeavour, about the importance of a sunny spirit. She took it as Frances's obvious duty to participate in prayer meetings at the Christian Chapel in Lygon Street and sessions of the Dorcas Society sewing circle. 'I feel almost coerced,' Frances told Isabella. 'There's an air of self-applauding rectitude about her that irritates me greatly.'

The church people she mixed with did, she admitted, alleviate her sense of isolation, and in general were less dour and inward-looking than those in the Tabernacle congregation in Dunedin. At the Lygon Street chapel the singing was hearty and the mood friendly enough, but the preacher, Mr Bignill, would never set the Yarra River on fire: a slow-speaking elderly man of benign disposition, he interpreted the Scriptures with meticulous attention to detail and seemed always to choose his words fastidiously, as if picking up each one between thumb and forefinger and holding it toward the light of exposition.

Frances told Isabella she had started to re-read *The Ring and the Book* in the melancholy knowledge that only through being read by others could Browning's voice now resonate – or rather, his many voices. What a strange restless ventriloquist he had been! *The Argus* had recently carried a report of his burial in Westminster Abbey.

Her walking, she confessed, was becoming a kind of compulsion. Some days she would stride along for miles, only half-aware of her surroundings, haphazard in the turnings she took. The tramway allowed her to venture to different parts of the city and suburbs at a whim, and to walk in an aimless fashion from wherever she alighted. And so she found herself in diverse places – the Flagstaff Gardens, or the markets, or the riverside, or sooty streets with huddled houses – without having consciously made her way there. She told herself that the exercise was beneficial for the body, and would lift her spirits, and that Melbourne was a fascinating city to be exploring in this way; yet she felt too that there was something unhealthy about all this meandering.

She closed the letter with 'Your unsettled friend, Frances.'

That evening she turned again to *The Ring and the Book*, where she had marked her place. Before beginning to read Pompilia's monologue, she stared trance-like for some minutes at the bookmark she had bought in Cole's Arcade, an advertisement for Pears' soap. It depicted a man's hand holding a quill and inscribing the phrase 'matchless for the complexion' on a parchment. Matchless, her mind murmured. Never met his match. Not a good match. No match for her.

The next day Miss Shacklock announced that they should spend the morning at the Temperance Hall with the Dorcas Society. Frances excused herself on the grounds of needing to attend to some banking and postal matters in the city, and wanting to read the latest newspapers from New Zealand in the public library. In truth her main reason was that an urge to roam alone had again become irresistible.

As the day remained overcast and cold she could comfortably keep up a steady pace for long periods, pausing only once for refreshment during the morning at a small Bourke Street tearoom, and once in the afternoon at the Book Arcade. Apart from those brief rests, she rambled on through the busiest streets and the quieter lanes, to and fro, never far from the centre of the city, engrossed in her singularity, as if in search of an address lost within herself.

The greyness of the sky made street scenes look like smudged charcoal drawings in a sketchbook. Despite the cold weather the stench from open drains was inescapable, and often she had to hold a handkerchief to her nose as she walked. Rats skittered furtively down alleys. The streets were filthy with dung and loud with the shouts of workmen. Teams of horses lumbered past her, leaning into the wind as they dragged wagons laden with huge blocks of stone towards the sites of half-shaped public buildings. From an elm tree in Collins Street a thick-necked crow watched her with an air of suspicion, reminding her of Wilkins, the saturnine black-whiskered deacon at the Carlton chapel: she could picture the way he always stood near its entrance after a worship service, chin sunk into his jowls and hands clasped behind him so that his arms were like dark folded wings.

The dismal prospect of a spinsterish future preoccupied Frances. She shuddered at the thought that perhaps some people already saw her as drifting into the same emotionally meagre state as Ethel Shacklock. Matchless, in the most pathetic sense. Perhaps she had been too quick to dismiss Donaldson's clumsy overture? But no – she could never have persuaded herself even to like him.

She walked on and on, this way and that, to avoid a life of waiting.

Nineteen

It was later the same day, in Bourke Street, as she felt the coal dust thickening in her throat and began to think wearily of returning to her lodgings, that she first encountered Bella.

What caught her attention was a group of young larrikins, banging on pieces of tin and shouting a raucous parody of 'Onward Christian Soldiers'. She saw that they surrounded a pale flustered young woman in Salvation Army uniform. As Frances drew nearer, the woman looked at her with a silent appeal, and Frances ran forward, calling out sharply to the gang: 'How dare you! Let her be! You should be ashamed of yourselves!' Their rude raillery stopped. They shambled away, scowling and muttering. One of them spat at the ground as he left.

'Thank you, Miss,' said the young woman, touching her on the arm. Frances saw that there were tears in her eyes. 'I suppose I must learn to bear ridicule from such…such scamps. I'm a new recruit – and I never expected the uniform would make some people so hostile.'

'Yet you belong to an army – and armies exist to wage war, do they not?' said Frances, smiling gently. 'War requires hostile forces, surely.'

'But Satan is the real enemy,' the woman responded, 'not our fellow men. My name, anyhow, is Bella – Bella Brotchie. Thank you again for coming to my rescue. I was so frightened.'

'I'm pleased to meet you, Bella, and very glad I came along at a useful moment. Frances Phillips.'

They found a coffee stall nearby and stood there together for some while, exchanging parcels of personal information. Frances sketched her own story briefly. In much more detail, Bella related how she had come to Melbourne a year previously from Geelong, just after her seventeenth birthday. Her father, she said, was an itinerant farm worker who for months at a time left them to fend for themselves; and although her mother tried hard to put food on the table in his absence by helping at the counter of the local store, the four children often went hungry. As the eldest, Bella had decided to move to Brighton, where a cousin knew of a place for her as a domestic servant. But this situation lasted only a couple of months: the man living next door to her employer had taken advantage of her, she said, and when her disgrace became known she was summarily dismissed. Too ashamed to return home, and desperate for money, she had drifted into a 'house of accommodation' frequented by men.

'This went on,' said Bella, 'until one night when I sought food from the Salvation Army shelter. The officers there persuaded me to abandon my sinful ways completely and give my life to Jesus. So here I am now, a soldier of the cross myself. I want to work with the Army to help others. They have a special Missing Persons office, you know – the "hallelujah detectives", looking into reports from families trying to trace a loved one's whereabouts. I hope they'll let me join that office when I've done the proper training for it.

'Anyhow, we held one of our marches this afternoon, and I was just starting to make my way homeward when that group of ruffians began to sneer and to revile me. I'm afraid one of them may have recognised me as someone who used to be...less respectable. It's terrible to think that my past wretchedness can reach out at any moment and grip me tight.'

Frances murmured some words of reassurance, hiding as best she could her perturbation at knowing that earnest simple-hearted Bella had been one of those women who let her favours become merchandise in ways that seemed hardly imaginable. For Frances it was a disquieting experience, and she found herself recalling her brother Edward's stern prediction of the dangers that a city like Melbourne presented to a single woman.

It would be several weeks before she saw Bella Brotchie again. Their next encounter was near the same spot in Bourke Street, but Frances did not at first recognise her. Gone was the uniform and the open manner; instead Bella wore a cheap gaudy dress and her cheeks were brightly rouged. When their eyes met, Bella at once lowered her head and turned quickly away, but Frances, though shocked, hurried after her and laid a hand on the younger woman's arm.

'Bella! It's Frances. I'm sure you remember. There's been a change in you. Are you no longer with the Salvationists?'

'You shouldn't be talking with me, Miss. It must be obvious I've returned to what I was. Your reputation will be harmed if anyone sees us together.'

'I'm less concerned about my reputation, Bella, than about what has led you into this backsliding. Just a couple of months ago you seemed to be happy in your calling as a Christian soldier. Tell me what happened, please.'

The girl's resistance was soon overcome and Frances took her into nearby tearooms, ignoring the murmurs of disapproval from some tables. Bella was silent for a while, eyes down, but having warmed her hands around the teacup and gratefully eaten most of a plate of cucumber sandwiches, she began to tell Frances what had come to pass since their previous conversation.

'It was loneliness,' she explained. 'Loneliness, and also seeing plainly that although Jesus may have wiped my sins away the people around me would never forget what I'd been and done, or let me forget. This was made all too clear to me one evening – just after you and I met, it must have been. I was standing with a senior Army officer, Major Barnes it was, outside a hotel, collecting money for our work with the poor and handing out leaflets. A rough-looking man came out of the hotel, very drunk, and walked right up to us. I knew who he was. He recognised me, and stood close to me and, laughing, grabbed my breast, right there in the street, saying very loudly something insolent about...about what I used to do with him. Major Barnes pushed him away and we left the area at once, but it was mortifying to know that the Major had been so crudely reminded of my past misdeeds.

'The incident made me lonely, Miss, desperately lonely. It made me see that I could never be quite accepted by decent people. And there was something else – I'm sure you'll think this utterly shameful, but it's the truth – I began to feel, too, that by cutting myself off from my life of harlotry I had lost the solace of physical contact with men. Since renouncing the sins of the flesh, I found my nights had become long and empty. Even ungentle hands can bring us a kind of pleasure, Miss Phillips.'

That evening, as Frances undressed in her sombre little bedroom, her thoughts remained fixed on what Bella had told her about the life of a streetwalker. Looking shyly at her own nakedness in the dressing-table mirror, Frances could not quell the image that came suddenly to mind: the shadow of a man standing close behind her own pale body, with one hand on her breast and the other holding gold coins.

Twenty

At Ethel Shacklock's urging, Frances accompanied her the next day to a Ladies' Endeavour meeting, and there, among the trickles of trivial chatter and gossip, she overheard a name that made her heart lurch.

'Did you know,' one stout dame asked another, 'that Brother Hammond – the doctor – is back in town? A most impressive preacher, he is.'

'Eloquent, certainly,' the other responded, 'and a striking presence – though a bit too severe in manner for my liking. Not much warmth that I could see. No, I hadn't heard of his return. It must be almost two years since he left here for New Zealand. So has he been called now as evangelist to one of our city's congregations?'

'Not to my knowledge. But Gladys Haberfield did tell me that her church in Brunswick has arranged for him to preach next Sunday morning. He has a number of admirers in that Glenlyon Road group.'

Frances kept her head lowered, feeling a sudden giddiness. It was an effort to breathe calmly but no-one seemed to have noticed her startled reaction. The conversation moved on past her.

Sunday came at last, a mild fine spring day, and with the help of a Brunswick cable tram she made her way to the sturdy brick chapel, arriving early and sliding into a rear pew. Only a few others were already seated, but the rows soon filled. And then there he was, the tall strong figure she knew so well. He entered with two women of about her age and they sat near the front.

The worship service began briskly with the usual sequence of prayers, hymns and scripture readings, after which the doctor was welcomed to the pulpit – 'our esteemed brother in Christ, Dr William Hammond, a world traveller, known to many here today as a gifted physician who ministers to spiritual as well as physical needs...'

All eyes were upon him as he began his address, the words unhesitating though he spoke without notes. His own eyes seemed to be on each person present, simultaneously holding them in that stern encompassing gaze she remembered so well. Frances willed him to look at her particularly, to see her as an individual, not just as one of the flock. Whether he recognised her sitting at the back she could not tell.

He took his scriptural text from the book of Ezekiel: the account of the wrathful message delivered to Egypt's Pharaoh, foretelling terrible desolation that would cover the sun and moon and stars with a dark cloud, making the people tremble in fear of their lives.

'Brethren and sisters, we are also living in a trembling world – a world riven by shock after shock. This is true of the sudden reversals that have lately afflicted our social order and our economic fortunes, but it is salient in our physical sur-roundings as well. Some of the most violent natural cataclysms in recorded history have occurred within the last few years, not far from where we are gathered at this moment. Our part of the planet has been profoundly shaken by the huge volcanic upheavals of Krakatoa just north of this country, and Tarawera to the east. The former exploded with such devastating force that thousands of people were hurled at once into eternity, and dark clouds of ash filled the skies over much of the earth. The latter destroyed instantly New Zealand's wondrous Pink and White Terraces, acknowledged far and wide to have been one of the greatest marvels of divine creation.

'Such terrible events must make each of us feel like John Bunyan's pilgrim confronted by Apollyon the Destroyer, and, as if echoing Christian's desperate cry, one's own inner voice exclaims in lamentation, *What shall I do?*

'Fellow disciples, do you have a personal sense of being perched precariously on the rim of a fiery crater? Are you anxious about your spiritual security? Is the very ground of your existence shuddering beneath you? That is the relentless action of God on the soul. He reminds us that, in the words of Paul's epistle to the Philippians, each of us must work out our own salvation with fear and trembling.'

To Frances it seemed that the doctor's words were coursing through her veins. Then he spoke more quietly, almost tenderly.

'My dear friends, let us remember also that this God of ours does not always manifest His power in such fearsome and formidable ways. Alongside that stern story from Ezekiel, we can now place a very different episode. Recall the experience of the prophet Elijah, when he stood upon the mount of Horeb before the Lord. Here is the passage in chapter nineteen of the first book of Kings...'

There was an expectant hush as Hammond opened the Bible that lay before him on the lectern, and found the page.

'I read from verses 11 to 12:

'And behold, the Lord passed by, and a great and strong wind rent the mountains, and brake in pieces the rocks before the Lord; but the Lord was not in the wind: and after the wind an earthquake; but the Lord was not in the earthquake: And after the earthquake a fire; but the Lord was not in the fire: and after the fire a still small voice.

'It was through this quiet voice of calm authority that the Lord then instructed his prophet Elijah what should be said and done. We should keep that always in mind. God has many voices, and we must be attentive to them all. Amen.'

As she watched the doctor standing on the platform, she thought suddenly – for the first time in many years – of her father. Hardly any specific memory of him had remained with her; she was only three years old when he died. But there was a shadowy image of a tall bearded man kneeling down beside her and placing his hand on her shoulder.

When the service ended the organ played a rousing martial tune as the worshippers followed the doctor out into the sunlight. Frances lingered to make sure she was the last to emerge. He was standing at the chapel door, looking expectantly towards her. The two women who had arrived with him were nearby.

'Miss Phillips!' His greeting radiated warmth, and there was an insistent pressure in his touch as he took her hand and continued to hold it, clasping it firmly between his palms in the way she remembered so well. 'I was sure it must be your face beneath the bonnet, there at the back. What a wonderful surprise to meet you again. Have you been long in Melbourne?'

'About a month. And you?'

'We arrived just last week.'

'Then Mrs Hammond is with you in Melbourne? I don't see her here this morning.'

'I'm sorry to report that Mrs Hammond passed away not long after our return to the United States. A sudden and severe illness; nothing could be done for her, alas.'

'I'm sorry to hear it. But I thought you said "we".'

'Indeed. I came here from the Cape, where I attended to an urgent business matter. Once that was transacted, I set out for Melbourne, and on the voyage I made the acquaintance of these two Dutch ladies,' – here he turned and beckoned them – 'whom I persuaded to accompany me to the chapel today so that they could share in the fellowship. May I introduce Miss Mathilde Reemst and her cousin Miss Henriette van der Velden? Ladies, Miss Frances Phillips from New Zealand.'

After a polite exchange there was a lull. Frances asked about their purpose in coming to Melbourne. Misses Reemst (exceedingly plump) and van der Velden (exceedingly thin) explained with tedious emphasis, often repeating each other's words, that they had decided on it as a holiday destination for two reasons: they had heard glowing reports of its Centennial Exhibition a couple of years previously, and then both had read Fergus Hume's celebrated novel *The Mystery of a Hansom Cab*, which 'everybody talks about', and which 'paints such an exciting picture of life in this city' that they felt compelled to visit Melbourne.

'I hope you won't be disappointed,' said Frances, 'if you find that Melbourne is somewhat less lurid than Mr Hume's narrative makes it out to be! Perhaps his is a typical New Zealander's view of Australian urban life. Mr Hume once lived in my own home city, Dunedin, and studied at the university there with my brother Edward, who told me that Fergusson Hume (who used his full name in those days) liked to say Dunedin was too small a stage for anyone with a large imagination. An understandable impulse.'

Not knowing how else to respond, Misses Plump and Thin merely repeated in duplicate their remark about Hume's 'exciting picture' of mysterious Melbourne.

'And you, Dr Hammond?' asked Frances. 'What brings you to Melbourne again?'

'I'm very keen to tell you about my reasons, but now is not the moment,' he replied, softening the refusal with an apologetic smile. 'I've promised to accompany these ladies back to our hotel in time for the midday meal. But may I call on you tomorrow afternoon, Miss Phillips? I would be grateful for an opportunity to share some information with you, and hear tidings of the folk we both know in Dunedin.'

Twenty-one

He arrived punctually. Watching from the window as he strode up the street, she thought how distinguished he looked, with his fair beard and broad shoulders.

The afternoon remained sunny, with a pleasant cooling breeze, and at his suggestion they walked to the Exhibition Building. Though it was only half a mile from her lodgings, Frances had not spent time there. Reports were unenthusiastic. According to the Dorcas Society ladies, the place now looked neglected and forlorn much of the time. All the glittering displays had been dismantled soon after the close of the Centennial Exhibition. A visit would hardly be worth her while, was the consensus. The once glorious Palace of Industry had become little more than an empty shell, they said, and there had been just a few miscellaneous small-scale attractions in recent months – a horticultural gala, an art show, a poultry competition, a concert in aid of the Trades Hall Council's strike fund.

But as they approached it, the sheer scale of the precinct quickened Frances's interest. Posters near the entrance announced that a carnival, grandly named 'Olympia', would be opening on the ninth of October – less than a week away. As they made their way along the main promenade past elaborate flowerbeds and a sculpted fountain towards the enormous building with its astonishingly tall dome, they could see gangs of workmen unloading carts at a side door, hauling large crates on trolleys and levering smaller boxes onto barrows. Preparations for the festival event were evidently in full swing.

'Are we permitted to look inside, do you think, with so much activity going on?' Frances asked.

'Let's assume so, unless told otherwise.'

With a purposeful air, he led her up the steps, across the vast foyer and through an ornate portico into the Great Hall. Its magnificence astounded her: the decorative panels, the arches with their gleaming wooden frames, the side aisles, the continuous first-floor galleries, the luminous octagonal drum of the dome itself, and around the dome a row of plaster heads representing the peoples of all continents. High up, in gold letters with black edging on a turquoise blue ground, was the solemn scriptural text, 'The earth is the Lord's and the fullness thereof'. The fullness: yes, she hungered after that, craved the experience of roaming the earth and seeing it in all its lordly manifold variety.

At one end of the hall, carpenters were constructing a large stage. At the opposite end they saw men wheeling boxes into a curtained-off alcove, carrying chairs, consulting lists and diagrams, measuring shapes chalked on the floor. In contrast to all the purposeful activity, they themselves felt conspicuously idle at first, but no-one seemed to pay them any attention, and indeed they were by no means the only casual visitors. Several couples and groups strolled around in a leisurely way, pointing at this and admiring that.

One party that walked past them was bubbling with chatter about panoramic views from the balcony. Hammond made enquiries, and a few minutes later they found their way to steep steps that would take them to the dome promenade. Frances preceded him on the climb and was secretly pleased, as she raised her heavy skirts, that she had worn her best stockings, and had a good pair of slender ankles.

They counted eighty steps before emerging breathlessly into the sunlight. On all sides there were vistas to make them gape, and apart from a few patches of factory smoke the view was wonderfully clear. Within and around the grid of central city streets it was easy to identify many notable features and they picked out several churches, the post office, Parliament and Treasury, and the Grand Temperance Hotel. Over there was the Yarra, flowing near the Botanic Gardens and then behind Flinders Street Station; and there stood the new Princes Bridge; and that majestic stone edifice would be the Town Hall. The ambitious scale of it all made her gasp. How cramped and cautious Dunedin was by comparison! Beyond the city in a broad arc stretched mile upon mile of suburban houses. To the south they could see the waters of Port Phillip sparkling in the distance, and hunkered far to the east were the blue-grey shapes of the Dandenong Ranges. You could spend years traversing this whole terrain, Melbourne and all its hinterland, and yet it was a mere corner of the world, a small portion of that unimaginable fullness.

'Truly an astonishing spectacle,' said Hammond, 'when we consider that in hardly more than a generation one of the great cities of the modern world has sprung into being. The march of civilisation has been more extraordinarily rapid here than anywhere else I've seen on the face of the earth.'

'I know your travels have taken you to many exotic places,' said Frances, 'and I wish I could hear all your stories. But what has brought you back to Melbourne? You promised to tell me that.'

'And indeed I'll do so. But let's return to the ground now, because your reference to the exotic reminds me there's something else I'd like us to see before the afternoon ends and the time comes for me to accompany you back to your lodging-house. Do you know about the aquarium behind this building?'

No, she did not, and had little idea what such a thing might contain.

'If what I've heard is no exaggeration,' he said, 'this one holds some very strange creatures, the like of which you will certainly never have seen in Dunedin!'

It was not a false promise. He paid a shilling each for their tickets, and soon after entering the aquarium at the rear of the eastern annexe they quickly agreed that it was a place of splendid spectacle. They exchanged stares with countless creatures: fish brought from all over the world to glide around in huge tanks; seals and penguins, slipping and spinning through the water in what seemed a cheerful game; tortoises, moving with much greater gravity; and most startling of all, alone in the largest tank, a massive crocodile. 'Man-eating', said the sign. Frances watched, mesmerised, as the scaly monster leapt at a large chunk of meat dangling at the end of a pole, ripping it with fearsome jaws. She shrank away, and Hammond placed a reassuring hand at her back.

'Tell me,' he said as they walked up Lygon Street towards her lodgings, 'how you and your brothers have fared since Mrs Phillips's sad passing. I confess that your elder brother's name escapes me, as I seldom saw him, but of course I remember Frederick clearly. I admired his devotion to the cause of the gospel, and particularly his conscientious attention to his tasks as Sunday School superintendent. What news of him? Is he well?'

'Very well. He married Mary Laurenson a few months after you left Dunedin and, as Fred likes to say, they are "happy as a box of birds". Mary is a sweet young woman.'

'I'm glad to hear it.'

'My other brother, Edward, still teaches Latin. I think he'd be happier if his pupils were more responsive, but no doubt his manner is too severe to bring out the best in them. He's very much a solitary. In that respect, at least, we're alike, he and I.

There we are – or were, until I came to Melbourne recently – two separate souls occupying one shared space, the house you know well. Strangers together.'

'You remain unattached yourself, Miss Phillips?'

She nodded.

He was silent for a while before speaking again.

'You mentioned the house in Half Way Bush Road. Did you sell your stake in that large family property before leaving for Melbourne? Presumably the three of you inherited equal portions.'

'Equal portions, yes – but no, the property remains intact. If I return to Dunedin I may perhaps go back into our old home. Edward is there alone at present.'

They had reached Miss Shacklock's place.

'There's more I wished to talk about with you,' said Hammond. 'May I call on you again soon? Perhaps the day after tomorrow?'

'That would be suitable.'

'Good. At three o'clock again?'

'Yes.'

Only after he turned away did she remember her unanswered question about his reason for returning to Melbourne.

Twenty-two

On the Wednesday, they took a tram into the city and spent a couple of hours sauntering among the crowds along wide, neatly paved footpaths, admiring the many grand buildings that lined the main streets. From time to time they paused while William pointed out this feature or that; he was well informed about construction methods and had a keen eye for the details of architectural style. Frances hung on his words. Every observation he made seemed apposite. She felt a pang of disappointment when he explained apologetically that he must cut short their time together because of a business appointment later in the afternoon. But as he accompanied her back to Carlton in the tram he suggested that they take another walk later in the week.

On Friday afternoon, with the mild spring warmth still holding, they strolled north up Lygon Street and then, with the gentle pressure of his hand at her elbow, he guided her past the crescent that edged the university colleges and on towards a pedestrian gate leading into the cemetery.

'When I was previously in Melbourne,' he told her, 'this was a place I came to often, for a meditative amble. There's always something instructive, it seems to me, about the way large urban cemeteries like this one combine the sequestered calm of a park with the crowded dwellings of a suburb.'

The grave markers clustered within the entrance were

distinctively Jewish. A few motifs that accompanied the portions of alien script conveyed recognisable meanings; a recurrent design showed hands raised as if in farewell or in blessing. Further along, outlined by rows of pine and cypress, was the Church of England section, and they paused to read the epitaphs of public figures whose names they knew: Hotham the governor, Barry the hanging judge and patron of culture, and Burke and Wills the hapless explorers.

But as they continued on through the curving avenues Frances took more notice of the poignantly modest memorials for the prematurely dead – infants, young mothers, goldrush miners who were hardly beyond boyhood. She lingered over lines that seemed to reach out to her directly from the grave of one youth in particular:

Warned by his sudden fate, learn heav'n to prize;
To Christ, the only hope of sinners, flee.
Death in one awful moment closed his eyes;
As sudden, reader, may thy summons be!

Frances liked the idea that a cemetery visitor was a kind of reader: a reader not only of engraved lines but also of buried lives, interpreting and imagining them as if they were characters in poems or novels.

They walked on in silence, inspecting other epitaphs. She was conscious of his quiet absorption in this theatre of remembrance, and on impulse asked why such a place engaged him as it did. He touched his palm as he spoke simply about the distant and lonely graves of both his parents. Sensing pain, she did not pursue the topic, and they emerged after a few minutes into the noisy streets of Carlton.

Hammond stopped, clearing his throat.

'You asked what has brought me back to Melbourne,' he

said. 'This city is actually not my destination. I was returning to Dunedin, and intended to make only a brief stop here. Encountering you has been marvellously providential, because I'd naturally assumed that you were still in Dunedin and it was to see you that I planned to travel there.'

'To see me!' Frances stopped and turned to him.

'Yes, Miss Phillips. Forgive me for being so boldly direct: I want you to know that in recent months you've been more and more in my thoughts.' He paused as she drew in a sharp breath and put a hand to her throat. 'I can see you're startled at what I'm saying. Nevertheless, Frances, I hope you will consider a future with me. As my wedded companion.'

For a moment she could not speak. His words churned in her ears. At last she composed herself, and looked up at him. His eyes had never looked so intensely blue.

'This is so...so sudden that I hardly know how to respond. It was only this week that our paths crossed again after a long interval, and the news of your wife's untimely death during that period is still fresh in my mind. Being asked so soon to take her place is quite a shock.'

'Naturally so. Naturally. My declaration has caught you by surprise, and of course you'll need time to think about it, and to let me explain my feelings and circumstances more fully. Can we meet again tomorrow afternoon to discuss the matter further?'

'I...I think so. Yes.'

They walked up to Miss Shacklock's lodging-house without further words being spoken.

Head crowded with questions, hands tingling, she stood at the door, watching him stride away into the twilight and turn the corner.

The next day he took her to the Botanic Gardens.

'Miss Phillips – my dear Frances, if I may speak as intimately as I wish – I trust you've been giving as much thought as

I have to the matter I raised so abruptly yesterday. It looms up at us now, and we must talk about it. But before we do, please tell me about your own purpose in having left Dunedin, as that may have some bearing on questions about the way ahead. Apparently you came here alone – something that many ladies would not be brave enough to do. There must have been a strong motive. What made you decide to travel to Melbourne?'

'Fred and others asked me the same thing insistently before I left home, and I had no ready answer for them. It seemed insufficient just to say that I began to be restless in Dunedin after my mother passed away, and my life there came to feel somehow incomplete. Whether Melbourne will prove to be a satisfying terminus or only a place of sojourn, I can't yet tell.'

'But you might contemplate favourably the prospect of further journeys?'

'I might, yes. Probably.'

'Then I want to you come with me, as my wife, to foreign lands. I know myself to be an inveterate wanderer, and I see that the same voyaging spirit stirs your blood. Be my travelling partner through life, Frances. Will you?'

'But where would we make our home? And how would we live?'

'There's time enough, my dear, to choose a suitable place to settle down. And we need never be anxious about means of support. I've always found it easy to secure employment as a medical man or as an evangelist, wherever I go. Besides, each of us has more than adequate resources, I think, to bring to the marriage. My material situation is quite comfortable, I assure you, and of course you're entitled to a share of your mother's estate.'

Her hopes of returning to Dunedin to be married were firmly quelled. He wanted it to happen here. And so a few days later they set the date for a month ahead, and made arrangements for a modest ceremony at the Christian Chapel in Lygon Street:

a Friday afternoon it would be, the seventh of November. It all seemed strange, and breathtaking in its suddenness, but William (as she must learn to call him in private) was very persuasive and she felt quickened by his eagerness that they should become man and wife as soon as possible.

She wrote brief letters to Isabella and to her brothers, knowing – but not caring greatly – that the lack of a customary courtship period would alarm them, and that the wedding would probably be held by the time they received the news.

The beginning of November came quickly. A festive atmosphere pervaded the city: newspapers carried excited predictions about the famous annual horseracing carnival, and shopkeepers could talk of nothing else.

'We should go to the Melbourne Cup this Tuesday,' said William. 'It will be a great occasion.'

Frances was disconcerted by his enthusiasm.

'I wouldn't have thought this the kind of event you'd wish to attend,' she said. 'Especially just before our wedding. Won't it attract crowds of gamblers and pickpockets and other people of low repute?'

'No doubt,' he replied with a smile. 'But we can avoid them. There will be many respectable folk there too. The annual running of the Cup is the highlight of Melbourne's social calendar, you know. A public holiday. Yes, our wedding comes close on its heels – but let's imagine that this year's gathering at the Flemington racecourse is a civic celebration in our honour!'

So they went. It seemed that all of Melbourne was going with them. On foot, in carriages, on trams, people converged from every direction like swarming bees. Several parades and processions held up the thick traffic with their displays of support for labour unions, trade associations and mutual aid societies. A brazen Salvation Army band raucously admonished those who thronged the last stretch of road towards Flemington.

Arriving at last, they were amazed at the spectacle – such a mass of humanity assembled in one place that Frances felt almost overwhelmed. Paddocks and adjacent slopes were already thickly populated. In every direction stretched a huge panorama of swirling colours and shapes. She could see, in a special enclosure set apart from the jostling multitude, an array of broughams and barouches, with ladies in expensive-looking silks and satins. Up on the hillside, countless couples and family groups were spreading out their picnic rugs. Bottles glinted in the sunlight. Some of the men near her were already drunk, and there were women circling through the crowd whose flashy attire and shameless manner proclaimed their willingness to make a commercial arrangement. Frances remembered Bella.

The surrounding babble became noisier by the minute. On everyone's lips was the name of Carbine – no mere horse, apparently, but a heroic creature, powerfully built and always finishing so strongly that it was being forced to carry ten and a half stone into this race, the heaviest weight ever. William interpreted features of the scene to her and explained how the gamblers placed their bets. The day was getting hotter. He removed his jacket and rolled up his sleeves. Frances stared at the fine long fair hairs, like corn-silk threads, on his forearms.

The horses emerged into an enclosure and were guided towards the starting-post.

'Look at the way their hind-quarters ripple in the sunlight!' exclaimed William. 'Magnificent flesh!' His arm brushed against hers.

And then a huge roar reverberated: the race had begun. William cupped a hand around his mouth as he leant towards her and raised his voice above the yelling that encircled them: 'That's the favourite,' he shouted, pointing, 'there on the rails near the back. The mighty Carbine! He won't stay in that position for long!'

She had never seen him so excited.

Hardly more than a minute later, thousands began chanting Carbine's name, cheering on the champion, louder and louder as he bolted to the head of the field and charged on towards the finish line. Jubilation erupted on all sides, as if the prowess of one superb animal could expunge entirely every anxious thought about the collapse of the building boom, the effects of the maritime strike, and the talk of a depression.

* * *

After all the hullabaloo of the Cup holiday, and the next evening's Guy Fawkes fireworks in the streets, Frances felt relieved that their little wedding service later in the week was so subdued. She had no great appetite for festive gatherings at any time, and all she wanted to do at this moment was to immerse herself quietly in the simple ceremony. It was, for her, of no consequence that the chapel held only a handful of people; they had not told many about the arrangement. Afterwards they went by hansom cab to Menzies' Hotel where William had reserved a splendidly furnished room for their wedding night. They took a walk up and down Bourke Street before returning to the hotel to dress for dinner. Frances, feeling ignorant and apprehensive about what would soon be required of her, could not eat much. When they retired to their room, William turned down the lamp, took off his jacket and with a self-confident smile began to unbutton his shirt.

'I don't know what to expect,' said Frances, colouring.

'There will be some blood,' he said, moving close to her, 'but don't be alarmed. Just let yourself yield to my hands now.'

Part 6

Franklin Falls, 1885–86

Twenty-three

Finally satisfied with his meticulous trimming of beard and whiskers, he stood back to scrutinise himself in a blotchy mirror on the wall of his hotel room. What he stared at was more than his present physical image; beyond it he saw a vista of remembered selves, scenes and transitions that had all contributed to the shaping of this person he now knew himself to be.

In the years since his release from Clinton Prison, young Will had turned into a personably middle-aged William – or rather, into a cluster of Williams, inhabiting each of them comfortably and often simultaneously. Their attributes merged now in his reflection. There was Dr William Hammond, versatile physician and herbalist. There was the Reverend William Hammond, itinerant preacher. And there was also, for a succession of well-to-do women, William Hammond the highly eligible prospective husband. Occasionally one or another of these Hammond personages would operate in a quasi-independent way, but mostly they came together as a trinitarian partnership for the shared purpose of soliciting other people's confidence.

Graduating from schemer to skinner had been an easy passage.

'This will help you, we trust,' Amelia Temple had said as she handed him the wallet, 'to make a fresh start. Members of our Aid Society have each been putting a little aside for you as your release date approached. But you'll need more than dollars to establish yourself; we pledge support through prayer as well, in the months ahead, and hope to see you thrive as a God-fearing hard-working free man. No doubt you'll remain in these parts, at least for some while, and you will of course be warmly welcomed into the life of our church here.' She lowered her eyes shyly and he observed the faint flush on her cheeks.

A week later he left town, having obtained from her – on a pretext of urgency – a personal supplement to the amount collected by the Society. He made his way south and then west, wanting to put as much distance as possible between himself and the good gullible folk of the Peristrome Church.

Now, some fifteen years later, looking at himself with satisfaction in his hotel room in Franklin Falls, New Hampshire, he could still remember in detail each stage of that westward journey, and how it took him to the mining towns north of Mt Shasta, close to the Oregon border. He had decided to pause for a while in Yreka simply because its Baptist church was in need of a pastor, and he could plausibly fill that role (with the help of some deftly forged letters of recommendation) and garner a modest stipend while looking around for further opportunities. Then the Modoc war erupted nearby, making it risky for anyone to travel in the area, and so he stayed on for a couple of years.

After the defeat of the Indians it became possible for him to make little excursions into the surrounding district. He did so with no particular purpose; there was contentment in simply wandering here or there at will, murmuring the words that Meikle used to recite: 'by road or pathway, or through trackless field.' He recalled clearly the day he rode to Tula lake to see the lava beds. Dark as dried blood, the rigid spate stretched before him. Its fissures and hollows spoke of slow erosion over the centuries, but he could imagine the explosive force that once sent torrents of molten rock across this whole expanse – liquid fire surging through the veins of the earth.

William stored in his mind the imagery of violent eruption, useful for sermons. His reputation as a powerful speaker continued to grow, and the Baptist church had become Yreka's most crowded.

Good fortune had come through a freakish accident. A stalwart of his church and prosperous carriage-maker, John Newton, was out collecting sweet resin from some of the tall sugar pines nearby when a huge hard green cone had plummeted down and struck him on the temple. That alone might not have killed him, but he had made the outcome certain by toppling backwards against a rock and breaking his neck.

On hearing the news, William had gone to Newton's widow with appropriate expressions of condolence, though his private thoughts were far from solemn. Mrs Vera Newton had been a perfect match for her husband: utterly vapid and vain. But having suddenly entered widowhood, she was also one of the wealthiest women in Yreka. Plainly it did not surprise her that young Pastor Hammond, so talented and so personable, chose to pay court to her. His attentions pleased her, even excited her and, though ten years older and not generally reckoned attractive, she was incapable of suspecting any ulterior design. He had gained her confidence with ease because she was so sure of her own charms.

She must have felt, then, a humiliating shock at finding herself abruptly and silently abandoned after less than a year's marriage. William had persuaded her to let him invest a substantial amount of her savings, supposedly in a project that would bring them swift and substantial returns. When Vera returned after staying a few days with a sister in Fort Jones, Pastor Hammond had vanished, along with the pocketed investment. He was already far from California.

* * *

Recalling that Yreka episode now, William saw it as the foundation for the material successes he had enjoyed in the intervening years. America was full of credulous souls, and of opportunities to fleece them. He had become the smoothest of swindlers – and remorseless in this vocation, as his chosen targets represented the sorts of people who had wronged him and his mother. To cozen anyone who reminded him of such contemptible souls as the La Chute churchgoers, Christie, Abernethy and Nellie Dixon was, in an intensely satisfying way, to exact justice. Where he could make fools of knaves, he did so with special relish; but where only fools were available, he would profit from their mere stupidity.

So here he was in Franklin Falls, drawn to this flourishing mill town because, reputedly, it was not only prosperous but also ingenuous. He needed to replenish his funds, and good pickings seemed likely in a place such as this.

But in his first week a chance encounter in a bookshop gave him a new perspective. Browsing in the poetry section he picked up Palgrave's *Golden Treasury of the Best Songs and Poems in the English Language*, and thumbed through the contents. Then, book in hand, he went up to the counter. 'I'll take this,' he said, drawing money from his purse. As the transaction was being completed, another customer, standing nearby, came up and spoke to him – a man of similar height and appearance to himself, but with longer hair and a fuller beard, and a little older, probably about fifty years of age.

'You've chosen well, sir, if I may presume to comment. An excellent anthology. I own a copy myself.'

'I confess,' responded William, 'that I'm buying it with the Wordsworth selections mainly in mind. Most of the sonnets and ballads that represent him in these pages are unknown to me, though passages from his *Prelude* have been familiar to me since boyhood. An enthusiastic teacher used to regale us often with sections of that great masterpiece.'

'A fortunate education for an apt young learner, I'm sure. Wordsworth's enquiry into the sources of thought and action can provide greater lucidity than cartloads of ordinary lesson books.'

The speaker introduced himself as Jonathan Harrison.

'New to this town, I take it?' Harrison asked. 'Then let me tell you, Mr Hammond, if you care to take an interest in our Unitarian Society, you can avail yourself of a splendid library. It contains many fine literary works along with books on philosophical, religious and other topics. We now have over two thousand five hundred volumes in all. Food for lively debate – and our members do exchange opinions vigorously, I can tell you.

'Now take Wordsworth, for instance,' he went on in a genial tone that William found engaging. 'There's dispute among us Unitarians about the value of Wordsworth's views. He accentuates some of our differences, you see. For my own part, much as I admire his eloquence, I see this poet as looking too much to the past. All very well to laud the dignity of a rustic form of toil, in harmony with the natural world, but it's a sentimental view, as his own words acknowledge: "Labour here preserves his rosy face" – remember that line from *The Prelude*? He gives no thought to improving the lives of workers in industrial towns.'

'Probably you're right,' William responded. 'But should we expect that? For me the power of that poem is inseparable from its inwardness.'

'True, true. Nicely observed, Mr Hammond. You're an astute reader, I see. As you tactfully imply, I want *The Prelude* to do something it doesn't profess to be doing – to turn its attention towards the social ills that vex us today. Quite unreasonable of me, but I do confess to wishing that Wordsworth had been more like his dear friend Coleridge, who was of course a Unitarian preacher, as I was myself until recently.'

There would be, Harrison added, a meeting of the Franklin

Falls Unitarian Society the following evening, in the hall next to the church; and visitors were always most welcome at these gatherings.

As he prepared to set out for the meeting, William had no elevated expectations. Jonathan Harrison seemed cordial enough, and intellectually active, if somewhat earnest; but in a small mill town there were unlikely to be many people with interesting minds. Nevertheless the evening might enable him to scout out an opportunity or two for some pocket-filling stratagem.

Twenty-four

Perhaps he had underestimated Franklin Falls; William began to see that now as the lively meeting drew towards its close. The speeches and debates had been intelligent, and unconstrained by any of the narrow religiosity that he had anticipated. Those seated in the hall – nearly a hundred people, at a rough count – were by no means passive listeners; their mood was one of courteous but animated participation.

Mr Alvah Sulloway, introduced as president of the Franklin National Bank and trustee of the Unitarian Educational Society, had signalled the evening's theme capably enough. Striding to the platform he tilted his head back, and spoke with self-assurance:

'Ladies and gentlemen, we can say proudly nowadays that Franklin Falls vibrates with ideas. The evidence of this is plain to see. There are many enterprising leaders in our midst whose creative thinking has led to innovation in our local industries, generating jobs for working people and capital for the development of schools, churches and other social institutions. Amongst us this evening is Mr Walter Aiken, acclaimed pioneer in the invention of knitting-machines, having taken out over forty patents. His latest machine makes a perfect stocking without seam in less than five minutes and works automatically. Besides that, he has created an ingenious device to make gimlet-pointed screws, and designed the locomotive for the Mt Washington Railway.'

A burst of spontaneous clapping acknowledged Aiken's productive ideas. Sulloway went on to mention other local leaders and their application of new thinking to business. More applause.

'But we are here this evening because our town also needs ideas of a different kind. There are now many people, attracted here by factory employment and related opportunities, whose lives lack the influences of Christian fellowship. The Unitarian Congregational Society may be unable to draw them all into the circle of worship, but our constitution speaks of a broader obligation – to promote fraternal justice, cultivate useful knowledge, and do our utmost to develop a serious and intelligent public spirit.'

Murmurs of concurrence rippled through the audience.

'Ladies and gentlemen, it is not my role to speak at greater length on this topic. The Unitarian Society of Franklin Falls is proud to be associated with Mr Jonathan Baxter Harrison, formerly our pastor, now devoting his considerable talents to the production of books and journal articles. Very recently his *Notes on Industrial Conditions* was published in our town, and many of us have read his most influential work, *On Certain Dangerous Tendencies in American Life*, which in just a few years has taken its place alongside the most durable commentaries on modern society. Mr Harrison, sir, would you be so kind as to speak to us now on the needs of our fellow-citizens?'

William was not easily impressed by public speakers but he was full of admiration at Harrison's extempore oratory.

'Let me raise with you, my friends,' Harrison began, 'in the most direct terms that I can find, the theme of mutual responsibility. Each of you will recall, from the Holy Bible's first book, that fundamental question posed by Cain many centuries ago: Am I my brother's keeper?

'Cain, with the shadow of guilt on his face, asked it in a shamefully disingenuous spirit, attempting to shrug aside what was on his bloodstained conscience. I put it to you that men and women of good faith must answer that age-old question with a resounding *Yea!* For we *are* indeed our brothers' keepers: the moral quality of any community is surely to be measured by the care its members extend to one another. And if, this very night, Franklin Falls were to be weighed in the balances, I say to you that it would be found wanting.

'You may protest that I speak too harshly. For this town already demonstrates responsibility towards our fellow man in a number of practical ways. Perhaps the most striking example is the New Hampshire Orphans' Home, providing charity in a healthy setting for children left fatherless and destitute by the Civil War, and great respect is due to those who have sustained that institution.'

He mentioned names, and appreciative sounds emanated from the audience.

'Yet is not that something of a special case? Plainly, most of our townspeople are not orphans. They have their own homes, their own family groups. And though it be a truism that charity should begin at home, every one of us has a bounden duty to help our fellow citizens conceive of *home* in its fullest meaning – ample enough to meet not only physical needs but cultural and spiritual needs as well.'

William shifted uncomfortably in his seat. Home. It was not an idea that he had allowed his thoughts to dwell on, not for many years. Too painful? Early memories of the little farm and of his parents tugged at him.

'When I invoke the term *cultural*,' Harrison was saying, 'you will recognise, my friends, that this is in no narrow sense. I have in mind the idea expounded with such cogency by Mr Matthew Arnold, whom I had the pleasure to meet during his

American tour. He contends that we need a larger conception of human nature, to lead us towards harmonious development of our best selves and of the cultural institutions that express our common humanity.

'To many of the working men of Franklin Falls, and to their families, these words would seem like a foreign language. Little in their lives could be described as harmonious. Hopes may at first shine brightly, but without cultural and spiritual nourishment they soon darken. Do you recall that sobering figure in Wordsworth's famous ode? – "Shades of the prison-house begin to close / Upon the growing boy". The shades of which the poet speaks may not literally signify a dungeon cell; they are most often cast by habits of idleness, trivial pastimes, vulgar talk, coarse behaviour and shallow thinking – which are, none the less, forms of narrow enclosure.'

As he referred to Wordsworth, Harrison had turned his gaze towards William, sitting near the back of the hall.

'How to conduct ourselves towards one another so that our shared place in the world seems more like a home than a prison: that is the question that we must answer together. Let us acknowledge that for too many working men and their families today, the church is no home. The fellowship of believers doesn't often make them welcome; it seems an exclusive group. I implore you, Christian brethren, to look into your hearts and ask yourselves what you can do, what we can do, to develop across our community an ideal of home that encompasses the full range of human needs.'

Twenty-five

During the next fortnight, William had two long conversations at Jonathan Harrison's home that would return to trouble him.

For the first conversation they sat together on a rough-hewn bench in a sunny garden nook behind the house, enjoying the cider brought out to them silently by Mrs Harrison. It was unseasonably warm and balmy for an October day. William did most of the listening while his host expatiated on several favourite topics: the miserable conditions of life in factory towns, the gradual abandonment of New Hampshire farms, the educational ideals of the Indian Rights Association, and the wanton destruction of forests. As he talked, Harrison's left hand cupped his right elbow while his right hand remained extended upwards in an admonitory pose, the thumb rhythmically stroking his long forefinger.

Although Harrison tended towards the sermonic, he punctuated his speechmaking intermittently with cordial questions.

'Tell me now, is that a Scottish burr in your voice?...Ah, from the Caledonian corner of Quebec! And what brought you here, Mr Hammond?...What vocation are you pursuing?...I see, a minister of religion! Which particular persuasion?...Well, well: much in common, much in common...Travelling alone, are you?...Unmarried, then?...Oh, a widower – sad misfortune to be left solitary at such an early stage...'

To any questions about his past or intentions, William responded briefly and selectively. He wished to steer Harrison back to the theme of social responsibility, keen to explore what it should mean in particular situations. Where did care for one's fellow man reach its proper limits, and care for oneself become a paramount duty?

As they talked on through the mild and cloudless afternoon, William found himself drawn towards the other man's view of the world, and began to reflect silently on the contrast between his own rapacity and the altruistic spirit that impelled Harrison's thinking. Having concealed his self-seeking motives, he was startled when Harrison suddenly posed a direct and personal question.

'Mr Hammond, may I speak frankly? It's not hard to see that you're a gifted man. I don't say this in flattery. You have a sharp analytical mind and an engaging manner. You use words well. Forgive me for asking something that you may think presumptuous: How do you plan to exercise your God-given talents in the future so that they bring benefit where it's most needed? I feel able to raise this question with you because I put it to myself a couple of years ago, and for me the answer was not to continue as a minister but to reach out to a wider circle through my writings. Of course, my answer implies nothing about what yours should be.'

William, for the first time in years, felt a flicker of conscience. Rubbing his fingers against his cheeks and running the tip of his tongue around his lips, he watched an osprey circling beyond the treetops, its predatory purpose belied by a plaintive whistle. He waited until it dipped and glided away.

'The work of a preacher,' he said slowly, still mulling over Harrison's words, 'though conscientiously undertaken, doesn't consume all one's time and energy. There's room to do more. I think that disorders of the spirit often affect the body – and conversely, injury to the flesh may underlie poor spiritual health. I would like,' he went on, and then paused to clear his throat. 'I would like...to do something to alleviate physical suffering. To become a kind of physician.'

It was a surprise to hear himself declaring this ambition, but as his words emerged he wondered how true they were.

'With particular emphasis on herbal cures,' he added.

'Indeed?' Harrison replied. 'Very interesting. Our society certainly needs healers of the body. So this is a field in which you have some knowledge and experience already?'

William nodded, involuntarily opening and closing his hand, with its jagged scar across the palm.

'I've studied the efficacy of various botanical remedies,' he said, 'and used to practise and write on the subject.'

'Excellent. I must introduce you to Harold Brockway. Prosperous man. Started out in millinery and fancy goods many years back, and then found he could make better money as a druggist. By the time I arrived here in '79, people were regarding him as a general-purpose physician. His own health has been poor lately, and I've heard he's intending to retire, so perhaps that may provide an opening for you. I'll arrange for you to meet him.'

A week later William sat facing Harold and Ethel Brockway across Harrison's dinner table. Harrison led the conversation as if chairing a meeting. His wife said only a few words all evening, content with the role of deferential helpmeet. Ethel Brockway, in contrast, spoke often, though her contributions had little substance. She seemed to want to make an impression of vivacity, but lacked enough wit to know how to do so convincingly. William judged her to be entirely unable to recognise her limitations. She smiled at him with indecorous frequency and with more teeth than he cared to look at.

The men spoke mainly of disease – physical and spiritual, social and individual. Brockway set them on that track, arriving somewhat late, looking pale and gaunt, full of grumbles about having been delayed by a case of typhus.

'Poor wretch of a child – high fever, mottled rash, blood from the mouth and bowels. Little chance of pulling through, I fear. Too far advanced. The unpleasant truth of the matter,' he announced, waggling his fork for emphasis, 'is that bad sanitation is the cause. Lice! Rats! That's how the typhus spreads, you know. Most of the factory workers don't keep their homes properly clean. Children suffer terribly because their parents don't know or care about simple principles of hygiene. There's nothing much to be done by the time they call me in.'

'Some years ago,' said William, 'when treating debilitated soldiers at Plattsburgh Barracks, I found that a herbal compound produced rapid improvement in some typhus cases.'

'Which herbs?' asked Brockway gruffly, sniffing a challenge.

'Prickly ash, if I recall rightly, and gravelroot...'

'Gravelroot?'

'I think it's better known around here as purple boneset or joe pye weed. To alleviate the typhus, gravelroot and prickly ash should be mixed in equal parts with wood betony, if you can get it, or wild indigo, and also vervain; then simmered in water, and cooled.'

Brockway frowned. 'A marked improvement, you say?'

'In several cases.'

'And you're sure it was indeed typhus that ailed these men?'

'Quite certain.'

Harrison intervened: 'There's a much larger set of problems, I believe, behind every such sickness. Since the Civil War, the whole body of society has been infected by serious moral diseases that are leading to the decay of our national character: a recklessly acquisitive attitude, abounding dishonesty, a passionate greed for riches. These things need stronger medicine than anything a druggist can dispense.'

'Well, there's no doubt,' said William, 'that post-bellum America faces many social problems, from pauperism to prison management. But are they all fundamentally moral problems? Some of them seem, rather, to stem from defects in the system of law, or of political economy.'

'No, no, I'm with our host on that point,' asserted Brockway firmly. 'You mention prison management for example, so let's consider that. It's a subject about which I happen to know a thing or two, through my cousin Zebulon.' He paused, watching for a sign of recognition. 'Zebulon Brockway, the progressive prison administrator. You've heard about his Elmira reforms, I dare say?'

William tried to disguise the automatic clenching of his hands and the flush of sudden anger through his veins. Since leaving Dannemora, he had never spoken to anyone about his bitter experiences there, but could not put the episode out of his mind. Some things were unforgettable: the filthy cells, the loneliness, the cruel punishments, the malice, the vermin, extremes of cold and heat, the stench, the coarse grey gruel, the arduous and demeaning daily labour. Any other prison could only be much the same, he was sure of that.

Elmira's reformatory had become famous as the place where prisoners were encouraged to exert themselves strenuously as they worked towards the prospect of eventual rehabilitation and release. Among Zebulon Brockway's innovations there, William knew, was the piece-price system: contractors supplied machines and materials, and then paid for the number of pieces (twine bales, shoes, hoes, etc.) that the inmates produced. The sentences imposed had an indeterminate duration: prisoners were urged to prove their fitness for liberty by labouring towards the gradual improvement of their status, earning marks for diligence and docility, and industriously working out their own salvation.

But William had heard the rumours of vicious punishments and corrupt practices at Elmira: floggings that inflicted injury but stopped short of damaging the offender's ability to work, arbitrary use of solitary confinement to break any spirit of defiance, favours extended to those who submitted to the depraved demands of guards. It was hard to listen calmly to Zebulon Brockway's cousin commending the Elmira reforms.

'Learning a trade, learning proper work habits – it's just what those young felons need,' the ignorant man enthused. 'Discipline. That's how to turn them into Christian gentlemen.'

'I don't think the matter is so simple,' said William, trying to keep out of his voice the emotion he felt rising in his throat. He looked down at his clasped hands and took a slow breath, knowing that if he turned his face towards Brockway his dislike of the man would show. 'No prison, in my opinion, can teach people how to become good productive middle-class citizens. It's an inevitably degrading institution, and calling it a reformatory or a penitentiary doesn't change that.'

Harrison remonstrated, 'But you wouldn't argue, surely, that prisons be abolished?'

'No, but we should recognise them for what they are – a necessary evil, and often administered more harshly and less honestly than they should be. This proclaimed ideal of attaining civic respectability through supervised effort and meted reward – it's quite delusory, in my opinion. Men who toil arduously without any independence, without any belongings of their own, without any social interaction, can never change their spots.'

'You speak with feeling,' said Brockway, 'but I can't share your pessimism.'

And I, thought William, don't wish to share your smugness.

He felt a kind of mordant satisfaction when, little more than a week later, Harrison told him that Harold Brockway had succumbed to the typhus and suddenly expired. William considered sending a note of condolence to Ethel Brockway, but his attention was engaged with an unexpected opportunity. Hearing that the town's Freewill Baptist Church was seeking a regular preacher, he made himself known to the officers of the congregation, who soon offered him a part-time position. While not handsomely paid, it covered the cost of room and board at a comfortable lodging-house and allowed him scope to supplement the stipend with what he might earn from other activities. Herbal medicine was the line of business he had in mind, but it would require some capital to purchase ingredients and dispensing equipment, and advertise. His pockets were nearly empty.

Before long, providence took material shape when the newly widowed Ethel Brockway attended one of his worship services. Standing afterwards at the door of the little chapel to extend the hand of Christian fellowship, William greeted her with due solemnity and murmured a few sympathetic words. Glimpsing the simper behind her dark veil, he continued to hold her hand and squeeze it gently. She returned the pressure.

In the months that followed, she came to every service. Sitting in the back row, she would raise her veil as soon as he stood up to preach, and he could see the naked longing in her stare. It was, he knew, an aperture through which his own needs could enter unresisted.

Twenty-six

His pastoral role gave him a licence to visit Ethel Brockway regularly and – within decorous limits – to console her in her widowhood. He could see that she was manipulable. But he had not forgotten the afternoon in Harrison's garden: cider sparkling in the sunlight, osprey circling overhead, and that long conscience-tweaking conversation about the mainspring of a person's actions and the responsibility to decide who should benefit from one's talents.

One evening, with this uneasiness stirring in his mind, he strolled through the streets in a southerly direction until he found himself some distance downriver from the falls. Looking back towards the smoky cluster of factories and houses, he could see where the two tributaries came together to form the Merrimack River that was now swirling past him. Along the western edge of the town flowed the urgent waters of the Pemigewasset, while the Winnipesaukee twisted its narrow way from the eastern side and then turned back on itself to surge under the Central Street bridge and cascade down beside the old mill. In a momentary hallucination, he imagined it all becoming topsy-turvy. It was as if the current reversed its direction so that it flowed back up the Merrimack to the junction and separated there into two distributive channels. And he pictured himself being carried upstream, brought back to that forking point and having to decide, uncertainly, which course to take.

As darkness deepened, he stood staring towards the tumble of rumbling water. He was not accustomed to feeling irresolute. For a long time now he had been sure of himself, confident in his ability to size up a situation swiftly and choose his way unerringly. Living by his wits, he had always known when to be cautious and when to be bold. This hesitation that now troubled him was something new. As to how he could tap Ethel Brockway's money, he was in no doubt. But the unfamiliar question was whether he had the heart to do what his head told him was easy.

Harrison's words lingered inconveniently in his mind. He *was* more capable than most men, endowed with great gifts – most conspicuously the power to persuade. He acknowledged, too, that there was a serious need for leaders. He could become such a person if he wanted to, someone who would be an influence for good. He thought back to his dedicated schoolmaster James Meikle, the decent and earnest chaplain Frank Bloodgood Hall, more recently Jonathan Baxter Harrison...He wondered whether Jeannie Hammond would be ashamed of the path her son had taken.

In recent years he had pushed her into the furthest recesses of memory. It was too painful to see her lying twisted at the foot of the stairs, or hear the cries of humiliation as she tried to ward off Christie, or relive his regular visits to her lonely grave.

In the surrounding shadows, he saw again the faces of people who had wronged him and his mother. He brought his fist down hard against a branch of the tree beside him. Damn them and their ilk! He had every right to retaliate.

It had been foolish of him to think, even for a passing moment, that he owed some duty to a society that had taken so much away from him. Let Harrison and other pious idealists wax eloquent about the needs of their fellow men. For his own part he had scores to settle, and would continue to seek quiet vengeance by parting the respectable from their surplus money.

Sooty air drifted down from a thousand chimneys and mingled with the dank smell of mist rising from the river. With his hands pressed into his armpits for warmth, William made his way back to his frowsty lodging-house in Peabody Street, reconfirmed in his determination to exploit Ethel Brockway.

* * *

'Divine providence,' he told the congregation in his sermon the following Sunday, 'has made available to mankind a wonderful variety of natural remedies for the physical ills that assail us. The first chapter of the book of Genesis records God's assurance on this matter: "Behold, I have given you every herb-bearing seed which is upon the face of all the earth, and every tree in which is the fruit of a tree yielding seed, to you it shall be for meat." From words such as these, one can derive scriptural authority for the botanic system of medicine.

'We cannot know precisely how human beings first learnt that by careful use of certain herbs they could cure their sickness, but in the course of time it has become evident that almost every member of the vegetable kingdom has some medicinal property. Ayer's Almanac wittily defines a weed as a plant whose virtues we have yet to discover. Although the first medicinal plant we read of is the Balm of Gilead, there can be no doubt from references elsewhere in the Bible and in later traditions that God's people have always known of the health-giving efficacy of leaves, roots, bark, flowers and seeds, when properly prepared and dispensed...'

In other public addresses and private conversations during the weeks that followed, William – Dr Hammond, as he now liked to be called – often mentioned the particular benefits of herbal medicine, and alluded to his previous experiences as a physician familiar with nature's fruits. From those who attended the church where he preached, word spread to others in the town. Growing numbers of people began to turn to Dr Hammond for advice about treating their ailments with certain infusions and decoctions.

To Ethel Brockway he began to talk expansively about his plan to set up a business that would produce and dispense botanic remedies. He was spending more time in her company these days. Barely four months since Harold Brockway's death, the widow had cast aside all formalities of the mourning period. The crimson feathers and gauze trim she now wore in her hat proclaimed publicly what William had already observed: she was a wealthy woman, who wanted to do some spending and acquire a replacement husband. On both counts William was happy to assist.

Their wedding was arranged without fuss and drew little comment apart from the tutting of a few envious gossips. Intimacy excited Ethel, which made it easy for William to engage her interest in his scheme to establish a botanic dispensary and herbal medicine factory in Franklin Falls.

'It's a very lucrative business opportunity, my dear – and one that promises to be a great boon to the community here, of course.'

'I'm sure you can make a great success of it. You're a clever man.'

'There's no doubt in my mind it will operate profitably. The real challenge is in getting the whole thing started. I'll need to purchase a suitable building, obtain the necessary equipment, organise a system for collecting the herbs from suppliers, advertise the manufactured products...It will all take a good deal of investment.'

Twenty-seven

'"Then I went down to the potter's house, and, behold, he wrought a work on the wheels..."'

As William's voice filled the little chapel with his reading from the book of Jeremiah, he saw his new wife lean forward slightly in her pew with an adoring expression on her uncomely face.

'"Cannot I do with you as this potter? saith the Lord. Behold, as the clay is in the potter's hand, so are ye in mine hand..."'

Later, as he was kneading Ethel's tremulous flesh and watching her mouth twitch against the pillow, he thought how easy it all was. You could stir blood in different ways: with well-chosen words, with well-timed gestures, with cunning hands.

Franklin Falls was brimful of money, albeit unevenly shared. He would do some redistributing. With the three thousand dollars that his wife had drawn for him from the Brockway inheritance account, and another twelve hundred borrowed from several enthusiastic townsfolk, William decided that he had enough in hand for his purposes. Having put down a small deposit on the purchase of a vacant shop in Central Street, he engaged a local architect to draw up plans for extending and modifying the building.

'And now,' he told Ethel, his hand palping the area between her shoulder blades, 'I need to make arrangements with some reliable suppliers. That means, my dear, a short trip to Concord. It wouldn't be prudent to sign any contracts before I speak personally with the people concerned. We must ensure that this business of ours is going to be on a sound footing.'

He could tell that she liked the way he said it: this business of ours. So she planted a kiss on his cheek and waved him goodbye at the coach station, smiling happily. Her infatuation was obvious: she might as well have been shouting to everybody, 'What a handsome and clever man he is, this husband of mine!' Of course he would be back, he assured her, in time to speak at the Sunday worship service.

But Sunday passed. A letter reached her a week later. Some complications had arisen, he said, and it was necessary for him to proceed a little further afield in search of suitable materials. He would write to her again as soon as possible, and return before long. She heard nothing more. Some accident must have happened, she told her neighbours and the church folk. When more than a month went by, still with no word from him, and with the whole town now aware of his absence through a report in *The Merrimack Journal*, she asked the police to make enquiries about her missing husband's welfare. They said they would do so, but expressed their doubts in bluntly sceptical terms.

'My guess, Mrs Hammond, is that it's more likely to be foul play than anything accidental,' said the officer in charge at Franklin Falls. 'But whether your husband is a victim or a perpetrator...' He implied his own view with a shrug, 'I'm sorry if that possibility shocks you, but such things do happen more often than they ought to.'

Some six weeks further on, chance intervened. Jonathan Baxter Harrison, visiting Boston to deliver a public lecture at the invitation of a group associated with *The Unitarian Review*, was startled to see the lost man loitering in the lobby of the Parker House Hotel, flanked by two loud-mouthed, loud-dressed women of dubious respectability. Having observed Hammond for a few minutes without making his own presence known, Harrison quietly summoned the police, who soon arrived at the hotel to apprehend the absconder.

'Larceny,' said Inspector Richardson, when William demanded to know why he was being arrested. 'Larceny on a bold scale, Hammond. We know about the circumstances of your disappearance from Franklin Falls. We know that you purloined large sums of money...'

'Purloined! Certainly not, Inspector. Any money provided to me was for an agreed and legitimate business purpose.'

'The business idea may have been legitimate in itself, but patently your real purpose was not. You obtained money from your wife and from a number of trusting citizens on a spurious pretence. If your motives had been honest you wouldn't be here in Boston now, long after you left Franklin Falls and long after you last sent word to anyone there. You can spare me any brazen protestation that your presence here in this city has anything to do with your ostensible reason for departing from that place.'

William's attempts to smooth-talk his way out of trouble proved unavailing. As his photograph was taken for police records, he reflected ruefully on the bad luck that had tripped him this time, just when everything seemed to be going according to plan. He should have erased his tracks more carefully, should have travelled further away from Franklin Falls, should have kept out of sight for longer. Next time he would be more discreet.

But for now might it after all be possible to get the police to drop the charge, or at least reduce the penalty, if he cooperated with them? Negotiations would allow him to reveal where he had stowed most of the Franklin Falls money. It could then be returned to those who had put such simple trust into his smooth hands. Perhaps the same skills could come to his aid once again. Was he not a consummate persuader?

Part 7

Dunedin, Melbourne, Honolulu, 1890–91

Twenty-eight

'She is certainly within her rights,' said Robert Stout. 'We must accept that principle, whatever we may think about the way in which the matter is being pursued.'

Edward frowned and tapped his hand on his knee. He had thought that Stout, renowned as a fiery debater in his parliamentary days, would show more vigour in helping him to ward off this attempt to fragment the property.

'So there's nothing we can properly challenge?'

Stout shook his head in reply.

'My greatest concern,' Edward persisted, 'is that Hammond is manipulating the whole thing. Frances was always wilful but she'd never have been so adamant about an immediate sale if he hadn't been pushing so hard, the greedy devil. When they came to me last week to announce what they wanted to do, I left him in no doubt about my view. I said to his face, "I can see your hand in this, Hammond." Of course Frances protested, claiming I've never treated her as an adult person in her own right, and so forth, but that's nonsense. He is pulling her strings, I'm sure of it.'

Tapping his fingers on the desk, he looked again at the two letters.

Adams Bros. Solicitors
Exchange Court, Princes Street
Dunedin
26 November 1890

Messrs Stout & Mondy Solicitors
Dear Sirs
Re: Phillips Estate

Our client proposes that the land be put up for sale in allotments. Mrs Hammond thinks they will sell as well now as they are likely to do for some time to come. We may, if you agree to this proposal, confer as to the precise plan to be adopted in the subdivision. Meantime we suggest that it be divided into seven lots, each house being sold with a piece of land and the strips extending from the town belt divided into two allotments.

As our client desires to return to Victoria next week we shall be glad to have your reply without delay. With regard to the money out on mortgage there need be no difficulty. An assignment of part of the securities and debts could easily be arranged.
Yours truly
Adams Bros.

Adams Bros. Solicitors
Exchange Court, Princes Street
Dunedin
27 November 1890

Messrs Stout & Mondy Solicitors
Dear Sirs
Re: Phillips Estate

Are your clients willing to purchase Mrs
Hammond's share at such value as may be placed
upon it by two valuers chosen in the usual way? If
so we are prepared to advise her to agree and then
arrive at a speedy settlement, or if your clients will
make an offer for the property we can consider it
and if sufficient would be prepared to accept it on
her behalf.

We have learnt this morning that there are
some Tramway Company shares belonging to the
estate, which were not mentioned yesterday. We
presume you did not know of them.
Yours truly
Adams Bros.

Edward handed the letters back with a sigh.

'Very well, Mr Stout,' he said. 'It seems we must comply.
Please arrange for the independent valuations.'

* * *

Sitting with Isabella in the D.I.C. refreshment room, Frances
felt a pang of disappointment that the expected responses
were not forthcoming. Instead, her friend was full of sceptical
questions.

'But Frances, how much do you *know* about him? About
his family, about his means? His professional background? If
he's a properly qualified doctor, where did he do his medical
training? And what exactly has he been up to in the years before
you met?'

'Isabella, you sound just like my brothers! Really, if those were the considerations that mattered most, I could have settled down with a safe bore like Stuart Donaldson! My William is a person of great intellect and charm and a wide experience of life. Quite simply, he's far, far more interesting than any other man I've met. I thought you would understand what I value, and accept my judgment.'

'Isn't it a wee bit strange that he doesn't wish to meet your friends?'

'That's most unfair of you, Isabella. Our complicated legal business had to take priority, especially as Edward has been so difficult about it all. Quite rude, in fact. And we've been very busy sorting out which of my things to take away with us, and which to discard. You shouldn't be offended now that we've had to decline your dinner invitation. William says we must get the Tuesday steamer back to Melbourne. He has some matters to attend to there.'

'But what can be so urgent? Why all this rush? He seems to want to hurry everything. The wedding was arranged and over before we knew anything about it, and now it's barely a week since you arrived back in Dunedin, and we've had only this one conversation, and you're leaving again. But Frances, believe me, if you're truly happy with this man I won't question you further about him. Certainly you deserve a companion whose mind is as lively as yours, and it would be impertinent of me to press any doubts about your choice.'

Frances thought this concession too qualified and belated to be altogether satisfactory, but let the matter rest.

'You will write to me, Frances? As often as you can? I'll want to know what you're doing, and thinking. What you're reading. How you feel.'

'Of course.'

After a pause they began talking of easier things. Isabella

told Frances about the progress of her two daughters, Charlotte and Nellie, students at Otago Girls' High School. Young Charlotte had no aptitude for study, sighed Isabella, but Nellie was showing every sign of sharing her parents' literary pursuits. She adored her new senior English mistress, Miss Fraser, and had become this year a voracious reader.

'Tell me, Frances,' said her friend, leaning forward, 'how you came to acquire such an uncommon knowledge of poetry, and such a lively awareness of the arts. For someone who left school so young, you seem to read more widely and deeply than many a person who's had the benefit of an extensive formal education. You're not entirely self-taught, are you?'

'Not at all. I was fortunate that dear old Angus Gordon, who'd been my father's friend and physician years ago, took a kindly interest in my welfare. I think he felt sorry for me, cooped up at home, having to help the maidservant and look after my sick widowed mother at an age when most of my friends were going on to high school. He had a sternly formal manner, like a pedantic dominie, but I grew to recognise the simple benevolence shining underneath. He'd come to our house every Friday afternoon, and insist I converse with him about whatever reading matter he'd left with me the previous week. He taught me to discriminate, explain, argue. Books were always the subject matter – books of all kinds. He loved the great poets particularly. He'd recite by heart, and with strong feeling, the whole of 'Tintern Abbey' and long passages from *Paradise Lost*. I can still hear him and picture him, his eyes closed and his cheek moistening:

'Some natural tears they dropped, but wiped them soon.
The world was all before them, where to choose
Their place of rest, and Providence their guide.

They hand in hand with wand'ring steps and slow
Through Eden took their solitary way.

'Dr Gordon was a wonderful instructor. Almost a second father, too, in some ways. He died just a couple of years ago, and I miss him very much.'

She did not add, but thought: I would miss him even more if it were not that dear William's voice carries some of that same power – 'Felt in the blood, and felt along the heart'.

* * *

On their last morning in Dunedin, while William was making arrangements with the bank, she visited the family grave plot and lingered there for half an hour, leaning against the wrought iron fence. There had been heavy rain during the night, and an unseasonable damp haze still hung around the trees bordering the cemetery. From somewhere in the misty distance a plaintive sound of bagpipes grizzled at the weather.

Sandstone inscriptions recorded only the barest of facts. She wished they could evoke more eloquently the particular lives that they commemorated in so few words. There was little she could associate with her father's name, and of her baby sister, dead at five months, she remembered nothing; Helen would now have been twenty-seven. About her mother, a kindly but ineffectual woman whose life had dwindled into despondency, Frances knew everything there was to know.

She walked slowly past the rows of gravestones, glancing at their epitaphs and carved motifs. Bereft families had chosen various ways of representing the consolations of Christian faith, and she was struck by the paradox that Jesus figured both as a sacrificial sheep and as a rescuing shepherd. The thought of being 'washed in the blood of the Lamb' had no appeal, but she found great comfort in being looked after by a guardian of the fold.

Twenty-nine

In the weeks and months that followed their return to Melbourne, there was not a great deal that Frances could find to say in letters to Isabella. It took some while to obtain suitable accommodation: at William's insistence they stayed again at the Menzies for a fortnight (Frances thought this extravagant, but her protestations were dismissed), and it was only reluctantly that he agreed to look for less expensive lodgings. The urgent business that he had cited as a compelling reason to hurry back from Dunedin seemed to have evaporated. When Frances asked him about it, he waved the question aside – it was just a tedious financial matter, he said, that turned out to be less pressing than it had seemed. He would explain it later, he assured her.

Meanwhile he had let the deacons at the Brunswick church know he was available should they require his services. A modest stipend was agreed upon and the arrangement soon settled. For Frances, there was intense pleasure and pride in simply joining the congregation each Sunday to listen to his eloquent sermons. As the preaching role carried few other obligations during the week, they could explore the city together in an unhurried manner. When the weather was clement, they would stroll through the Botanic Gardens, or take a tram to the magnificent Public Library, or revisit the cemetery in Carlton. In the evening there were sometimes entertainments, and although William was seldom given to mirth he laughed merrily when they went to see *The Mikado* at the Princess Theatre.

'But that burlesque world,' she said as they returned from the theatre. 'Do you think it resembles modern Japan in any way?'

'Not in the least, I'd say. I want us, one day, to see Japanese society at first hand, but we shouldn't expect to encounter anything like the ridiculous Town of Titipu.'

'So the reality will be less strange?'

'Probably more strange. Whatever we find there, I think it's likely Japan will turn out to be a very peculiar place. Although I've yet to visit any oriental country, my journeying in various parts of the world convinces me that the most common mistake we make is to assume our views and values will be shared elsewhere. Other people, especially from other places, are often much more opaque than we generally suppose.'

It was a conversation she would recall more than once during later travels.

None of their Melbourne activities seemed sufficiently noteworthy to warrant recounting in a letter to Dunedin; and besides, Frances was finding it difficult to pay much attention to anyone but William. She loved to hear his deep voice, and to watch his gestures, even his ordinary actions – the fastidious washing and drying of his hands, the care he took in trimming his beard, the way he gripped his knife and fork tightly as if at any moment they might jump from his grasp. She wanted to touch the hair above his knuckles and the veins that stood out on the back of his wrists. Above all, it was the hardness of his body, his sinewy vigour, that fascinated her. She became more and more eager for his nightly embrace, and wondered how lustfulness could be deemed sinful when it was between man and wife. She loved the sensation of his hands as they moved all over her, and then, as he shifted his weight on top of her and the riding and rippling began, she could hardly distinguish the heavy thud of his pulse from the loud echo of her own body.

During the daytime a kind of lethargy would often come over her. Melbourne itself had lost much of its attraction. It was difficult for her to regard it, now, as more than a transitional space. Words came to her from the last chapter of Paul's epistle to the Hebrews: 'For we have here no continuing city, but we seek one to come.' Although they had found a well-equipped house to rent in Brunswick, it was just a temporary arrangement. There were moments when she would have liked to feel more settled here, make this busy metropolis her home, this place where she and William had joined their lives together. Yet it was really just somewhere to wait, pausing for a few weeks or months until they received their proceeds from the Dunedin property sale. And then their adventuring would begin.

'The Pacific first,' William said without hesitation, when she asked about the travel plans he had in mind for them. 'We must see that great expanse of ocean, and some of the many islands scattered across it. I've especially wanted to visit the Sandwich Islands – a paradise, by all accounts. We'll take a steamer to Auckland and from there to Honolulu.'

* * *

'What utter claptrap!' William slapped the booklet irritably with the back of his hand. 'Do these building society publicists think we're all fools?'

Frances raised her eyes enquiringly from her volume of Browning.

'I picked this up yesterday – left on a seat in the tram. Not surprising that someone had discarded it. "Home Truths for Home Seekers" it's called, but a more truthful title would be "We Want Your Money". A special publication of the Australasian Building Societies and Mortgage Companies Gazette. It would have us believe that respectability depends on buying a house! People who prefer to move around are all shiftless nomads, apparently. Just listen to this supercilious nonsense:

> 'A notable feature of our Australian cities is the frequency with which certain of their inhabitants move from one place of abode to another. We refer to that class of people, forming a large portion of our suburban population, the family heads of which astonish their necessarily few friends if they remain two or three years in the one suburb...'

William snorted with derision. 'Hardly a year since the Premier Building Association collapsed, with its secretary now in jail – and yet these marketeers, posing as moralists, hope to convince us that the settled life of home ownership is the only virtuous life. Here's another clever bit of mesmerism: "The working man who continues for eight or ten years to pay his contributions" – into the coffers of a building society, they mean – "becomes thereby an improved man..." An *improved* man! Hah! How much *improvement* will that man enjoy when the boom subsides and he must default on the repayment of his loan? When he's out of work and his family is put out of its home? This whole economy, built on the idea that everyone must have a settled domicile, is already showing signs of collapse. It's a house of cards – that's the irony!'

He tossed the booklet aside contemptuously. Frances was pensive, remembering the dinner-table conversation a year earlier, at the Morrisons' villa, when she had first tried to express her own thoughts about the elusiveness of 'home' and the allure of mobility. There seemed no doubt that William was the perfect companion for a restless woman. Yet she felt some undercurrent of uneasiness, too, at the prospect of being on the move indefinitely, almost like a gypsy.

* * *

By the time the money came through in the first week of March, she was certain that she was with child. This condition made her both joyful and apprehensive.

'Shouldn't we tarry here until after the baby is born?' she asked.

'But why?' William spread his hands in a rhetorical gesture. 'Surely it doesn't matter to infants whether they happen to be in one place or another. And you, Frances, you can be just as good a mother on the high seas or the open road as in a Melbourne suburb. If we postpone our travel plans now, merely because of an imagined inconvenience, there will always be something to justify further delays. The world is out there waiting for us to make its acquaintance, but we must seize our opportunities while they're available.'

His energy and decisiveness carried her along. Yes, of course she wanted to travel with him; she shared the sense of urgency, and was just as eager to see the world as she had ever been. No doubt the baby would be adaptable, she told herself, and indeed would probably thrive in response to the changing scene.

It was on her thirtieth birthday, a few days later, that she saw for the first time how quickly William could become vexed by even a trivial matter. He announced that he wanted them to celebrate her birthday and the pregnancy with a special meal at the Menzies, but she was feeling nauseous and told him that she could not face the thought of dining out grandly.

Frowning, he stared at her.

'I hope, Frances,' he said coldly, 'this doesn't mean you'll wish to turn your back on social pleasures from now on. A prospective mother you may be, but your primary duty is as my wifely companion.'

Feeling the sting of this rebuke, she began mildly to explain: it was probably just a temporary indisposition, but for the time being she would be poor company for him and a misery to herself if they were to try to celebrate in that way. The fine food would be wasted on her.

To her astonishment, these conciliatory words somehow exasperated him. Scowling, he struck the table with the palm of his hand and left the room abruptly. It was such an excessive and almost infantile reaction that Frances sat for half an hour trying to make sense of it. She decided it must have been no more than a delayed outburst of pent-up tension over the estate claims. Edward had been quite hostile towards William, and even Frederick's attitude to his new brother-in-law had hardly been cordial. She could excuse her husband for this moment of ill-temper now.

Nevertheless she became a little more cautious towards him, a little more inhibited, a little more inclined to pause and choose her words. It was the first shadow over her contentment.

On the other hand her admiration for his intellect remained unabated, and nowhere was this more evident than when he spoke. The precision of his language was masterly, not only from the pulpit but in the most casual conversation as well. Compared to William, most men of her previous acquaintance seemed to fumble with their words, and privately she had always been confident of her superior verbal skills. But William was exceptionally articulate. In part, she knew, this reflected his greater maturity: it had transpired that he was some twenty years her senior.

She felt an intense curiosity about this strange man she loved, prodigiously eloquent and yet often oddly brusque. Even when in a good humour he seldom spoke of his past without some reticence. Several times, during this period in Melbourne, Frances asked him to tell her about his younger self – how he had developed his gift for public speaking or acquired his knowledge of medical matters, where his early education had taken place. Usually he brushed such questions aside – tersely or playfully according to his mood; but now and then he would talk of people from whom he had learnt and places in which he had shaped his skills. He spoke with special warmth of his schoolteacher in La Chute, Mr Meikle, 'an uncommonly decent man with a spellbinding voice and a compassionate heart' who had instilled into his charges a sense of the power of poetry and storytelling. He mentioned a jovial good-natured fellow, Jerome Davin, who had become 'a sort of stepfather' when the family moved to Owen Sound. There were passing references to Jesuit teachers – this must have been at a later stage, she supposed – 'admirable in their passion for disciplined learning but naive in their view of human nature, and tainted by the vile corruption of the papist church.'

About personal aspects of his adult life she could draw little from him. What experiences had he passed through in the years before she knew him? There were only snippets of information and Frances wondered about his parents, the brothers he had once mentioned, the scarring across the palm of his left hand. He had alluded to travels in different parts of North America, and beyond – at least, she knew, to Malta and South Africa as well as the Antipodes – but what had taken him from one place to another? She knew of the now deceased Mrs Hammond who accompanied him to Dunedin when Frances first met him, but he had also been widowed, he said, as a young man in La Chute. Frances wondered about the years between those marriages, but did not feel bold enough to enquire directly. Facts would be more likely to emerge, she thought, if she did not press for them.

Thirty

William took charge of all their plans. He would return alone to Dunedin, he decided, 'to tidy up some of the legal matters'. From there he would proceed to Auckland to await her arrival from Sydney, where she would spend a fortnight before boarding the *S.S. Mariposa*. They would have a few days in Auckland together while the steamer was being prepared and provisioned for their onward voyage to Honolulu.

Anxiety at the thought of being separated, even for two or three weeks, and having to face the Tasman crossing without him, was lightened by the pleasant prospect of staying in Sydney with the Bruntons. Though it was a long while since they had left Dunedin, she remembered them fondly and knew that their kindness to her family went back to an earlier stage than her memory could reach. Her mother had often sung their praises: they had been generous when she was struggling, as a young widow, to manage three children. 'Of all the church folk,' Mrs Phillips used to say, 'it was George and Ida Brunton who helped me most, in all sorts of practical ways. Good people. Such good people.' After their move to Sydney, letters arrived regularly, and as her mother's eyesight gradually failed she would get Frances to read and re-read Ida's letters aloud to her.

Writing to them now from Melbourne, with news of her marriage and mention of her impending visit to Sydney, she was confident of being invited to stay with them. Indeed Ida's postcard reply came back quickly: 'We *insist* that your time in Sydney be spent with us. Expect to see us on the wharf when your boat comes in.'

What Frances did not expect was the change in George Brunton. He had always expressed his opinions vehemently, but after a weekend cooped up in their small Newtown cottage she was finding his manner quite overbearing. He would talk loudly at her, jabbing with his forefinger, a constant tic at the corner of his mouth.

'He often gets like this now,' said Ida apologetically when at last he was out of the house. 'It's all the reading that does it. Makes him so agitated these days.' She gestured towards the little table beside his armchair, where there was a pile of books. 'I blame the man he works with, his business partner – not a godly man, and he gives George some radical literature, full of troubling ideas. George won't attend church with me these days.'

Frances managed to dodge and deflect most of Brunton's attempts to hold forth, but even the mildest topic could provoke a harangue, as it did on her last evening. It was an exciting prospect, she was saying, to travel overseas with her husband.

George Brunton frowned. 'Where to?'

'Well, we haven't made plans beyond the Sandwich Islands, but probably Japan and China.'

'What's the purpose of your travels?'

'George!' his wife remonstrated. 'Don't be such an inquisitor! Frances doesn't have to tell you her reasons for what she chooses to do.'

'But she ought to know her reasons,' he replied gruffly. 'If there's nothing more to it than the idle curiosity of the tourist, that's a lost opportunity for an intelligent young woman.'

'Opportunity?' As soon as she uttered the word, Frances regretted giving him this cue.

'The opportunity to learn, of course!' he almost shouted. 'To learn what human progress really means. To understand how civilisation goes through stages – at different times in different places. Listen!' He snatched up one of the books beside his chair, flicked through some of the pages towards the end, and read in a declamatory tone:

'The great Turkish and Chinese Empires, the lands of Morocco, Abyssinia, and Tibet, will be eventually filled with free, industrious, and educated populations. But those people will never begin to advance until their property is rendered secure, until they enjoy the rights of man; and these they will never obtain except by means of European conquest...'

He broke off, wrinkling his forehead. 'Civilisation continues to evolve, y'see, and evolution means that each created thing, sooner or later, needs to be discarded when a stronger thing comes along to push it aside.'

George was perspiring with passion. His cheeks shone bright red and there were flecks of foam on his lip. He read on relentlessly:

'In all things there is cruel, profligate, and abandoned waste. Of all the animals that are born a few only can survive; and it is owing to this law that development takes place. The law of Murder is the law of Growth. Life is one long tragedy; creation is one great crime.

'Pain, grief, disease, and death – are these the inventions of a loving God? That no animal shall rise to excellence except by being fatal to the life of others – is this the law of a kind Creator?...Pain is not less pain because it is useful; murder is not less murder because it is conducive to development. Here is blood upon the hand still, and all the perfumes of Arabia will not sweeten it.'

He clapped the book shut and shook it at her. 'Y'see! Reade is one of the great travellers of our time, but one of the great thinkers too. That's what you need to remember when you go from country to country. Just looking isn't enough. You have to ask yourself what it all tells you – about why people suffer, about what drives mankind forward.'

'It's a terribly bleak view of the world,' said Frances.

'You probably find it shocking too, and yet it's the truth,' he retorted.

* * *

When at last she saw William again, Frances wept and clung to him. Her journey from Sydney had been uncomfortable, and she was unsure whether to attribute the biliousness to the rough winds or to her own condition. Their stay in Auckland would be short and he agreed that they should spend the time quietly, resting in their harbourside hotel.

The weather was changeable: a fine morning could yield suddenly to squalls that churned up the water and drove spray high over the wharves. On their second day, one of these storms on the harbour caught some pleasure boats unawares. From their hotel window Frances witnessed a yacht capsize, flinging people into the turbulent water. A lifeboat was launched from a ship anchored nearby, and as it gradually approached the upturned hull she thought she saw someone dive into the water with a lifebelt. Then heavy rain obscured her view. The next day's newspaper confirmed her fears: Henry Talbot, a young officer from the *Persian Empire*, had drowned along with two of the three he had tried to save.

The report troubled Frances acutely.

'Why should the accidental death of strangers affect you so much?' William asked, with a hint of irritation.

She twisted her handkerchief.

'I'm not sure I know,' she confessed. 'Perhaps it's simply the piteous nature of that poor young man's sacrifice – losing his life in an attempt to rescue others. Or perhaps it's the violent way they all died, so cruelly sudden – sucked under the surge. I can't bear to imagine what that must have felt like.'

But afterwards, when he had left the room, she said to herself: 'It's more than that.' What exactly was stirring in her heart? It felt something like the mixture of emotions that seized her after Grace Hutton's accident. In part, she thought, it was stark fear at the prospect of her own eventual death. But mingling with that was a different feeling, more staunch: a determination to surmount the fear and press on.

Lines learnt long ago welled up, and she whispered them to herself.

No voice divine the storm allayed,
No light propitious shone
When, snatched from all effectual aid,
We perished, each alone:
But I beneath a rougher sea,
And whelmed in deeper gulfs than he!

It's a dreadful truth, she thought. We do perish, in anticipation, whenever we know that somebody else is perishing. Each alone. This trip across the Pacific will frighten me, I feel sure. But the knowledge makes me all the more resolute about travelling.

Thirty-one

It had been a long voyage to Honolulu, sometimes monotonous, and she felt relieved to be on firm land again, in a good hotel with a comfortable bed waiting to ease her fatigue. The morning sickness had disappeared, though now that the baby was quickening so vigorously inside her Frances craved rest and liked to retire early. But this evening, despite her lassitude, she would write a family letter. Pulling a sheet of paper from the writing desk, she leaned towards the lamp and cleaned the nib of her pen. She told Fred and Mary about the flying fish, thick as sparrows; the natives whose canoes met them at Tutuila, selling handiwork and diving for silver coins but disdaining coppers; the fruit trees – banana, breadfruit, mango, cocoa nut – growing outside the hotel as abundantly as grass grew in Dunedin. Hardly informative, she thought as she sealed the letter, but it would reassure them that she was safe. She would reserve more considered reflections for Isabella, when she could find time and energy.

During the next few weeks there was no opportunity for leisurely correspondence. William was like a coiled spring. They must travel up the newly completed Tantalus road, he announced. One of the hotel guests had told him it was a magnet for tourist business: it would take them through a lush rainforest and give them wonderful views on all sides.

She protested. She was tired, she said. But it would do her good, he insisted, to get out and see the countryside. There was no resisting his determination.

He went to a livery stable that was said to be the best in Honolulu. In a light rockaway carriage, Frances and he set out the next morning, first for a sweep around the city and then towards the summit of Punchbowl Hill; but, taking what turned out to be the wrong road, they drove up Nuuana Valley until they came to a standstill in the midst of a big sugar farm. The road was so narrow that they had to get out of the rockaway while William, with great difficulty and much muttering and sweating, unhitched the horses and turned the vehicle around by hand. By this time Frances was trembling with anxiety and feeling faint with the heat. As they returned to town William was in an ill humour and hardly uttered a word.

She had come to know that there were times when his mood could change abruptly. He would withdraw into a cold dark silence, and Frances felt as if their marriage had turned a street corner into a sudden bitter wind.

A week later he found someone to drive him to the lookout but Frances declined to go this time, pleading a stomach disorder. He returned with lyrical descriptions of what he had seen – an old volcanic crater, huge plantations, a panoramic vista that included Diamond Head and Waikiki. Though glad to see him so animated, she demurred at the suggestion that she accompany him on a repeat excursion. Nor did she want to be looking around the town with him, or even attending worship services on Sundays. No, she said, in her condition she'd be a hindrance. But he shouldn't think of curtailing his activities on her account.

He did not hesitate, after that, to spend several hours each day away from her, usually on unspecified 'business opportunities'. Much as she loved his companionship, and longed for his hand on her shoulder, the hours of solitude seldom dragged. She read for long periods, looking up often from the page to reflect on some phrase or to follow a tangential thought.

Now and then she tried capturing some of these reflections on paper for Isabella, only to discard most of the pages. In the end the letter she despatched was mainly about the little stack of books she had bought in Auckland. Her special delight, a new discovery, was Robert Louis Stevenson. How was it, she asked her friend, that this wonderful writer – a Scot, too! – was hardly mentioned in Dunedin except as a spinner of boys' adventure yarns? An Auckland bookseller recommended Stevenson and she had devoured several of his stories during the voyage. The steamer had taken them close to Upolu, Stevenson's home in recent years. Had Isabella read his *Strange Case of Dr Jekyll and Mr Hyde*? An extraordinary tale of good and evil wrestling for a man's soul, and cleaving his personality in two. What a dreadful thought – that someone with every appearance of respectability could perhaps be the epitome of evil!

She described for Isabella the people she had seen in Honolulu: all colours and sizes and shapes, just like the fruit and blossom trees, the women with their loose-fitting dresses of taffeta or dimity, the native men so powerfully built, big-chested and strong-limbed, the Chinese workers scrawny in comparison. The trade in sugar, she wrote, seemed to dominate everybody's lives. Some local people were worried about the big American warships that came to the Pearl Harbour naval base. There were rumours of a plot to overthrow the monarchy. According to William, it would be in the best interests of the natives – most of them fishermen and farm labourers – to be governed as an American state, because their ruler lived so extravagantly in the Iolani Palace.

And yet the United States didn't seem to have imperial aspirations like those of Britain and some European nations. Frances remembered how the world map at the front of Edward's

Cyclopedia showed in crimson all countries of the British Empire, scattered across the face of the earth. And on the voyage from Auckland, when they dined at the captain's table, he talked about the 'All-Red Routes' linking every colonial territory to London: the lines of shipping and telegraph criss-crossing the world like arteries and veins. It seemed unimaginable that any other country would ever try to emulate Britain's colonising mission.

Thirty-two

As the September rains thickened and the time approached for her confinement, Frances felt the first sharp pangs in her swollen belly. William had found a local midwife to assist with the birth, and a druggist's store where they could obtain imported herbs. When Frances went into labour he insisted she drink copious infusions of dried burnet stalks and leaves. It was a day of steamy heat, and the bowls of hot water in the small room made the air seem muggier. Sweat ran down her face. The sudden clutching pains frightened her, and as her groans became more frequent William administered chloroform. Suddenly she was being roused and encouraged loudly, the slippery little body was emerging from hers in a confusion of blood and tears, and her own cries of relief gave way at last to the plaintive squeaking of a daughter.

They named the newborn after her mother, but seldom spoke of her as Frances: she would remain 'Baby'. In the weeks that followed, almost everything seemed to be dictated by the irregular rhythms of feeding and sleeping. Although Frances had not anticipated that Baby would rule their lives so imperiously, she revelled in the rituals and routines of mothering.

Strange at first, the sensation of suckling soon became comfortable and then intensely pleasurable. She came to love the way the little mouth would clamp around her nipple and tug with greedy pulsations. Occasionally, while nursing, she felt a delicious tingle running from her breast to her groin. Sometimes William would sit with her, smiling quietly, and watch her feed their child. She imagined the three of them as a picture painted by Millais, with a caption like 'Contentment'. But at other times, returning from one of his afternoons in the town, he would be in an irritable mood, brow wrinkled and lips pursed. Mischievous gossip had spread mistrust, he said. When pressed, he told her about stories he knew to be circulating.

'Your forbearance amazes me,' she said. 'How can you let them sully your name like this?'

'I do feel indignant, naturally,' he replied. 'False witness is hateful. But God's messengers have often had to contend with worse. I think it will soon be time to leave this place. My path is blocked here.'

While this occupied her mind, Frances penned several pages to Isabella, but it was partly for herself that she wrote:

It pains me to say that many of the protestant
missionaries in these islands are small-minded and
mean-spirited. One can understand their jealousy
towards the success of the papists here, but they are
also hostile towards some of their own kind. William
has encountered this exclusive attitude, finding
them very resistant to his offers to preach. Evidently
wanting to keep their little paradise to themselves,
they are quick to disparage and even defame others
who dare to carry out the Lord's work here.

I've learned about an episode involving my
hero Robert Louis Stevenson that reflects this hostile
atmosphere. He was here in Hawaii just a couple
of years ago, and during his stay he visited the
government's leper colony on Molokai. His aim

was to uncover the truth about the famous Catholic missionary to the lepers, Father Damien, who had died only a month earlier. There had been scurrilous rumours that this priest contracted leprosy through intimacies with female patients. RLS (himself a Presbyterian) questioned the people of Molokai closely, nuns and lepers, who left him in no doubt that the stories were utter falsehoods, and that Father Damien was a person of remarkable integrity.

Then last year, while in Sydney, RLS read in a Presbyterian newsletter another attack upon Father Damien by a Dr Charles Hyde, former missionary to Molokai, who maintained these rumours were true. RLS was so provoked that immediately he published *Father Damien: An Open Letter to the Reverend Dr Hyde*. I read it on the boat, just before our arrival, stirred by its passion but never guessing my husband would become the object of similar aspersions.

There has been a lot of nasty gossip here about William. It would be generous to say that the stories stem from misunderstandings but it's more likely that envy and spite are the causes. I know about these matters only because I asked him why he stopped attending our Church's worship services, and seemed angry towards the deacons. He explained that there have been two incidents in which he was blameless but has been traduced.

The first arose when one of the church families appealed to him provide an opinion, as an experienced physician, on the health of their maidservant. This young native Hawaiian woman had been complaining of intermittent abdominal pains. My William duly examined her and diagnosed

ovarian inflammation, for which he prescribed
salicin grains in water and a liniment to be rubbed
above the groin area. As she seemed slow to
comprehend precisely what this latter treatment
required, William had to show her, and it appears
she subsequently mentioned something to her
employer that was taken to mean William had
undressed her and laid his hands on her private parts.
This slander then spread among the church folk, as
he discovered when they began to shun him. In vain
did he protest that he had done nothing wrong.

The other matter concerned an elderly lady
whose acquaintance he had made. William talked
with her about the preaching he wanted to do
among the people who have come here from several
nations – especially the Chinese and Japanese
immigrants brought in as field labourers for the
sugar industry or the new pineapple plantations.
Well, this old Christian widow, Mrs Holcroft, was
stirred by William's earnest dedication to this task
and soon became an enthusiastic supporter. Being
a quite wealthy woman, she was happy to provide
some funds. The money was primarily needed for
employing assistants and training them, so the
Lord's work could continue after we left Honolulu.
Teaching is a slow business, and William has spent a
great deal of time with his recruits. Meanwhile old
Mrs Holcroft suddenly turned somewhat strange
and confused – senile, I suppose – and started
complaining that William had tricked her into giving
him that money.

The way this calumny has circulated around
the town is so unfair. Naturally William feels

indignant, and I don't think we'll be staying in
Honolulu much longer, though with our sweet
little baby less than three months old I'd prefer to
build up her strength before we do much further
travelling...

Recalling Isabella's earlier questions about William, Frances put
aside the pages.

* * *

Frances stroked the back of her baby's hand. The skin's texture
was like a rose petal. Their steamer to Yokohama was leaving
at noon the next day and there was packing to finish, but she
sat back reflectively for a while, thumb under her chin, index
knuckle against her lips. How did she feel, really, about the
strenuous itinerary that William was proposing? Yes, a year earlier when they were poring over maps together in the Melbourne
Public Library she had shared his enthusiasm about touring from
country to country. But motherhood was changing her own
priorities. Japan, China, and the rest – why the plan to go on to
such places at this stage? They were a family, not adventurers
or writers. Would the sampling of exotic places and people
continue to seem a sufficient rationale, or was it becoming for
them an addictive kind of drug, like laudanum? Was it enough
to observe and admire new and strange things, and keep moving
on towards the even newer and stranger?

Questions, too, were forming in her mind about William.
Some matters had always puzzled her. She wondered now whether
his behaviour was as entirely innocent as she wanted to believe.
Could there be, despite denials, some truth in the accusations
that had blighted their time in Honolulu?

The questions would have to keep. She packed them into
the luggage.

Part 8

Japan, British Columbia,
Alaska and beyond, 1892–94

Thirty-three

Within a few weeks of arriving she began to see Japan as something more than just an alien culture. Without becoming less singular, it took on unexpectedly another dimension, personal and disturbing: there were moments when this country seemed a kind of theatre, an extravaganza in which her own half-dormant apprehensions assumed surprising shapes. Things that at first struck her as merely picturesque soon came to embody and enact the troubles of her heart.

Yokohama bustled. On entering the harbour they could see at once, despite the patches of wintry haze, that this was a place where multiple sea-roads converged in a hurly-burly of different purposes. Jostling for elbow room were all sorts of vessels: steamers coming or going with passengers, mail and commodities; a few navy gunboats, rust-blotched; a variegated miscellany of junks, schooners, luggers, tugs, and the smallest oblong-sailed fishing sampans with their mat awnings. Stacked at the dockside stood masses of boxes and crates. Countless little wagons were being rapidly unloaded to augment the piles of merchandise awaiting export.

As their *jinrikisha* took them along the teeming port city streets to their hotel, they were surprised that Japanese people seemed to be outnumbered. This Kannai district abounded in the familiar faces and shapes of westerners. Yet everything was made strange by the peculiarity of noises, colours and smells. Frances remembered Melbourne's reeking alleyways, but the pervasive stench in Yokohama was oppressively different, seeming to waft from a rotting carcase. If it is like this on such a cold winter's day, she thought, it must be unbearable in the hot season.

She sent a brief letter to Fred and Mary, telling them where she now was and providing a few dashes of local colour, but felt displeased with what she had written. It was facile. A picture postcard could have conveyed more. Her underlying dissatisfaction, she knew, was with her own ignorance about Japan. What did she really know of it?

Yet through a chance encounter she soon began to see Japanese society through more experienced eyes. On the third day after their arrival she and William decided to take a ride to the main shopping precinct. Under a lean-to near the hotel, around a charcoal burner, a group of *jinrikisha* coolies crouched like skinny squatting frogs. One of them was summoned and instructed by an imperious hotel officer. Frances and William climbed on board the cart as their runner clutched the handles and quickly set off. Under a clear sky the afternoon felt perceptibly warmer than on previous days. Baby seemed glad to be carried in her mother's arms.

Frances had expected more exotic-looking shop fronts. Apart from the blue cloth that draped their doorposts, some of them – with their signs written in English – would hardly have looked out of place in the streets around the centre of Dunedin. Evidently they catered for foreign visitors. Inside, everything was clean, neat and bright. Cheap curios of little interest to Frances filled many of the shelves, and pictures on the walls were predictable and undistinguished: cherry blossom boughs, river barges, street lanterns. The snowy cone of Mt Fuji reminded her of the white hat of a *jinrikisha* runner.

What did attract her attention in one shop was a glass

cabinet containing an array of small, meticulously crafted boxes: cardboard, bamboo, bronze, wooden; some with carved sur- faces, some with inlaid designs, some painted and lacquered; some with hinged lids, some open; a few cylinder-shaped, most rectangular, often with inner compartments. Engrossed by this display of ingenuity and precision while quietly rocking Baby, she was startled when a loud American voice spoke to her.

'All such beautiful objects, aren't they?'

Turning, she saw a thickset, dowdy, grey-haired woman approaching her, all smiles.

'And what an even more beautiful young creature you have there in your arms,' the woman continued, coming closer and putting a fleshy thumb-tip gently against Baby's palm, so that the little fingers instinctively encircled it.

Frances murmured a proudly maternal platitude as William strolled towards them from the other side of the shop, where he had been inspecting some silk cushions.

The American woman introduced herself to them as Mrs Abbie Higgins, 'now in my tenth year as a resident of Yokohama'. She had come from Nashville, Tennessee, she said, soon after being widowed. The missionary calling was loud and clear, and so she gladly put her shoulder to the wheel of Methodism's work in Japan. William mentioned his own experience as an evangelist, and there were brief exchanges of other information before Frances interrupted apologetically to say that she must return to the hotel without too much delay because the baby was hungry and tired.

'Yes, of course, of course. Let me not detain you a moment longer. But Mrs Hammond, do please call on me at my home if you find yourself with time on your hands. While the doctor attends to matters in the city, you mustn't stay enclosed in the hotel all day, my dear. It would be delightful to talk with you further over a pot of good local tea. In fact I'll make the invitation more specific – could you pay me a visit about three tomorrow?'

So it was arranged, and for the first time in well over a year Frances had a long leisurely conversation with a woman – a woman who, it turned out, had many compelling stories to tell about life among the Japanese. Frances needed no persuading to return, and the ritual of tea with Mrs Higgins became a frequent pleasure during the next few weeks.

Evidently a person of substantial means, Abbie Higgins lived in a blue and white bungalow up the winding Bluff Road, a house on the closely built-up hogsback of land that looked out over the harbour and across the hills in the other direction. Her neat little garden was edged with tall oleanders, camellias and magnolias. She spent each morning at the Methodist Mission office, and most afternoons visiting friends or being visited. As Abbie loved to talk, Frances was happy to prime her with questions. On a wide, glassed-in verandah, they sat among the fan-leaved palms for two hours or more at a time, one talking loudly and gesticulating vigorously, the other listening quietly as stories and opinions flowed.

Abbie's late husband had been an importer of tea from Japan, and tea for her was much more than a refreshing drink. She spoke with enthusiasm about the place of tea in Japanese life, not only its ceremonial consumption but also the elaborate process of cultivating, picking, transporting, drying, packing and shipping. Rocking slightly this way and that as she shifted her weight from one heavy haunch to another, she told of having gone one evening at the invitation of a tea-merchant friend to see the spectacle of the leaves being put through a sequence of machines in a *godown*, a tall warehouse in the business district. She was dumbfounded, she said, by all the clamorous activity, as barefoot half-naked sweating coolies – women stripped to the waist, and men with hardly a stitch on – rushed around amid an inferno of steam and heat and noise. Huge quantities of tea leaves cascaded down chutes and spread along troughs, disappearing into firing machinery before emerging to be sifted and shaken in broad flat baskets and packed into large foil-lined wooden crates.

As Abbie described the gleaming bodies, the hot dust-filled air and the flares that lit up the building, Frances visualised it all as a garish stage spectacle, and was startled to catch herself imagining furtively the shapes of the toiling women and the glint of ruddy light on their small firm breasts. She had never seen any adult female form that was not fully clothed, except her own, and the pictures that now came unbidden to her mind were disturbingly lascivious. She pushed them away; but later, when her baby's lips were sucking at her nipple, the same imagery returned. That night she woke to find her skin glistening with sweat, and lay in a fever of desire until William, responding to her tentative hand on his thigh, loomed over her and slaked her thirst.

Thirty-four

'There's no doubt they're a very clever and industrious people,' declared Abbie. 'And, yes, they've made great educational progress since the constitutional reforms came in. You can see it plainly in the way the government works now. Look at the Meiji cabinet – largely composed of men trained in the heritage of Christendom. A wonderful advance. But I tell you, my dear, Japanese civilisation will always be held back until it discards the elaborate picture-writing system they adapted from the Chinese. Those brushstrokes may look pretty but the long process of acquiring the knowledge and skill to write like that is a terribly tedious business. One of the great benefits our missionaries have brought here is the alphabet. When our form of lettering becomes widely accepted, democratic learning can develop properly. And then the Christian religion will flourish.'

Having no opinion about the relative merits of ideographs and alphabets, Frances simply nodded and let the conversation pause while she took a piece of cake.

'Everyone seems so very polite here,' she remarked, sipping the tea that Abbie had poured ceremoniously into a little bowl. 'In the shops. At the hotel. It *is* sincere, I suppose?'

'Well, I wouldn't say insincere, quite,' replied Abbie. 'But it's not really about sincerity. In this country, etiquette is everything, from sandal to topknot. The Japanese people find all these courteous conventions necessary to...not exactly to disguise, but to *control* what underlies that reticent surface.'

'What does underlie it, then?'

Abbie slowly dispensed more tea, and looked out the window before responding.

'A concern – no, it's more than that – an *obsession* with status. The whole intricate set of relationships between people. Strictly ordered, you see. They need to keep the populace in their proper station, and especially to make sure women remain subordinate.'

'The local women at our hotel do seem very meek, it's true. Perhaps timid?'

'No perhaps about it. You've seen the tiny trees, toy trees really, that people here call *bonsai*?'

'We have, yes. There are some on tables in the hotel lobby.'

'That's just what it's like for the women in this country. Boxed in, tightly enclosed, trimmed back. They're given no choice in life. Marriage is arranged for them – and that's if they're lucky; the alternatives, often, are even more demeaning forms of servitude.' Abbie punctuated her narration by smacking the knuckles of her right hand into the palm of her left. 'You've heard about the tea-houses, no doubt? Let me tell you my dear, they don't have much to do with tea. Some of them are little more than whorehouses!'

While Abbie talked on about the work that the Women's Christian Temperance Union had been doing in Tokio, Frances found her thoughts drifting back to Bella Brotchie in Melbourne – to their first encounter, when Bella was a new recruit in the Salvation Army, full of hope that she could put her shameful experiences behind her; and then the later meeting. Bella had seemed almost defiant in what she said about the physical solace of being with men again.

A week later Frances, William and Baby were travelling

towards Tokio on a jerky train. Sudden departures and new itineraries, she had begun to understand, would be regular features of her life.

'Why Tokio?' she had wanted to ask. But knowing that, for him, abrupt resumptions of journeying, this way or that, needed no particular justification, she packed their bags without complaint and they made their way to the railway station. The Yokohama to Tokio line, someone in the hotel had told them, was Japan's first, opening just twenty years earlier. At a stall beside the platform they bought *ekiben* for the journey – neat little *bento* lunch boxes of leaf-wrapped rice balls, pickled apricots and salty titbits. The dainty precision of these packages, and of so many other small items she had seen in the shop windows and the hotel rooms, matched the descriptions that Abbie had given her of the compact interiors of Japanese homes. Domestic space, Abbie said, at least in the households of well-to-do families, was beautifully ordered, with simple but elegant furnishings.

That was one Japan, but there was another. Looking through the carriage window as they rumbled along beyond the town limits, Frances saw recognisable signs of civilisation begin to disappear, giving way to rough farm huts and the small shiny rectangles of irrigated rice fields, with peasants bent into animal shapes and up to their knees in thick mud. A picturesque setting, yes – the emerald enclosures, knobbled hills, patches of forest with dark blue pines – but seemingly a brutish existence. What family graces, she wondered, could those people possibly enjoy, perched on their dirty little patches of ground? What relevance did the WCTU notion of a companionable home, centred on a common dining table, have to the hardships of the toiling peasantry?

It was an odd paradox, she thought, that the more she travelled the more she encountered heightened apparitions of home, of family, of intimacy. Scenes glimpsed from the train, or described by Abbie Higgins, or played out in the streets and hotels and shops, were presenting to her, as in a pantomime or tableau vivant, half-recognised aspects of her inner life. The changeful relationship with her husband, particularly: as smooth-surfaced and bright as a painted box, yet sometimes a glimpse of something sombre and shapeless underneath.

After enduring a few dismal days of Tokio rain they made their way down towards Kobe, travelling through many miles of devastated countryside where a huge earthquake had gashed open the fields and roads, precipitated landslides and shattered countless houses. They had heard about this cataclysm, which came just a few months earlier, sending great ripples and jolts through a vast area from Sendai in the north to Kagoshima in the south. To see now for themselves the starkness of the damage was to be reminded how perilous and pitiless the natural world could be.

Was this ravaging of the landscape and its people to be understood somehow as God's handiwork? She thought of William's sermon in the Brunswick church – it was hardly eighteen months ago, and she could hear again his sombre voice speaking darkly of a world riven by shock after shock. She remembered the tremors that his words had evoked, and had sent through her veins, harbinger of the quivering pleasure that his body would later transmit so intimately to hers.

In Kobe the cold weather continued and weariness overtook them. Frances came down with a fever, and then William and Baby. Influenza, he said; it would take its course, and meanwhile they could only rest. They were miserable for a week, lost all appetite and became silent except for occasional whimpers from the child. Their aches receded at last, but as they sat in a damp eating-house waiting for a meal they did not expect to enjoy, William announced that they would abandon the idea of going further west into China by way of Korea.

'We've sampled quite enough of oriental life,' he said firmly, 'at least for now. I think we should return to Yokohama and then, before long, take the steamer to Canada. I'd like you to see something of my native land.'

Frances's response was cut short by an outburst of angry yells from the small open kitchen area, and then a scowling man emerged, flung his large chopping knife to the floor and walked quickly past them to the doorway, still shouting over his shoulder at someone in the kitchen as he rushed into the street. It was like a histrionic performance, an extravagant eruption of over-acting.

William shrugged. 'Whatever that was about, it doesn't bode well for our meal,' he said. 'But I suppose we should be thankful he didn't choose to disembowel himself in front of us.'

Remembering the *Mariposa* captain's stories about barbaric local habits of ritual suicide, Frances shuddered. An incomprehensible race, the Japanese, full of enigmatic contradictions. Seemingly perfect manners, ruptured now and then by flashes of exaggerated ferocity. The filthy conditions seen from the train window out in the countryside, and then the fastidiously crafted objects that filled the city shops. In Tokio they had bought an exquisite Kutani bowl. She resolved to keep it with her always, to the end of her life, when it perhaps would hold more material meanings than she could yet imagine. For the time being it was simply a marvel of artistry.

In its delicate design the bowl surpassed any piece of porcelain Frances had seen in New Zealand or Australia. It was broad, about a foot in diameter at the rim. Inside, a powdery spray of speckled golden foliage fell across a spill of bright redness, like the foam-flecked breaking of a bloodshot wave – and then, meticulously detailed, a linked fringe of curlicues around a tilted circle of whiteness; and etched within that, a cluster of pink and gold flowers, dark leaves and crimson berries, all threaded on a fine-lined gently bending branch. On the outside, bold slabs of colour alternated with panels showing birds perched or flying among blossoms. She had seldom come across any object of such wonderful subtlety, and it revived her love of images, making her more alert to the appearance of things, to their patterning and placement.

Thirty-five

On their return to Yokohama she saw her surroundings with a painter's eye. The inescapable smells that had slapped their noses when they first arrived a month earlier no longer seemed so unusual, and initially curious sounds such as the nocturnal booming of temple bells were losing their strangeness. Now it was the brilliance of different colours that struck Frances, and the shapes of things: large clumps of yellow-green bamboo, or the extravagantly bright fluttering flags of butterflies, or the slate-hued robes of merchants as they stood smoking their little brass pipes. For the first time in more than a year she opened her old sketchbook and made pencil drawings of what she saw. With William away from the hotel each afternoon – he liked to stroll around the business district, he said – she could draw while the baby slept.

William seemed impressed by her skill. He nodded under-standingly when she said with a sigh that she wished she could stay long enough in Yokohama to learn something about local artists. He had just met a wealthy merchant, he said, a Mr Joseph Foxton, who collected Japanese art. He would ask him where they might find some pictures to look at. But she was unprepared for the pair of woodblock prints that he brought back to the hotel a couple of days later.

'I think these may startle you, Frances,' he said before

putting the two sheets on the table in front of her. 'You'll find them very wanton, no doubt. They'd shock respectable people in our own society. But I've purchased them because they can help us to appreciate Japanese taste. All classes here, I'm told, including housewives, openly enjoy them. *Shunga* is what these prints are called. Carnal subjects, but finely done. Foxton assures me that artists of the highest repute have produced drawings in this style without the slightest opprobrium, and the pictures continue to circulate widely despite official attempts to discourage vendors in recent times.'

Whether through nonchalance or tact, he moved away and warmed his hands at the fireplace as she picked up the vividly coloured pictures, and she could stare at them without needing to affect modesty. In each of the bedroom scenes the man and woman, crouching in an oddly contorted embrace, both wore brightly patterned traditional costumes – but these were pulled back shamelessly to reveal hugely swollen private parts.

Not knowing what to say about the prints, she asked about their supplier.

'This Mr Foxton: What kind of man is he?'

'Wealthy merchant. Single. Well connected here, apparently. He's been some ten years in Yokohama. He collects porcelain, paintings, unusual photographs, various art objects.'

'How did you meet?'

'Just a chance encounter at the herb doctor's shop on the port road. Foxton was there asking for a stimulant for certain discreet purposes and I engaged him in conversation. I told him about my own experience as a physician, and we continued talking at his club – the United, in *Kaigan-dori* Avenue.'

Frances said nothing about the *shunga* but their depictions rose up in her mind later, at bed-time, when William put his hand under her nightgown.

It was also through Foxton, a little before their departure

from Japan, that they bought Ada. Frances was never sure exactly how the arrangement had been negotiated, or how in the first place Foxton came to know the girl. William, in his usual way, made the decision suddenly and presented it firmly: Frances would need help with the baby and help, too, with other practical matters that required attention because of the further travelling they intended to do. Here was this girl, providentially available, and just mature enough to take on some domestic responsibilities under Frances's direction. The perfect little maidservant, and inexpensive for the purpose. She was a lovely creature, twelve years old, a half-breed who spoke enough English to understand their expectations. For six hundred dollars her needy family would let her be indentured to William and Frances, accompanying them on their journeys and living with them until the verge of adulthood, when she could return to Japan if she chose.

'The arrangement will not only suit us very well,' William explained, 'but will also be a fine Christian service that we can provide for this hapless waif – an opportunity that other young mixed-race girls would envy. Their usual fate, Foxton tells me, is to be sold for a paltry sum to work in houses of ill repute for three years, and at the end of that time no-one else wants them.'

Although Ada seemed docile and pleasant, Frances felt a vague uneasiness, troubled at the prospect of taking such a young person away from her familiar surroundings, but knew better than to question William's judgement or motives. Still, her unspoken thoughts went on tugging at the knotty thread that linked so many women with commerce. If the prostitutes of Tokio were a kind of merchandise, so were those of Melbourne. If there was something even faintly dubious about buying Ada's services, then a similar question must arise with any maid employed anywhere in domestic service. If the oriental idea of arranged marriages implied a material transaction, was this really so very different from the exchange of goods that often accompanied, albeit less openly, marital contracts in the society to which she herself belonged? After all, William had acquired wealth along with a wife. But then, what did that matter? Were they not spending her money together, as part of the agreement to spend their lives together?

Thirty-six

'Yes, we have become real gadabouts,' she wrote to Isabella, 'but in this Age of Travel, as the newspapermen keep calling it, there are many globetrotters who are much more notably energetic than ourselves. That headlong hero Phineas Fogg is hardly an egregious case! You mentioned that Mr Rudyard Kipling was in New Zealand just a few months ago; well, on the point of departure from Yokohama we must have nearly crossed paths with him and Mrs Kipling. According to a newspaper report they were due to arrive at our hotel, in the course of their honeymoon, on the very day we left!'

She described the comfortable twelve-day journey to Vancouver on the Canadian Pacific liner *Empress of India* ('two fat funnels, one fat captain, sixteen knots of speed, and accommodation for six hundred passengers, though most of them were down in the third-class cabins') and made a few observations about Vancouver that she thought Isabella would find witty. But although she felt less restricted than when writing to Fred and Mary, there was still a sense of inhibition. Impossible even to hint at any of the misgivings that stemmed from William's recent behaviour. Having rebuked Isabella so sharply for raising sceptical questions about him when they had last been together in Dunedin, Frances could not bring herself now to admit to feeling somewhat troubled.

Several things, just little things, were contributing to her sense of discomfort. There was the matter of young Ada. William paid her more attention than Frances thought proper, and she was particularly unhappy with the way he often placed a hand on the girl's neck, almost like a caress, when he was speaking to her. On one occasion Frances discovered Ada sitting on William's knee, as if she were his own child rather than a servant. Then there was that odd incident on the steamer from Yokohama when William snubbed an American man who greeted him by name. He explained this to Frances afterwards – a little awkwardly, she thought – as a wish to avoid being pestered by a bore who must have confused him with 'some other Hammond'.

A few months later she wrote to Fred and Mary. 'We have moved inland,' she explained, 'and purchased a grand place of a hundred acres in the country, close to the town of Vernon, with plenty of hunting, shooting and fishing on it. Two beautiful streams running through, with three waterfalls, one of them fully thirty feet in height, almost rivalling the Niagara in beauty.' Large salmon, she told them, would soon be coming up the rivers in such numbers that – according to neighbours – people would be manuring their fruit trees with them.

In every visible way their property near Vernon was, in Frances's eyes, just as idyllic as her letter painted it to be. It lay in one of the most beautiful parts of the North Okanagan Valley. She liked to picnic with William and their year-old daughter on the northeastern side of Kalamalka Lake, above one of the small bays, and walk along its rocky indented shoreline. In the other direction acre after acre of dry bunchgrass rangelands sloped up towards forested ridges – Douglas fir, said William. The play of dark and light made her yearn to convert what she saw into washes of colour on paper, but these days her daughter demanded so much attention that there was never a spare moment to take up a paintbrush. The images would have to be stored away in a corner of her mind, and summoned later when she had more time. Her eyes absorbed the landscape and everything that moved in its shine and shadow. She caught glimpses of creatures she had never seen before, squirrels, marmots and once, distantly, what must have been a black bear. This was a land of wonder.

Yet something was missing: a clear sense of their purpose in being there. If only William could be coaxed into candour about what he intended! Even when they were sharing something as pleasant as a little excursion to their favourite lakeside cove, he often seemed abstracted, almost remote. If she tried to ask what he was thinking or feeling, his answers were evasively brief. There were business matters, he said, that didn't concern her. Perhaps, she thought, he was tiring of her. Perhaps he was less happy than she herself with the fact that they were now expecting another child, due at Eastertide. She would have liked to be sure that Vernon would remain their home until at least a year or so after the birth – longer if possible; would it not be the perfect place to bring up two infants? But he brushed such questions aside.

She guessed he was speculating in land. When she went with him to see the new branch railway terminus at Okanagan Landing, he left her to stroll around while he talked at length to Joshua Greenblatt, the Vernon real estate salesman. Several times William made trips into the town without explaining his business there. She supposed he knew what he was doing. There had certainly been an influx of settlers into the region, and cattle ranchers like O'Keefe seemed to want to buy up as much pasture land as they could before prices rose any further. She had heard neighbours talk optimistically, too, of the great scope for making orchard holdings more profitable through irrigation. There had been a favourable report in their newspaper about experiments at the Coldstream Ranch in channelling water for fruit production.

For the shrewd and the well informed, it was no doubt a propitious time to watch for land sale opportunities. While William seemed to have a nose for profitable transactions, it was faintly annoying that he wouldn't discuss any of this with her. If some financial uncertainty was involved, might not the residue of her inheritance money be at risk? She knew there was no point in asking. William would fume with resentment.

Then, with the fall season (as she was learning to call it) now moving sharply towards winter, William came in from a visit to the town and announced that they were going to leave at once for Victoria. He had decided, he said, that they should take immediate advantage of a very fair offer from Mr Greenblatt, and dispose of their property while the going was good. And besides, he didn't care to spend a winter so far inland.

'But William,' she remonstrated, 'this is our home and in my condition I'd much prefer to stay here until after the baby is born.'

'No possibility of that,' he said shortly. 'The contract I've just signed obliges us to vacate the place without delay.'

* * *

Her fine son arrived on 5 April, in Victoria B.C. They called him William Ewart Hammond – William after his father and Ewart after Gladstone. His middle name would make him distinctive; there seemed to be so many William Hammonds in the world.

* * *

A short letter came from Isabella, the first in several months. It seemed uncharacteristically subdued in tone, listless, and the handwriting had developed a tremor. 'I have been quite unwell lately,' she wrote, giving no details. Most of the letter was about a lecture on Birds of Passage that she just had attended at the Athenaeum, in which a visiting American ornithologist spoke of the great annual pelagic migrations of petrels and shearwaters – including the mutton bird, whose astonishing flights were now thought (he reported) to extend northwards from the Otago peninsula all the way up the western Pacific to Japan and even to Alaska, then down past California as far as Patagonia. The lecturer had quoted, said Isabella, a wonderfully evocative passage from Mr Darwin's *Voyage of the Beagle* that described huge flocks of petrels, hundreds of thousands of them, skimming past his ship for several hours near the coast of Chile, blackening the surface of the water and making a noise that sounded like a great crowd of humans talking at a distance.

Isabella finished with some snippets of local news. Mr Donaldson, glum as ever, was still in search of a companion. Poor Grace Hutton was permanently crippled and her mind had turned in on itself: she could not be persuaded to take an interest in anything, not even to resume the sketching that had once given her such enjoyment. Mr Larnach had again been unsuccessful as a candidate for parliamentary election and a knighthood was no longer considered likely. His third wife – more than twenty years younger than he – was described as demanding and opinionated. Indeed, Mr and Mrs Larnach now spent most of their time away from Otago, and his great stone manor had ceased to be truly a home.

Frances called to mind that grey castle-like edifice overlooking the steep sloping valleys of the peninsula. It seemed to belong to another life. Dunedin was so remote now in every sense that the idea of ever returning to the city of her birth had become doubtful, though where her peregrinations with William would ultimately take her she could not guess.

Thirty-seven

'Must we always move so restlessly from place to place?'

Her question seemed to annoy him. He smacked the newspaper into shape, and went on looking at it rather than her as he replied.

'I thought you were enjoying our travels, Frances. This is the kind of life you used to say you wanted.'

'It isn't the travelling itself that troubles me. There just seem to be sudden changes of plan, so that we leave places sooner than expected, or take quite abruptly a different direction.'

'To my mind that's a large part of the pleasure of mobility.'

There was an implacable hardness in his tone that made it clear he would brook no further discussion of the matter, just as he had recently shrugged off her query as to why he abandoned their plan to visit his brothers in Manitoba.

And so they set out for the latest place to have caught his attention: the Alaskan Panhandle. Perhaps it's for the best, she thought, to be leaving Victoria with so much sickness around. There was fear of an epidemic in the town, and their own neighbourhood no longer felt safe: only a few days before, a child from the big house along the road had died after violent fits of vomiting.

Packing for previous journeys had made her an efficient supervisor of the process. She could now trust Ada to sort and stow properly the children's things, and as they had not accumulated many household chattels it was an easy matter to arrange for these to be shipped or stored. But there were a few items that required her personal attention. One of these, the most cherished object bought during their travels, was the Kutani bowl. With great care Frances prepared to swathe it in tissue paper, admiring again the perfection of its shape and the decorative patterning of crimson and gold against the concave field of white. She held it high to look again at the detail of the figures depicted in panels on its outer sides. There was the bird that soared above the curving bough, like a blossom that had taken wing to float in air. At first she had regarded the whole set of scenes as evoking that kind of freedom, but when she looked more closely, the birds perching on branches in the other panels seemed to be trapped there, as if their feet were stuck fast in the gluey lime once used to catch small birds. She remembered familiar Shakespearean words:

O limèd soul that, struggling to be free,
Art more engaged...

It was a poignant image, one that returned to trouble her mind for a long while afterwards.

* * *

Juneau
Alaska
13 October 1893

Dear Fred and Mary,
I received your letter just the day before we were
called to part with our darling Frances, the joy of
our hearts. Baby took Cholera Infantum one week
ago today. We did all in our power for her, but to
no avail. It has been very hard for us. She was her

father's pet. He made so much of her, but at the
same time, I must say, did not spoil her. No doctor
could have done more or been more patient and
attentive than her papa was. She was always so
delighted when he took her up. Our hearts are full
of grief at this our great loss. Everyone who saw her
said she had 'the handsomest face' they had ever
seen. She certainly had fine features and lovely fair
skin. The photo I sent really did not do her justice.
She would not sit still or keep her hand from moving.

Our darling was two years and nineteen days
when she died and measured 2 ft 11 inches in height,
very tall for her age. We laid a piece of ourselves
aside with her in the cold grave. Just before we left
Victoria the death rate among children with the same
disease was about sixty per week.

We came up to this land of the midnight sun
about a month ago. We are uncertain how long we
will stay here. It is certainly a go-ahead place, though
rough around the edges. The largest gold stamp mill
in the world is near our house. Hundreds of men are
engaged in gold mining.

Tell Edward about the death of our darling.
Doctor joins me in love to you all.
Your affectionate sister,
Frances
P.S. Our baby William is six months old and weighs
26 pounds. He has been creeping since he was five
months old, and calls for papa and mama as plain
as any person can do. Everybody says he is quite an
exception for his age.

* * *

When they had first arrived in Juneau, the weather was mild and they thought the Panhandle was among the most impressive places they had ever seen. Across the Gastineau Channel a broad belt of islands sheltered them from the Pacific. For a week or two Frances imagined that she could be happy there. A sense of exhilaration enlivened the town, with scores of miners moving through noisily on their way to the new strike at Birch Creek.

But cloudbanks soon loitered overhead and the rain set in for days on end. Between the downpours, fog hung thickly in the air. Their daughter's sickness had come on rapidly, prostrating her small body with exhaustion. Her temperature kept rising but the skin felt clammy. William gave her a compound powder of ginger and leptandra fetched from a local doctor, but nothing seemed to help. They could not stop her spasms of vomiting. Her face turned pale and her lips darkened. Her death was dreadful. Throughout that night, Frances wept without pause.

After the burial, colder weather closed in and winds snarled along the streets. Snow began to pile up in the gulches. Just as her hands, when she walked to the store, soon became numb even through the two pairs of thick woollen gloves, so too did Frances feel her spirit stiffen, despite all her husband's condoling words. Standing for long periods by the window, wrapping her arms around her ribs, she would stare with apprehension at the snow-topped mountains that rose steeply behind the houses. Behind them there was, she knew, a huge icefield. She sensed its invisible menace.

Winter deepened. People said it was the harshest season for years. The mountain walls funnelled the wind, and at night great gusts came roaring down around them like wild animals. Juneau seemed little more than a puny assemblage of logs propped anxiously against the rain bursts, the drifting snow and the sense of utterly blank desertion. Even the tall City Hotel and the Decker Brothers building began to look fragile. The men had lost their swagger and the women pulled their coats tightly around their bodies.

Slush surrounded the house they were renting, and a depressing odour of dampness clung to everything inside. The new year arrived with no promise of relief. Almost every day, William chopped and stacked blocks of wood to fuel the stove heater. He seldom spoke much to Frances. Sorrow had brought a slab of silence between them.

Ada, their impassive little helper, was kept busy not only with the cooking and cleaning but also with the care of the remaining baby. Frances had lapsed into despondency since the death of her firstborn. She sat for hours on end, hands folded, imagining that small body in the frozen ground at the end of the township.

For the first time in a long while she thought of that other graveyard on the far side of the world, where her parents and infant sister lay. It was nearly thirty years since her father's death. Although some memories of him seemed clear enough to be her own, she knew they probably drew on what her mother and brothers had told her. But there were a few distinct impressions she could be sure of having retained directly from the time when she was three years old. Sitting on his knee, she could smell and feel the texture of his brown woollen jacket as she snuggled against him, his big warm hands enclosing her tiny fists. Through his long beard, which gave him such a serious air, she could hear that deep dark voice of his with its rich burr, singing:

> There was a little minister who had a little horse;
> He saddled it and bridled it and threw his leg across,
> Singing Hey Johnny Ho Johnny, come along with me,
> Hey Johnny Ho Johnny Johnson!

Just before they left Alaska a letter came from David Morrison. After suffering a degenerative palsy for several months, Isabella had been carried off by a violent apoplexy. Frances felt stricken not only with this further grief but also with an intensified sense of extreme isolation. Isabella had been her closest remaining friend, the only person – apart from William – in whom she felt able to confide.

Thirty-eight

With her arm linked tightly again to her husband's she had spent two long wet days at the Midwinter Fair, glad for once to leave young William in Ada's charge. Though the large exhibition site in Golden Gate Park was decked with thousands of palms and other plants, this was not a time for strolling along the garden pathways; steady rain and cold winds kept the crowds inside. The five huge halls contained countless exhibits. Frances had fully expected to admire the display of ingenuity and innovation, knowing that this San Francisco fair had selected most of its items from Chicago's greatly acclaimed Columbia Exposition, which had closed just a few months earlier. But in fact she found little to excite her interest, and William seemed similarly unimpressed.

'Why is it, do you think, that we feel so dissatisfied here?' she asked him as their second day at the fair wore on and their curiosity began to flag. 'Only a few years ago, at the South Seas Exhibition in Dunedin, I seemed to be in a wonderland that was all asparkle with specimens from a widening world. And when you and I went to that great Palace of Industry in Melbourne, even though the exhibits had been dismantled, we still felt a sort of exhilaration. Are we just sated now with all the travelling we've been doing? Have we had a surfeit of modern marvels?'

'Or perhaps,' he responded after a pause, 'it's simply that so much of what we're seeing here appears speciously contrived, even false? This Egyptian temple, for instance: yes, there are some fine things, grand things, in its art display, but the building strikes me as a showy caricature. And the rest of the fair is like that, too. The banners flying from every roof, and the national "themes", as they call them, jostling one another – the Chinese theatre, the Eskimo habitat, the buffalo paddock and so on – all just entertainment for the undiscerning. Nothing much more than razzle-dazzle and flag-wag.'

Frances smiled and nodded. She could imagine how David Morrison, with his pride in the civic architecture of Dunedin and Edinburgh, would have derided this meretricious array of buildings, with the tall skinny tower in the centre of them and the electric fountain sending jets of water a hundred feet high in so many shapes and hues. But it was not just the visual vulgarity that grated. Above all, the Midwinter Fair seemed to epitomise the illusion of progress, the vanity of commerce and industry, blowing their brassy trumpets as if to drown out any acknowledgement that most of the western world was now in the grip of a serious economic depression.

* * *

Granada
Nicaragua
Central America
20 April 1894

Dear Fred and Mary,
We have been called to part with our darling boy. It's impossible for me to convey what great grief we are in and what a sad parting it was. I sent you a card about the whooping cough, but we never thought

it would come to this. He was such a charming, loving, beautiful child. The cough went hard with him, though that didn't bring about his death. Apparently his teeth were the whole cause of the trouble. He had only one tooth through (canine) and the gums and cheeks became red and swollen. When we arrived in Puerto San Jose we took the train to Guatemala. Our lad was quite better of the cough on arrival, but too weak to stand the teeth trouble. The doctor thinks there were abscesses that poisoned the blood. It was enough to touch the heart of a stone to see our darling child knocking his head against the plastered wall and not a cry out of him, except to call 'dink, mama, oh mama, dink!' (for drink).

We would rather see all we have in the bottom of the sea than have lost our dear little William. His papa often said that he was too smart a child to live. We have this consolation: he lies in the prettiest cemetery we have ever seen. In Guatemala they do not bury their dead, but deposit the bodies in beautiful sepulchres. We bought one for our darling boy and saw his body placed in it while Christian service was being held.

We hope to spend a few months in Nicaragua before going to England. We are both in good health and hope you are enjoying the same blessing. The doctor joins in kind love to you all.
Your affectionate sister,
Frances
P.S. Our darling boy passed away on 13 April – twelve months and eight days old. Just six months to the very day that our darling Frances was buried.

Despite her matter-of-fact mention of England, the prospect of going there for the first time held little appeal now for Frances. Her heart was utterly haggard and she could see no meaning in further journeys. Even the knowledge of being pregnant again could not lift her out of the slough of despond. She remembered detachedly the spirited young woman who had left Dunedin just four years earlier with such eager longing for new scenes, new experiences. Unsure what exactly she was seeking then, she could not tell whether she had found it. Indeed she had ceased to care much.

Now that she and William were a childless couple again it was their relationship with each other that increasingly preoccupied her. But while the love she felt for her husband remained intense, it became further clouded with anxious doubt as he withdrew almost sullenly into indistinct corners of his mind. William Hammond had turned out to be a much more puzzling man than she could have known at first. Intimacy had failed to disclose everything.

Frances felt most alone when they were in the same room and he sank into one of his moods of silent, wounded seclusion. It appeared that the loss of their babies was weighing heavily on his mind.

She felt ill in her stomach; but the cause, she thought, was unlikely to be physical. A fatigue of the spirit had weakened her. Weary lines from a well-remembered poem came unbidden to her mind:

For, what with my whole world-wide wandering,
What with my search drawn out through years, my hope
Dwindled into a ghost not fit to cope...

Part 9

Dunedin, Melbourne, 1888—91

Thirty-nine

To the newly arrived evangelist and his American wife, Dunedin appeared to be a curious blend of the strange and the familiar.

As their boat emerged from a scud of showers offshore and steamed into Port Chalmers under a brightening sky, the angular headlands might just have risen freshly from the ocean that morning, with sharper contours than William had seen anywhere else in his travels; but the huddle of buildings around the wharf looked hardly different from those of several coastal settlements he knew in other places. And while the town's business activities, he soon found, had something of Melbourne's rough vigour, people here seemed subdued, and tended to act more diffidently.

A lilt in some of the voices reminded him of the Caledonian farmers he had known near La Chute, but others spoke in a slow, muffled, flat-vowel monotone, their lips hardly moving, as if words were costly and expressiveness smacked of extravagance. Yet the brethren and sisters of the Tabernacle congregation appeared to be doing their earnest best to make the pair of newcomers welcome.

'My impression,' said the doctor to Clarissa Hammond after his first meeting with the deacons, 'is that these folk would like to be more cordial if they knew how. Their tone strikes me as dour and guarded, but I think it may be just a habit of reticence. When they come out abruptly with a curt unsmiling question like "Settling in all right?" or "Getting to know your way about?" they mean to show kindness, really.'

She nodded and returned to her knitting. His observations, when he shared them with her, seldom drew any lively response. Clarissa was not much of a talker, except when occasionally propelled by one of her own tiresome stories about herself; and Dunedin taciturnity suited her well enough.

The Sunday School superintendent, Frederick Phillips, invited the Hammonds to a midday meal after the worship service on their second Sunday in Dunedin. As he drove them in a comfortable wagonette through the town belt towards the family home, they sat facing his sister, Frances. William thought her a handsome woman, with her grey-blue eyes and fair hair, guessing her to be in her late twenties. Along the way she pointed out signs of the small city's expansive ambitions.

'Over there, look – the cleared strip of land running up the hillside – that's where the famous cable tramway is being extended,' she told them. 'Civic pride swells with every additional mile of cable.' Mild irony flickered at the corner of her mouth. 'Most people can talk of little else. I suppose you've already heard about the ingenious pulling and braking methods invented here in Dunedin to make the carriages safe on the steepest of our curving streets?'

'No,' replied William, with an amused smile. 'I confess to complete ignorance about the secret mechanisms of your cable tramway.'

'And I lack the knowledge to explain them properly. But the newspapers have carried lyrical reports about a dolphin brake, I think that's the term, and other gadgets too, devised by a clever young local engineer. It's because of his inventiveness, we're told, in adapting the machinery to our local conditions that Dunedin was able to follow San Francisco's example and become the second city in the world to install a cable system for public conveyances. They say he's now employed in Melbourne, supervising their tramway development.'

The road began to climb. Outside the central city area most of the box-like weatherboard houses and shops looked as if they were not made to last. But as the wagonette trundled into the Upper Kaikorai district, William saw that some buildings betokened prosperity. That large one, he learnt from Frances, belonged to a wealthy architect, and the one beside it to an accountant. The Phillips home, though not ostentatious, was a substantial dwelling on a large section of land. Dark native trees sheltered it on the southern side, and William asked Frances what they were, but the Maori names she used meant nothing to him.

There were tensions in this family, not far below the surface; he soon saw that. At the table, Frances and Frederick were pushed to the margins of conversation by their querulous mother and by an elder brother, Edward – a teacher, whose lessons William felt sure would be tedious.

William steered the conversation towards the topic of property, asking about the cost of land, of rent, of house construction.

'We intend to move out of our hotel,' he said, 'as soon as we can find a suitable place to live.'

'There's a vacant house not far from here along City Road,' said Frederick, 'that may be available, I believe, for tenants.'

Within a few days the Hammonds had become neighbours of the Phillipses, quickly establishing a pattern of regular visits. Old Sarah Phillips was ailing fretfully, and wanted the attention of this new minister with his mellifluous baritone, charming accent and ready supply of reassuring phrases. Her daughter was a more rewarding conversationalist, shy but intelligent, showing glimpses of an independent mind. Frederick, though stolid, seemed good-natured enough.

As far as other church families were concerned, William felt that he was still on probation. A number of them made hospitable gestures but remained watchful. While the deacons, he knew, had appointed him on the strength of an unhesitating recommendation from Houchins, some probably had reservations about the smoothly self-confident style of an 'American' preacher. He would have to win them over patiently.

One of the senior deacons, Samuel Eckersley, combined a beaming manner with an insistent inquisitiveness. As he and his wife sat in their little parlour with the Hammonds, he plied William with strong black tea and a series of probing questions.

'What kind of medicine have you practised, Dr Hammond?'

'Oh – various kinds in different places, according to need and opportunity.'

'Including surgery, perhaps? There's a shortage of good surgeons in this city.'

'No, that's something I've avoided. I saw too many distressing results of clumsy knife work when I was working in a military hospital. Plattsburgh – aftermath of the Civil War. I just don't have the stomach for anything as gory as that.'

'So what doctoring do you like to do?'

'Herbal medicine has been my particular interest.'

'Well now! Are you acquainted with Mr James Neil's botanic dispensary in George Street?'

'No, I've not seen it.'

'Then you must go there, you must. A clever man, Mr Neil. Does a lot of his manufacturing on the premises, and has a wonderful range of powders and potions. He'd like to meet you, I'm sure, because although he's a true Scot he did his medical training somewhere in the United States. Chicago, I think he told me. Is that where you studied?'

'No, Canada. I'll certainly visit Mr Neil's establishment.'

A series of inconvenient questions followed about William's

past experiences as a preacher, but he managed to deflect them smoothly. Eckersley turned to Clarissa.

'So, Mrs Hammond, did you meet your husband through the church?'

'No, it was his work as a doctor that brought us together. Just a few months ago.'

'A few months ago! You're very recently married, then?' Eckersley's dark little eyes were like beetles.

'Oh yes, September.'

'Well, well. I had no idea you were newlyweds.'

'Love at first sight for both of us, it was,' she declared, with a noisy inhalation. William winced; her sniffing habit was getting worse. 'Married just a month after meeting!' she added complacently.

William could imagine Eckersley's thoughts. In anyone's eyes, Clarissa must seem ill-favoured, by no means youthful, and an utter dullard.

'We met in Atlanta, you see,' she said. 'Atlanta, Georgia. I'd fled there by train from Florida, with dozens of others, because of a big outbreak of yellow fever. Very severe, especially in Jacksonville, where I was living.'

William could anticipate every detail ahead. She had only a handful of stories. This was the most familiar, and once wound up she would tick along as loudly as an Ansonia clock.

'...like a plague in Bible times. People were talking about digging mass graves. I saw a corpse in the street, flies all over it, horrible. I was panicking, I don't mind telling you, desperate to get out of there before quarantine could stop me. Crowds of us crammed the carriages of the northern train. Well, the authorities in Atlanta were afraid the fever would spread, you see, so when we arrived at the railroad station there they had doctors on hand and made every passenger submit to a medical examination. And that's how I met this dear husband of mine. He was so kind, and wanted to know all about me, why I was travelling alone, and got me talking, and I told him what had made me so terrified of disease, because of the way my husband – my first husband, Mr Lawrence – had died, and...'

'Oh!' Eckersley exclaimed. 'So you'd just been widowed?'

She rattled on mucously. The late Mr Lawrence, she explained to the Eckersleys, was an orange grower near Sanford, Florida. They had prospered, but all their fruit was the Parson Brown variety, which was becoming less popular in the market – too many pips – so he had the idea of importing seed stock of Maltese oranges, with their rich blood-red pulp. Not much more than a year ago she had accompanied her husband to Malta and he bought a share in a large sunny orchard in the middle of the main island. But while they were there, cholera had broken out in the rural districts, where there was no sewerage. The disease caught him suddenly.

'...There were scores of others dying all around the countryside. Terrible. But God protected me from the contagion, mercifully. Back in Florida, I put a manager in charge of the Sanford property and moved to Jacksonville, but you can imagine my fear when the yellow fever struck that part of Florida just a few months afterwards!'

She paused to check that the drama of it all was not lost on the Eckersleys.

'But all that sadness and worry,' she went on, 'is behind me now, praise the Lord. If it hadn't been for the yellow fever I'd never have gone to Georgia, and met this fine man of mine.' She turned to William with a doting gaze.

'And what took you to Melbourne after your wedding, Mrs Hammond?' asked Eckersley.

'Well, we didn't travel there directly. William wanted us to go to Malta and sell the share in the orchard property, you see, so we did that. Then we came to Melbourne on a whim, really. We just fancied – didn't we, my dear? – that it would be interesting to see this go-ahead part of the world. And I was particularly curious to see Melbourne, because there's a little township called Melbourne where I come from. And Dunedin, too, has its own little namesake in Florida! Amazing, isn't it!'

* * *

The months passed, and William grew tired of Dunedin. His irritating wife, too, wearied him. It was time, he thought, to persuade her to convert those orange groves in Florida to cash.

Although his sudden resignation startled the Tabernacle worshippers, more than a few were not sorry to see him go. For all his eloquence and charm, there was something disconcerting about this man, something that made them uneasy.

Forty

Arriving in Melbourne for the second time more than a year later, he was sure it would be a safe refuge. As far as he knew, his wife's sudden demise had aroused no suspicions. He himself had certified that the cause of death was heart failure after the onset of liver disease. She had no kinsfolk or close friends. In the unlikely event of police interest in the matter, they would not find it easy to track him on the other side of the world.

He had plenty of money for the time being, but much of it remained for safe keeping in a Florida bank. He would soon need to think about new sources of income. It would also be necessary to disencumber himself of his two Dutch companions, who had turned out to have very few assets.

They had sought his company after a stirring sermon he had preached during the voyage. A week out from the Cape, their ship *Damascus* was tossed around alarmingly in roaring winds, its newly fitted electric light system failed, and most of the passengers were sick and frightened. When the tempest subsided William led a thanksgiving service at the captain's request, reading expressively from the Psalms: 'They that go down to the sea in ships...'

William went on to speak of spiritual dangers, more fearsome than any physical peril: 'It's only natural, my dear companions, that we all should feel great alarm when storm clouds thunder above our heads and the pitiless ocean surges around us as if charged with malice and menace. But in the perspective of eternity our frail bodies are of little consequence. What matters is the salvation of our souls. The terrors of the deep that surround us now are as nothing compared with the terrors of hell. The psalmist goes on to speak of those condemned to "the wilderness, where there is no way". Wandering forever in a trackless spiritual waste is the dreadful fate of the damned. Brethren and sisters, when we think of a desired haven let it be the one that lies beyond any port in this present world of ours. Let it be that ultimate destination awaiting the company of the redeemed at the end of all mortal life.'

These dire admonitions, and more like them, had the pair of Dutch ladies snivelling into their handkerchiefs. They came to him straight after the service, still dabbing at their eyes, to introduce themselves and thank him for his pastoral support. That they were foolish creatures was obvious. Judging them also – incorrectly, as he later found – to be wealthy, he did not hesitate to cultivate their acquaintance.

* * *

Despite the pricking of the land bubble there was still fat money in Melbourne if you knew where to look for it. A shrewd person could seize opportunities swiftly, and move on.

During his previous stay, the Centennial Exhibition had dominated the city's mood. Other grand new buildings, too, had fed the sense of exhilaration. Now, less than two years on, William found that the huge ornate coffee palaces were no longer packed with people – but he thought there was a good chance, nevertheless, of cultivating a useful relationship with some gullible person at one of these gathering places for the temperance movement. He would frequent the Federal and the Grand for a while, and perhaps join the rooftop promenade at the Queen's in

247

Carlton, relying on his wits to open a door or two.

Cole's Book Arcade, he thought, was another likely spot: a convenient hunting ground for skins and sharpers. Immense crowds swarmed every day under the rainbow signage of this merry circus of letters, drawn not only by the amazing range of publications on display but also by the splendid balconies and arches, the music, the red-jacketed staff, the costumed entertainers, the ready supply of food and drink. With all those hearts leaping up, childlike, it would be a simple matter to broach a few cheerful conversations about books.

Meanwhile he would try to reinsert himself into the local circle of the Disciples of Christ. Most of them were fairly simple souls, and their readiness to respond to specious slogans should prove easy to exploit.

He had developed such a plausible facility for pious performances, adapted to different situations, that he seldom felt any need to ask himself what he really believed about religious matters. He could embrace the tenets of one creed and then, when expedient, switch to another without discomfort, like an actor stepping overnight into a new role on a different stage.

When had he first developed this dexterity in slipping from one imaginary self to another? Had it come from his reading? Those stories of stealth in the backwoods, of shape-shifting scouts who could imitate to perfection the shadowy arts of the Red Indians: were they the wellspring of his guile as an actor?

Only once, and with reluctance, had he ever spoken candidly to anyone about religion. It had been some four years earlier, but he remembered well the details of that conversation, which took place the day after his arrest in Boston. Remanded in custody for absconding with the Franklin Falls money, he was startled when his warder announced a visitor. It was Jonathan Baxter Harrison, with his long beard and long words.

The two men stood awkwardly on either side of the grated door to William's cell.

'You may not welcome my intrusion, Hammond,' said Harrison, reading the other's face, 'but I do want to talk with you.'

William shrugged, muttering an ungracious response.

'I haven't come to remonstrate,' Harrison went on, 'or make your shame more painful. Let's simply acknowledge that you have done something seriously unjust, and say no more about the misdeed. I'm here because it troubles me to see in you a man who appeared to be devoting exceptional talents to the welfare of others but suddenly took a downward path. I wonder whether I can somehow help you, as your brother in Christ, to cleanse your spirit and hold fast to the company of the faithful – if not back in Franklin Falls, then (once the law has exacted whatever retribution it must for your offence) in some other place, beginning afresh. The Lord needs you to re-enlist in the cause of social justice.'

Though characteristically orotund, Harrison's phrasing was free of glibness. William recognised an irony in the fact that he himself, a master of deceit, could admire – albeit grudgingly – the sincerity of this man's appeal to him.

'You speak eloquently,' he said.

'Pah!' Harrison waved the words aside. 'Eloquence is nothing in itself. "Though I speak with the tongues of men and angels..." You know the rest.'

'But you're assuming,' said William after a pause, 'that I share your convictions about religion and justice.'

'You don't, then?'

'Much of what the churches preach is false.'

'I agree!' Harrison had adopted the posture that William remembered well: one hand cupping an elbow, the other hand raised, its thumb and forefinger rubbing together. 'But what is fatal in the unbelief of our time is not the rejection of one church creed or another. It's a failure to recognise that the fundamental forces of the universe are hostile to injustice. Self-interested individualism is abnormal, destructive. The work of making this country a wholesome dwelling-place is required by an order that human beings did not make and cannot change.'

'You're a good man, Harrison, and I'm not. But those high-sounding abstractions of yours are far from persuasive. Tell me, how is it possible for an intelligent person to regard the universe as inherently just, when all around us every day we see evidence of a cruel mismatch between deserts and fortunes?'

'Justice may work in mysterious ways...'

'That's the usual facile answer from men of religion – pardon me for being so blunt – to any inconvenient question about the lack of a moral order in life. Invoking mystery is tantamount to acknowledging tacitly that the reason why God's hand is invisible may be because there's no such hand.'

Harrison drew in his breath sharply.

'Do I shock you?' William asked.

'You sadden me. Evidently the world in your eyes is very bleak – and that must make you feel utterly despondent.'

'A bleak world, yes. But despondency? No. "Not without hope we suffer and we mourn."'

'Wordsworth?'

'Wordsworth.'

'What loss are you mourning?'

'It's not so much the fact of loss that matters. When loss occurs through injustice...' He fell silent.

'Tell me.'

'You're a relentless inquisitor, Harrison.' William dropped his gaze for a moment, clenching his fingers around the bars, and then went on. 'I had decent and loving parents. Both were snatched away in my boyhood. My father's death was a cruel accident, but my mother's was caused by the malice of others. By pillars of the church and the community.'

'And the sense of injustice still rankles, I see that and understand it. Yet whatever happened to your mother surely wasn't inflicted on *you* in any deliberate and direct way?'

'Nonetheless I've also suffered personally from the spite of others. False testimony, unprovoked, put me into a filthy, wretched prison for many years. It was a large part of my life, utterly wasted: the time when other men could use their talents to establish themselves. That wrong, that deep wrong, makes me impatient with any talk of fraternal justice. Taking money from respectable people is a mere trifle, a peccadillo, compared with what respectable people have done to me and my family.'

'But not the same respectable people. The folk of Franklin Falls did you no harm.'

'Retribution by proxy can be better than none.'

William turned away from the door and sat on the stool in the corner of his cell, as if there was no more to be said.

'I, too, am mourning a loss,' Harrison called out to him.

William looked up questioningly.

'The loss of the great contribution you could have made to a better and fairer society. You're squandering your uncommon abilities. Letting your spirit be consumed, corrupted, by this bitterness.'

William shook his head and made no response.

After a few minutes, Harrison had left, calling over his shoulder: 'You deny feeling despondent, Hammond, but I don't believe you. A naked individualist is utterly devoid of hope.'

forty-one

Idly browsing the shelves in Cole's Book Arcade one wet afternoon, William picked up a handsome album of New Zealand landscape photographs, produced by a Dunedin firm whose name he recognised, Burton Brothers. In the magnificence of the scenery there were hints of menace. He remembered spectral shapes from *The Prelude*: 'huge and mighty forms that do not live / Like living men moved slowly through the mind'. What seemed to give the images fixed on these photographic plates an uncanny aura was a faint suggestion of imminent movement behind the apparent solidity. One of the most spectacular scenes, captured by the camera only few years ago, showed the famous Pink and White Terraces, since destroyed by the fearsome Mt Tarawera eruption. Looking up from the page, then closing his eyes for a moment, he remembered the lava beds of Tula lake. Volcanic cataclysm, he thought, would be a powerful figure to use next Sunday, when he was to be guest preacher at the Brunswick chapel of the Disciples of Christ.

Earthquakes and other shocking upheavals, yes, he could work up something rousing on that theme for the sermon. He called to mind a passage in Ezekiel that would do nicely as a text.

He had never found it difficult to impress the adherents of 'primitive Christianity', as these groups liked to call their kind of faith. In their scheme of things, the role of evangelist was not a prerogative of an ordained group. That gave William an opening. He had more than enough knowledge and skill to make him a popular choice to preach at their services. He could slip into the phrasing they liked to hear as easily as slipping his arms into a shirt.

Sunday morning came and he made his way along Glenlyon Road to the squat little brick chapel, no less dowdy for being newly built. Old Luke Haberfield, having arranged the invitation, was there to greet him and introduce him to others as they arrived. Haberfield had now become even more obese than a couple of years earlier; his huge belly jutted out in front of him and he kept his arms stiff beside him as walked with shuffling steps, like a human wheelbarrow pushing himself along.

There were a few people William remembered from his association with the Lygon Street congregation when previously in Melbourne. He supposed they had transferred their membership from Carlton to Brunswick. Briscoe, the grinning grocer, shook William's hand with his usual exaggerated cordiality. The Norris sisters, an unforgettable pair of fussy sparrows, bobbed and twittered at him in a pantomime of salutation.

When the time came for his sermon, William felt the usual surge of energy and self-assurance. Few things gave him as much pleasure as wielding over an audience the power of words. Pitch, volume, pace and pause – he knew how to deploy them all for cumulative effect. Within a couple of minutes he had everyone in his hand, he could see that: each as still as a waxwork, some with mouths ajar as if unsure whether to inhale or exhale.

As his eyes raked the pews he was startled to glimpse, under her pale blue bonnet, a familiar face near the back of the chapel. It was Frances Phillips, surely. But what was she doing in Melbourne? When he spoke to her after the service he lost no time in discovering she had travelled alone from New Zealand. More venturesome than he would have thought. He had underestimated, apparently, her capacity for independent action. Perhaps this encounter with her could prove propitious.

* * *

Their conversation during the next day's visit to the Exhibition Building quickened his interest. Though it was not an unusual experience to have someone absorbing whatever he said, the situation seemed slightly different with Frances. While entirely attentive, she let his words hang between them and turn this way and that like leaves in the wind before responding. She was, as he already knew from his time in Dunedin, shy, and perhaps impressionable, susceptible; but no fool. Unlike most around her, she valued exactitude in language. He remembered how, talking with him during those earlier days, she would sometimes pause and deliberate with a slight frown until she found the precise phrase she wanted, occasionally summoning an apt line from Browning's poetry, in which her mind seemed to be as thoroughly steeped as his was in Wordsworth's.

He was careful with her now about his choice of words, and particularly about the way he touched on the matter of her inheritance. Gaining access to her trust, and so to her assets, would pose an interesting challenge. Interesting, yes, and also agreeable: in her case he anticipated more pleasure from the process of inveiglement than her predecessors had provided.

For their afternoon walk later in the week, the Carlton cemetery was a spur-of-the-moment choice. The mild warmth of the spring day seeped into them. Head inclined towards him, saying little, she appeared to listen closely to everything he said during their stroll between the glum rows of monuments. But as they made their way back towards the gate she caught him by surprise with an abrupt question.

'I have the impression that this place, or something connected to it, has been much on your mind. Why is that?'

Her directness startled him into a frank reply that lacked his usual fluency. He spoke with effort, as if drawing heavy phrases up by bucket from a deep well.

'To die is one thing; to be uncommemorated is another. A more sorrowful fate. I often think about my parents' graves. Both remote, separately remote, on the other side of the world. No headstone for either of them.'

He stood still, head bowed, before going on.

'When I left La Chute – that's the small township where I grew up in Canada – when I left there as a young lad with my mother and brothers, soon after my father's burial, only the name scratched on a makeshift wooden cross showed where his body lay. And by the time I returned to La Chute a few years later, the cross had disappeared. Perhaps someone took it to kindle a fire. My mother's grave is in Owen Sound, another little settlement, much further west. We went there from La Chute. Her grave, too, was unmarked, just a miserable mound in the corner of a small enclosure, but I can picture the spot exactly. I used to visit it every Sunday for years.'

He opened his hand and looked at the familiar scar.

'I'm very sorry,' she said, 'to have intruded on difficult memories.'

He shook his head silently, shrugged, recovered his poise and changed the subject.

Then, just a few minutes later, it was his turn to catch her off balance. His proposal of marriage was sudden but by no means impulsive. He had calculated the moment, could tell her emotions were enkindled, and felt confident she would yield. The next day, taking her to the Botanic Gardens and pressing her for an answer, he was unsurprised that she gave her assent so readily.

He knew to proceed with caution, modifying or hiding some of his habits. It was clear to him that she was much more observant than other women he had known. His immersion in the carnival atmosphere of the day they spent at the racecourse made her uneasy, he noticed. Laying his bets on this occasion, and any future occasions, had to be surreptitious; his penchant for gambling, which had grown in recent years despite a signal lack of success in picking winners, was not something he wanted to reveal.

Persuading her to expedite their wedding and keep the arrangements simple was not hard. Beneath her quiet and reticent manner he sensed an eagerness, tinged perhaps with apprehension, to become his wife and join her flesh with his.

For his own part, there was genuine and unprecedented pleasure in the prospect of matrimony. He had been through nuptial ceremonies several times before, but never until now with someone who had an agile mind or such a comely face. Frances Phillips would be an unusually attractive woman even without her wealth. While still mindful of his main purpose, he found himself anticipating their union keenly.

Forty-two

The circumstances of his return to Dunedin caused him a little discomfort, though he took care not to let it show. He had been expecting the raised eyebrows, the sidelong glances. Less than eighteen months ago he left the place with one wife, and now here he was again with another, someone he had met when in this city previously: no doubt the gossips would be busy with that, and even busier when Frances informed her brothers she and the doctor wished to sell her share of the jointly owned property, and then leave Dunedin without delay.

As soon as they arrived they went to see Frederick. After the greetings and formulaic pleasantries, Frances broached the matter of the property.

Her brother was taken aback. 'But neither Ted nor I could afford to buy your share from you!'

'Then it may be necessary to put it all on the market.'

'But it's the family home!' he exclaimed. 'Our father was so proud of establishing it, and our mother lived here with us for all those years after his death. They would never have wanted it to be carved up and sold to strangers.'

'You look at this house with warm sentiment, Fred. I look at it more coolly – as the place where for so long I was nursemaid, and even shared at times the tasks of cook and scullery maid.

Year upon year, while you and Edward were out in society, I was cooped up with an invalid.'

'I thought you accepted your role. I had no idea you felt so resentful about it.'

'Resentful? No – just very clear in my mind that this place now belongs to my past, not to my future.'

When William insisted that the sale be quickly arranged, Frederick flinched. 'I'll need to talk to Ted, and then we'll see what legal procedures have to be followed.'

'We intend to meet with Edward ourselves,' said William. 'We'll also be appointing lawyers to act on our behalf in this matter after we leave Dunedin. We'd be grateful if you could let us know as soon as possible who your representative will be, so the necessary documents can be prepared on both sides.'

Frederick rubbed his hand slowly over his forehead. 'Must we do things so suddenly, and in such a cold and impersonal way?'

'In a case like this,' William replied, 'where one of the parties isn't intending to reside here, there's a special importance in making sure that all the formal paperwork is swiftly and properly completed.'

'Then your decision to go back to Australia very soon is quite firm?'

'Absolutely definite, yes, though how long we stay there remains to be seen. We both want to travel further abroad.'

* * *

Back in their hotel room, Frances asked him whether they must really be in such a hurry to return to Melbourne.

'There are people here I'd like you to meet before we go. I've told you about my friend Isabella Morrison and her husband the architect. An intelligent, well-educated couple. You'd enjoy their company, I'm sure. And I want them to see what a fine husband I have, after all. I think they'd begun to believe I was consigning myself to permanent spinsterhood.'

He resorted to smooth compliments to deflect her question, but she persisted.

'What is it in Melbourne that's so urgent, really? We've just arrived here. I know this business with the lawyers is vexing, William, but can't we linger a while, and be sociable?'

He frowned. It was impossible to explain his reasons to her. In truth, tension over the property settlement was only a part of the problem. His past could catch up with him at any time. There had been that tricky moment during his earlier sojourn in Dunedin when James Neil, the town's shrewd purveyor of botanical potions and powders, began to probe too far into how much William really knew about herbal medicine. Meeting people with professional expertise could pose a particular danger. Frances herself, though quick-witted, was not worldly-wise; but if her friends the Morrisons were as clever and knowledgeable as she stated, they might be capable of asking awkward questions and seeing through his veneer of respectability.

'I'm not obliged to go into every detail with you,' he said bluntly. 'You should trust my judgment. Some business matters need my prompt attention in Melbourne, and I don't have the time to loiter here. If you aren't ready to return with me, I'll need to go on ahead and you can join me later.'

It was obvious that his brusque words had stung her, but he knew she would not resist further. Silence fell between them. After a few minutes he tried to make amends, gesturing towards the book on her bedside table, a small well-worn volume that she took with her everywhere.

'What is it about Browning's poems that keeps drawing you back to them?'

Frances tapped her knuckles against her chin, a habit now familiar to him, and took time to consider a reply.

'Isabella asked me that once. She said his lines often seemed jerky and jagged. I told her it's not music I seek, or at least not the kind of soothing melody she admires in Tennyson. I don't want poetry to lull me or hypnotise me. I turn to Browning because he invents such fascinating characters, and finds a different voice for each of them, a singular voice – rough or not – that conveys obliquely some strange story.'

'Isn't that a more appropriate thing for a playwright to do? Or a novelist?'

'No, I don't agree. Browning's poetry absorbs drama and storytelling, because its subject matter is human variety – men and women of every imaginable colour and shape. A clever corrupt rascal like Bishop Blougram, a cold villain like that Italian Duke surrounded by artworks, Karshish the Arab truth-seeker, and the philosophers, painters, all the rest of them. That's what I miss in your beloved Wordsworth – for all the impressive rumbling of organ pipes there's precious little sympathetic curiosity about anyone other than himself.'

'You're judging Wordsworth too severely, my dear, but I won't argue the point with you. You defend Browning well. When it comes to poetry, let's agree to differ.'

As an oblique response she picked up the book and began to read aloud to him: 'Where the quiet-coloured end of evening smiles...'

For several minutes he listened intently as she read the poem in full, her calm voice moderating the uneven lines and the intrusive rhymes. The pictured scene rose clearly in his imagination: ambling sheep on twilit hillsides, the lovers' tryst, the crumbling tower, residual stones of an ancient city now covered with grass. The layered countryside evoked by 'Love Among the Ruins' was far distant from the small southerly corner of the world in which William and Frances found themselves, but as the bucolic phrases floated he looked out through the window towards the mottled hills and wondered whether this place, so recently settled by migrants from that other side, might also have a hidden past of its own.

When she finished, he asked: 'Could there ever have been anything like that here, long ago? Some half-buried, half-forgotten civilisation?'

'You mean a Maori city?' She looked puzzled.

'Not a city, I suppose. But perhaps traces of the way they lived in ancient times, before the Scottish settlers came. I remember hearing, when I was last in Dunedin, some tale about fortified native villages that used to be on the peninsula in years gone by. Might that be true?'

'I don't know much about it, but there were certainly native tribes all around this region – I've seen some of their ornaments and weapons in the museum – so yes, there are probably still signs of what they constructed. But nothing really ancient. They were settlers, too. The museum says that while Maori people have lived in these parts for a few centuries, according to their own legends they originally came from overseas in big canoes. They were seafarers.'

'From where?'

'Perhaps from the Sandwich Islands, some say, or another group of islands out there in the far reaches of the Pacific.'

'Astonishing! All that way in canoes? What a migration! It makes our steamship travel these days seem very prosaic.'

'I wonder what impelled them to set out,' Frances mused. 'What their journey meant. They can't have been sure there was any land at all in this direction. It must have been a brave voyage of exploration – purely a venture into the unknown, with little chance of returning safely to their home country.'

William tried to imagine what it would have been like, day and night, for weeks, months, in hand-built boats with puny paddles, out on the vast expanse of the ocean, swept by storms and scorched by the sun, knowing only that their most likely destination was death.

'But it may not have been the heroic spirit of discovery that drove them,' he said. 'It may not have been a voluntary choice at all. What if they were a group of exiles, banished after tribal warfare, or desperate to escape from famine or disease? Not everyone who travels abroad does so because of wishing to leave home.'

Forty-three

For the first time in his life, William was experiencing the delight and disquiet of genuine intimacy.

Previous wives and associates had served his material purposes, and that was all. Objects of calculation, instruments of profit. But Frances was unexpectedly interesting: he liked hearing her talk, and her manner had a charming directness about it, an unaffectedly tender warmth. While conversation with her could be lively, she also seemed comfortable with silence, and spent hours at a time reading or drawing. While they were at a theatre performance or a gallery exhibition she would usually stay quietly abstracted, but afterwards the comments she made would often surprise him. Her mind had subtle recesses. She was never dull.

Just as he had not imagined until now that a woman could be a stimulating intellectual companion, so too it was unprecedented to discover such a friend of the flesh. Though a little reserved at first, she had not been bashful; and before long she was encouraging his caresses and clasping him ardently. Whenever he looked at her during the daytime – at her shapeliness, her soft pale skin and the shine of her hair, at the graceful way she moved – it was with a sharp tingle of sensuality as he anticipated that night's interlocking and threshing.

Keeping his emotions calmly detached had never been a

problem for him in the past. There was something uneasy in the fact that she could stir in him this mixture of lust and affection. Occasionally, too, there would be a remorseful twinge at the deceitfulness that governed his whole way of life, and a fitful desire to be more fully what she thought him to be.

When she told him that she was with child, he felt disconcerted, ambivalent. Elation, which he could express to her, mingled with apprehension, which he could not. Fatherhood was a condition he had never contemplated, and children had no place in his schemes, but as he strolled along to the street corner to buy a newspaper, picturing a remarkably handsome and intelligent infant, William was whistling a merry tune that came to him from his boyhood. It had been years since he whistled.

* * *

Back again in Dunedin to complete the legal paperwork and collect the proceeds of the property sale, he stayed not a day longer than necessary. As Frances had authorised him by letter of attorney to act on her behalf, there was no need for her to accompany him there. Instead he sent her on ahead from Melbourne to Sydney: there she would stay with the Bruntons, family friends, and proceed from Sydney to Auckland, where he would join her.

Of course they could have travelled together all the way, but he arranged things like this as a kind of test, a private test of his own intentions. Quite simply, though he was careful to give her no hint of what was in his mind, he wanted to find out whether he could bring himself to dispense with her. Once the money was in his pocket it should be possible, if he had a firm enough resolve, simply to abandon her, board a ship travelling westwards, make his way to Cape Town and then on to some British port. He would never be traced. In the past, he would not have hesitated to seize his profit and quietly disappear. Now the situation was more complicated. By the time his ship crossed the Tasman, a swift passage with a boisterous westerly behind him, he knew that he would not leave her. At least, not now. He missed her smile too much, her grey-blue eyes, and her conversation. And although a baby would be inconvenient, it might provide some satisfactions, too. He would meet up with Frances in Auckland, as arranged, and embark on a Pacific voyage with her, and see how he felt in a few months' time.

After finishing the transactions in Dunedin he made his way up the coast to Auckland. Despite the fierce weather she was there waiting at the wharf, clutching her bonnet and shawl and waving to him as he braced himself against the rail.

They were both tired from their travels, and content to spend their time in Auckland resting and relaxing. It would have been an uneventful few days but for the fatal accident that Frances witnessed out in the harbour. The drownings seemed to affect her deeply, and her distress made him think about his own attitude to the power of the ocean.

He was certainly capable of pity and fear, and there were few things as terrifying as being tossed by a storm on the open seas. But for him deep water meant other things as well. It provided him with ways of escape, allowed him to shed ghostly shadows of himself beside the shoreline and to make a swift departure. The image of a trackless waste was not always desolate.

Part 10

To the ends of the Earth, 1892–97

Forty-four

'And your brothers?' she asked him, as they sat in the cabin of the ship that was taking them slowly along the narrow, misty channel towards Juneau. 'What of them? There's never any exchange of letters, and I don't understand why you called off the plan to visit them in Manitoba. I'd have liked to meet them. Don't you want them to make your wife's acquaintance? Don't you want them to see your beautiful babies?' He was dandling their daughter on his knee.

She waited for him to answer. He averted his eyes but still sensed her gaze. By the time they left British Columbia he had been well aware how much his fits of moodiness were distancing him from Frances. They made her worried and insecure, he could see that. His occasional ill-tempered outbursts were part of it, but more harmful was his lack of candour. She seemed to know when he was dissembling or withholding, and it became obvious that his refusal to explain himself puzzled her, blighted her trust.

In silence he carried their little girl on his arm across the cabin to the porthole, peering with her through the thinning patches of mist and pointing towards the glimpsed Alaskan shore.

Some things had been bottled up for so long, like little embryos, pickled curls of tissue, that he could not bear to take them down from their dark shelves and look at them, or let her look at them. It had been difficult enough to tell Frances about the harsh struggle of his early years, let alone disclose the full story of his ruptured and ruined family life, fragment by pathetic fragment. He still baulked at describing the terrible deaths of his father and mother; Frances was the only person who had come near to hearing any of the details. But it would be even more difficult for him to talk about his brothers, because something like shame flickered around the lapse of contact with them.

He mulled it over now. Did he simply feel shame? That wasn't quite his feeling, though there would have been a kind of embarrassment in trying to tell Frances that, when last heard from, George was drifting aimlessly from one unskilled job to another while Stewart had become a drunken recluse after his seduction by the Jesuit priest. There was something else. When he thought about his brothers, William's sense of shame was more tangled: it included a chafing realisation that *they* would be ashamed of *him* if they knew how selfishly he had used his talents and opportunities, knew that he himself was in fact a worse kind of vagrant than they, an unscrupulously clever vagabond. George and Stewart had been injured by life, as he had; but they kept their wounds to themselves, each man wrapped morosely in solitude. In contrast, what he had done with his own wounds was to transfer them to others, inflicting pain on gullible people.

He earnestly wished he could surrender himself to the contentment that floated near his fingertips. Living with Frances had brought new satisfactions, reviving and refining dormant emotions, turning him towards a better self. He no longer wanted to be a charlatan, no longer wanted to be acting the part of a physician or a minister. Pretence was not gratifying any more. Yet he found himself now in secrecy's trap. Unable to reveal to Frances that the man she fell in love with had been a cunning, swindling, heartless impostor, he could never rinse his conscience clean; nor could he explain to her why from time to time it was necessary to abandon some place where she felt comfortable, and sidle away suddenly to escape the consequences of past actions. But there was a deeper discomfort when he asked himself who he really was. He was imaginary, a fictional character. He was, in fact, nobody at all.

So here they were now, nobody and wife, arriving at this inchoate far northern frontier, their ship gliding towards the flimsy cluster of waterfront docks and the untidy spill of little township buildings that seemed as insubstantial as a scattered pack of cards, with dark mountain slopes looming behind and lifting bony shoulders into drifts of cloud.

* * *

The house they found to rent in Juneau was shabbier than they would have liked, and sparsely furnished, but there was nothing better available. William left the unpacking to Frances and Ada while he went looking for food and kitchen supplies in the downtown shops. After the evening meal, Ada put the children to bed, and he sat by the fireplace with a newspaper, angling it towards the candlelight and firelight, and glancing now and then at Frances as she moved various objects into different places on the shelves beside the chimney corner.

He watched her pick up – as she so often did when pensive – her most prized possession, the Kutani bowl. Since buying it in Tokio she had kept it close at hand wherever they went, wrapping it with reverential care every time they moved on to another place and setting it in a conspicuous position within each successive home.

Now she held it up high in both hands to look closely at the panels on its side, and her gesture seemed to him almost votive, as if the bowl's deep concavity of red and white and gold could somehow contain her being's heart and home.

'You cherish this bowl,' he remarked. 'It's a truly beautiful object, but I think it means something more to you than that.' His tone made it a question.

Tilting her head, she kept her eyes on the bowl as she responded: 'Not easy to put into words. Every time I look at it there's some new detail that catches my attention. Or I see part of it from a different angle and it leads my thoughts off somewhere else. This pattern on the inside, now: it hadn't struck me before, but the long red curving shape here, with a frilled edge like a scatter of spray, doesn't it suggest the curl of a wave breaking against the shore? And the rest of the interior surface – that's the solid ground and what grows out of it. And then this bit across the middle, just a lightly shaded outline, suggests the same border between land and sea, but in another way. It reminds me of the line you get on a map to mark the coastal fringe.'

He wanted to hear more. 'And that dividing line – what does it mean for you, then?'

It seemed she had not heard, or was not going to answer. Then, after a minute, she recited:

'Oh, which were best, to roam or rest:
The land's lap or the water's breast?'

Browning, he supposed.

Letting the conversation lapse, he turned back to the newspaper. But Frances spoke again. 'It must always be in the minds of the Japanese, that line.'

'That line?' He had lost the thread.

'Their coast. Whichever part of Japan they live in, even high up on those hill-slopes, the sea isn't very far away. Surely there's a kind of tension in that.'

He nodded. 'Any islander might feel it, I suppose.'

'But for the Japanese it's probably inescapable,' she said. 'Each piece of their country is so narrow, just a sliver on the map, it could hardly let them forget what surrounds them so closely. All those earthquakes and tidal waves – every time the ground shudders under their feet or the ocean rears up over the strand, they'll be reminded yet again.'

As he thought about her words it occurred to him that of all the other places they had visited, hardly any significant residue remained among their possessions; but traces of Japan continued to travel with them. It was not only this bowl. There were the curious *shunga* pictures, too. The pair of woodblock prints, with their brightly coloured and uninhibited depiction of bedroom scenes, sometimes served to stimulate their own intimacies. He would take them from the folder and show them to Frances as they lay together on their own bed, coaxing her into the positions of the painted figures.

forty-five

Another part of Japanese culture that went with them everywhere, more opaquely, was their young companion.

To Ada, William thought, Juneau must be a very strange town indeed, as unlike Yokohama as almost any place could be. But then the scenes of Canadian life would also have seemed surprising to her, he supposed, though she had never shown what she thought of them. He could seldom be sure what was going on in Ada's mind. Her face was not exactly expressionless; there were fleeting smiles, and even the occasional brief whispery chuckle, especially when baby Frances said or did something amusing; and William sometimes glimpsed the hint of a little frown, too, if he happened to speak sternly. Yet she kept her own counsel.

Ada was the first girl – the first at her stage in life – that William had been able to observe at close quarters since his classroom days in La Chute forty years earlier, and she was utterly unlike those ungainly raw-boned farming lassies. Ada had a demure manner, a quiet poise, and a slender form that was already becoming elegant. Her small dark eyes seemed constantly watchful.

Wanting her shyness to melt, wanting her to feel almost part of their family, he developed a habit of patting her on the shoulder. He thought it would soften the consciousness of servitude. As she wore her hair in braids, his fingers sometimes touched the nape of her neck, and in an absent-minded way he would stroke its soft honey-coloured skin.

Then, one evening in Vernon, he had come upon her unexpectedly in the scullery when she was leaning over a tin basin and washing herself, stripped to her tiny waist. She turned towards him in the candlelight, and he could not stop himself from staring at her small wet breast buds as she slowly wiped the soap from her armpits with a sponge. There was a cloth spotted with crimson, and she pushed it quickly behind the basin. It struck him that her menses must have begun already, and he wondered whether her real age might perhaps be more than twelve years, despite what Joseph Foxton had told him when she was sold.

The image of light and shadow flickering on her body stayed with him afterwards. A few days later he was sitting in a balcony armchair, turning the pages of Cook's *Boston Monday Lectures* while Frances was busy inside the house, when Ada suddenly came up beside him and seated herself on his knee, placing one of her hands against his chest. Startled at the unaccustomed familiarity, he tried clumsily to move her away so that he could stand up, but disengagement became awkward as she nestled against him, and both were still linked in an intimate sitting position at the moment when Frances appeared in the doorway. From the expression on his wife's face as she swung around and went straight back inside, he could tell what she was thinking, but there seemed no point in following her with what would surely seem a lame explanation.

Probably Frances was already recalling, he guessed, the uncomfortable earlier episode in Honolulu. There would still be at least some doubt in her mind as to what had really happened there, though he had brazened it out at the time. Lies came fluently to his lips when he needed them, and in that particular situation they had been necessary. About the misdemeanour itself he felt no onerous guilt. It wasn't that he had gone looking for trouble. If Frances hadn't been so heavy with child, preoccupied with her condition and unresponsive to his desire for her, he wouldn't have yielded to temptation. He hadn't planned to touch the Burnetts' servant – but when she seemed slow to understand how to rub the liniment into her groin, and wanted him to show her what to do, he felt suddenly an aching, like an acute kind of thirst, irresistible.

The scene came back to him again. The young servant woman (her name escaped him) had taken his hand in hers and moved it up under her loose *holoku* dress, holding his fingers tightly, rubbing their tips between her thighs, and pulling him closer. But as he tried to climb on top of her, she rolled quickly aside and pushed him away. Then she was holding out her hand, and the meaning was unmistakeable: not an invitation but a demand. She wanted money. When he shook his head she scowled, straightened her dress, and flounced out of the room.

Within a week he was snubbed and shunned by the Burnetts and other church families, and he soon found that a story was circulating in which his role was cast as a predatory one. In stoutly denying it and representing himself to Frances as blameless, he had to suppress a double anger: anger that this shameless native woman had made him out to be the instigator of indecency, and anger that he had let himself be enticed into caressing her.

Since leaving Honolulu, Frances had never mentioned the incident and he had seldom thought of it. Only because of what Ada did that day in Vernon had it resurfaced in his mind. He could not be sure whether Ada's action had any seductive intent. What had she seen and heard as a young girl in Yokohama? When Foxton arranged for William to buy her as a maidservant there had been more than a hint that some form of prostitution would otherwise be her fate; but had she, perhaps, already been precociously introduced to vice?

As the Alaskan daylight began to fade at the edge of their second afternoon in the Juneau cottage, he and Frances watched and listened while Ada now cradled the infant in her arms and their other child played noisily at her feet.

'Has there ever been such a prodigy as your little namesake?' he asked his wife, as their daughter conducted a solemn three-way conversation with her new china doll and Ada, using a special dolly voice to respond to her own remarks and Ada's. 'Just listen to her chatter! A ventriloquist, too! As clever as she is beautiful.'

Frances smiled indulgently. 'Do you remember how anxious you felt when I told you we were going to have a baby?'

'Anxious? I suppose so. I'd never imagined myself as a parent.' Yes, he did remember his mood when she announced her pregnancy, more than two years ago now.

But as baby Frances turned into a person, and her babble turned into intelligible words, affectionate pride stirred in him. He looked lovingly at them now – Frances and Frances – eyes and hair of identical colour, the same shapely mouths, but two different creatures, each uniquely winsome. Fatherhood, he reflected, held out to him the promise of something near to contentment.

forty-six

As he stood at the courthouse door, the piquant irony of the situation was no less amusing to William for being invisible to others. Having made a career of pretending to be what he was not, there was much for him to relish here in this ridiculous pageant of impersonators: a crowd of upright citizens in outlandish fancy dress, none of whom could have guessed that a master of disguise was in their midst.

During his first week he had walked into a little photography shop and studio in Juneau's main street, wanting to arrange a family portrait sitting. Now that young Frances was nearly two years old and young William just reaching six months, it would be timely to have their group image captured – all four of the Hammonds together. Winter and Landerskin, said the sign, Photographs and Curios. He spoke to Landerskin, an affable fellow with ears like batwings, who reserved a time in his appointment notebook and on a card that he handed to William.

'Next Wednesday, then, at ten.' He inclined his head smilingly. 'Thank you, Dr Hammond.'

Overhearing these words, a man who had just entered the shop stepped towards William and spoke up.

'Pardon my intrusion, sir,' he said, 'but Mr Landerskin addressed you as "Doctor" and I thought I was the only physician in this town, so let me introduce myself: David Henderson.'

'William Hammond.' They shook hands. 'I'm a recent arrival,' William explained. 'Here with my family. We don't know how long we'll be staying in Juneau,' and he added in a tone of jocular reassurance, 'but I'm certainly not intending to set up a rival medical practice!'

'I'm glad to hear it,' said Henderson, with a theatrical gesture of relief. They exchanged a few brief pleasantries before he added, 'Now let me extend an invitation to you and Mrs Hammond, for next Saturday evening. My wife and I are hosting a ball for any of the townsfolk who'd like to come. A fancy dress ball, at the courthouse. There'll be quite a crowd, but plenty of space for dancing. The sale of tickets will raise funds for the new native church building. Perhaps you've heard about this construction project?'

'Nothing at all.'

'Well, it's stirring up a lot of interest here. Talk of the town. Right, George?' Landerskin nodded vigorously, beaming like a cherub.

'Native church? You mean for Eskimos?' William asked.

'No, no,' said Henderson. 'It's a different group of Indians around these parts: the Tlingit. People of the coasts and islands.'

'And they're Christians?'

'Some of them. Converted by Russians. Eastern Orthodox. In Sitka, the Tlingit have had their own chapel for some while, since the days before Russia sold Alaska to the United States. The Russians always conducted worship services for the natives in the Tlingit language. But then our American missionaries tried to get rid of native language and customs, and make the Tlingit use English. Well, some of the Auk Bay Tlingit visited Sitka...'

'Auk Bay?'

'That's the old name for this area hereabouts, where we are. Anyhow, they went over to Sitka and got themselves baptised there, and last year they invited an Orthodox bishop to come here and instruct them. Next thing we knew, they'd decided to build a church, and it's all moved very quickly over the last few months. They bought a site in the middle of the town, just up that road...'

'The natives bought land themselves? How could they afford that?'

'Oh, they've put their savings together. Scores of them have been earning good wages for years. Gave up their hunting and fishing, moved to Gold Creek to work for the miners as diggers and carriers and woodcutters, and now they're providing much of the labour for the church, with the help of half a dozen Serbian miners. I've seen the plans: it's going to be a handsome little octagonal structure, as different from everything else in Juneau as it could possibly be. The architectural drawings came from Russia, along with two hundred silver roubles, so I'm told, but they need more funds.'

'So you've organised this ball. I suppose you have some particular connection, then, with the church? And with the natives, perhaps?'

'Neither. I'm not a religious man of any sort, to be frank with you, and I seldom have any contact with the Tlingit. When they get sick they rely on their own medicine man.'

William raised his eyebrows in an unspoken question, to which Henderson replied: 'Just a whim, really. I decided to help raise money for this project because I'm delighted at the wonderfully incongruous prospect of having an ornate Russian chapel, with all its ancient trappings, built by and for the local Indians in a rough American mining town. What a splendid medley of cultures!'

William smiled. 'Or a mere muddle of beliefs?'

'In my estimation, Dr Hammond, all beliefs about God and so forth – what people like to call the spiritual realm – are more or less muddled. I hope I don't offend you, but I must say it seems to me that most human beings, regrettably, are suckers for superstition. Not that I scorn them for that. It's a fortunate weakness, because it produces beautiful things. Foolishly beautiful, I'd say, but beautiful nonetheless...'

Henderson broke off. 'I should apologise,' he said, 'for chattering on like this. You were on your way and I've imposed on you. But I do hope you'll come along on Saturday evening. The courthouse. Tickets at the door. Prizes. Must be fancy dress, mind you – whatever garment or guise you like.'

* * *

By the time he arrived, half the population of Juneau seemed to have packed itself into the little courthouse. With a small group of musicians straining to make their tunes heard above the noise of tapping feet and boisterous voices, couples spun around the floor in eddies of exhilaration.

Frances had stayed back at the hotel. Their daughter seemed to be coming down with a nasty cold, and although Ada could be trusted to watch over both the children, a sick child would want her mother on hand. So William came to the ball alone.

A smile plucked at his mouth as he surveyed the motley attire of the dancers and loungers. A large man with a thick black beard and heavy boots wore an outrageously bright scarlet dress, with cheeks rouged to match, and laughed uproariously as he twirled to and fro in time to the music and held in his arms a much smaller fellow whose huge Red Indian feathered head-dress seemed about to slide down over his eyes. Someone else, wearing an even grander hat, a metallic mitre, and holding a crosier, stood apart from the throng in the embroidered vestment of a bishop; or perhaps he *was* a bishop.

William felt pleased with his own garb, having managed to find a hunting frock, a broad-brimmed scouting hat and a pair of fringed buckskin leggings. The fur pelts hanging on the porch of the Decker Brothers store in South Franklin Street had attracted his attention: he was looking for clothing reminiscent of Fenimore Cooper's pathfinder, and this general store had just what he wanted – for a good price, too.

A roughly lettered sign suspended above the musicians promised Prizes and Surprises for the best dancing display, but William did not intend to dance. He had come because, infected by Henderson's irreverent enthusiasm for this Tlingit vagary, he wanted to make a contribution to the building project; and because, curious as always, he was glad of an opportunity to see so much of Juneau's population at one time under one roof. Though the wind was cold outside, the room had become warm with all the exertions and exhalations. Near the door was a stall selling ice-cream, and he bought one at what would have been an outrageous price anywhere but at a fundraising event. Licking the sticky confection as it dripped on to his whiskers and sleeve, it occurred to him that he probably looked devoid of dignity – but so did everyone else, and there was something agreeable about it all. He caught himself smiling.

At that moment he was startled to see little Ada standing in the crowded doorway, shivering and looking around anxiously. He pushed his way towards her.

'Ada! Ada!' He had to raise his voice. 'What is it? Something wrong?'

'Must come, sir,' she said. 'Baby Frances – very sick. Very sick.'

He strode back to the hotel, Ada hurrying behind him.

As soon as he entered the room he could see, even by the dim candlelight, that the wee mite was feverish. Her tiny hand clutched her mother's. Her limbs were twitching. Sweat stood out on her temples, and her trembling lips seemed to be darkening: a bad sign, he knew. It was all too likely to be the cholera they had left Victoria to escape. She would need an emetic, a syrup of lobelia or something similar, but he had no medicine with him, nothing at all. Where could he find any on a Saturday night in a place like this, a rough mining town?

He rushed back to the courthouse and searched for Henderson, finding him at last beside the stage with a loud-speaker in his hand.

'Dr Henderson!' William called out.

Henderson greeted him. 'Lively crowd,' he said cheerfully. 'Good takings. I was just going to announce that we'll be able to hand over more than four hundred dollars to the building fund.'

'Please, Henderson, I need your help. It's urgent. My infant daughter has suddenly taken very ill. I think it may be cholera. I'm sorry to be asking you now, here, but I don't know where else to turn. I desperately need something to empty her stomach. Perhaps lobelia?'

'Come with me.'

The cold air bit his throat and nostrils as he hurried with Henderson up unfamiliar streets, buffeted by rising gusts of wind. It seemed half an hour before they reached Henderson's house, where he was given a small jar of powder.

As soon as Frances opened the door he saw the fear in her eyes. 'It's worse! She was groaning terribly for a long time, and now she's gone into a faint.'

'Get me some boiling water and a cup.'

He felt the pulse: rapid and feeble, like her breathing. Frances brought the kettle and he poured some of the water into the cup, stirring in a measure of the powdered blackroot and ginger until the mixture became milky. When it had cooled enough he roused the child, drew her into a sitting position, and held the cup to her dry, darkened lips. He continued to hold her upright in the cot, his arm around her thin little shoulders. Within a few minutes, violent retching seized her. When at last the spasms abated, her head flopped forward. Her breathing became more and more subdued. And then it stopped.

Part of his own spirit expired with her at that moment. For the first time since boyhood, William shed tears. Language crept away from him like a wounded animal. He was almost wordless, solitary in his inexpressible grief.

The formal phrases he murmured a few days later, when they stood together at the edge of the hole in the miserably swishing rain and began to lower that diminutive coffin, gave no comfort to either of them. The act of burial seemed to draw other things into the cold wet ground with her: he was interring not only his daughter but also much of his faith, much of his hope, much of his love.

Faith? Never before had he needed to ask himself what he trustingly believed in. The 'wisdom and spirit of the universe' that animated the poetry he knew so well was too diffuse to have any tangible influence on his personal creed. So what was that creed? He was as intimately familiar with the scriptures as with Wordsworth's lines, but had always regarded them as mere material for sermons whose persuasive power did not depend on any convictions of his own. But now he knew most assuredly what he did *not* believe in: he did not believe that there was any justice, goodness or mercy in the shaping of events. He had no faith in a divinely ordered scheme of things. 'The evidence of things not seen'? There was none. There was good fortune and there was calamity. There was kindness and cruelty and vengeance. But these did not extend beyond the human world. Only in himself could he have faith. In his judgment of things.

Hope, too, was gone. Jonathan Harrison had been right. William was indeed nothing but a naked individualist, and as such could never ultimately be hopeful about anything, not in a fundamental philosophical sense. Though he might sometimes feel flickers of optimism, even immortal longings, there could be no rational or religious basis for them.

Love persisted, but it seemed to him now a poor, sadly diminished emotion. To lose a daughter was to know how flimsy any loving tie would always be.

Forty-seven

After the death and the burial and then the eventual departure from Juneau, while that small body remained behind in the ground, everything was different. Tender feeling for his wife and son remained, but its entanglement with sorrow made it deeply painful.

Even his tongue was numb. He could sink into silence for hours, only half attentive to a newspaper or book in his hand, lifting his eyes at times to stare blankly at something or someone unseen.

One of these moods was on him as young William crawled crabwise along the floor towards him. He felt a small sticky hand on his ankle, and looked down.

'Da!' said his son. 'Da da da.'

William shook himself out of his brown study and put a hand on the child's head. 'Hmmm? What are you saying, my boy?'

'Da!'

'I thought so. Quite right. Off you go then. Let's see you crawl over to Ada.'

The little fellow, frowning with discomfort, pulled and pushed himself around the floor – but stopped suddenly to rub his hand against his nose and cheeks, whimpering, then wailing piteously. This had been happening for a couple of months. The skin on parts of his face had turned bright pink, not a healthy ruddy colour but a sore rash. There was something wrong, but what? Very few teeth had come through. Perhaps his gums were abscessed, poisoning his bloodstream. William was uncertain about treatment, and in a place like this there seemed little chance of getting good medical attention for his son.

Choosing Guatemala had been impulsive, like nearly all their travelling. Frances was reluctant, pleading fatigue and low spirits, but yielded to his pressure. He had insisted, quite arbitrarily, on coming here for no more specific reason than its exotic lure: scraps of information about this middle part of the American continent, edged by the Pacific on one side and the Caribbean on the other, made it enticingly strange. He had read about Guatemala's former capital, Antigua, half deserted after earthquake damage, resting in handsome disrepair between smouldering volcanoes and coffee plantations. He had seen photographs of solemn men with top hats perched above their leathery faces, and trousers that stopped short above their knees. And there was the fascination of stories he heard in San Francisco about the relics and rubble of a once great civilisation deep in the Guatemalan rainforest, a legendary city of stone temples where rituals of human sacrifice were said to have taken place long ago.

But any plans of journeying beyond Guatemala City were now dismissed. Worried about his little boy's pain and weakness, William thought that the calomel powder they had been rubbing on his gums day and night for a couple of months was probably insufficient. He made a strong mercury solution from the powder and administered it as a bedtime drink. But after a week of this regimen the boy's condition deteriorated. His heartbeat was alarmingly rapid. He had been salivating, but his mouth seemed dry and his tongue looked swollen. He kept calling for water. Redness covered his fingers, palms and soles. He had become feeble, no longer crawling around and not even able to sit without sagging.

One morning his breath was shallow and he seemed unable to swallow. The drink they held to his lips dribbled down his chin and neck. He closed his eyes, gave a last sigh, and died in William's arms.

The place where they laid him was unlike any cemetery they had seen before. There were many crypts set into walls beside the tree-lined pathways, and his tiny coffin slid smoothly into one of these *nichos*. William tried to take some comfort from knowing that his son would remain above the ground, above the encroachment of the water table. But he could not stop thinking about putrefaction.

When they returned from the cemetery to their hotel they found that Ada had disappeared, and taken a purse in which Frances had been keeping American dollars. The porter told them he saw the girl set out in the direction of the railroad station hours earlier. There was a note, clumsily lettered: *VERY SAD GO HOME.*

'What does she mean?' Frances muttered as they looked at the scrap of paper. 'Is she apologising for her theft, and for deserting us? Or wanting to express sympathy? And does she really intend to find her way back to Japan, all alone? She's hardly more than a child. What a reckless thing to do! If she wanted to leave us, now that there's no role for her in helping with the children, why didn't she speak to us and let us work out something? I wonder if it's even legally possible for such a young person to travel to another country without others.'

'Very sad go home,' William repeated aloud. 'Could it have a more general meaning? It almost sounds like a maxim, perhaps a translated Japanese saying: people who are sad should go home. A statement not just about what she wants to do but also about what she thinks we ought to do, being so bereft.'

'But William, we have no home to return to.'

Her tone was flat, dispirited. He looked at her sharply: was she reproaching him? But he did not respond. He knew she was so smitten with grief, as was he, that it was no time to be arguing.

Why Ada left them, and what happened to her, they would never know.

* * *

With no particular plan or purpose apart from an unspoken wish to get away from the small footprint of mortality, they moved on southwards into Nicaragua, stopping in Granada.

Their hotel window looked directly across the huge lake, and they talked of hiring a small boat. From out on the water, they were told, there would be wonderful views of the volcanic peaks. But within a few days, Frances fell sick and took to her bed. At first it was an intermittent discomfort, apparently no more than an unsettled stomach, and they attributed it to the local food; probably, they thought, some of the pork in the *nacatamales* they had bought from little stands in the market-place was tainted. Then her condition seemed to worsen: she began to suffer bouts of nausea and felt jabbing pains in her abdomen.

'I think I may be with child again,' she told him. 'But it doesn't feel quite the same as before.'

The weather was oppressive. Every day brought another heavy downpour, and the steamy heat invited mosquitoes and other pesky insects into their grimy rooms.

After a week she declared herself more comfortable, though still weak.

'Can we go somewhere else now?' she pleaded. 'Move on to a cleaner place, somewhere less humid?'

'Yes, time to move, and not just because of the climate. We

want more reliable food and lodging than we can get here.'

'And more people who speak our language,' she said.

'Besides,' he added, 'if we stay long in Nicaragua there's a chance of getting caught up in civil disturbances. This new President of theirs, Zelaya, is stirring up conflict. I'm told he wants to annex the Mosquito Coast, and there's a lot of unrest here in Granada about that, and about other things he's doing. I was looking at the *San Francisco Examiner* yesterday in the lobby. It says the American navy has sent ships to the eastern seaboard. A show of support for all the whites who work there – mine managers, engineers, merchants, people like that, and their families. Marines came ashore at Bluefields and they've calmed things down. I think we should make our way over there while protection is available. It's a busy port, Bluefields, and I'm sure we can soon get a ship to Jamaica, and then on to England.'

The jolting rail journey was slow and unpleasant. When they opened a window the carriage would fill with pungent smoke from the engine, and when they closed it the heat was stifling. The food they bought at the station before leaving was inedible, the only water they could get had a brackish taste, and their seats were hard benches. While Frances slept fitfully, William reflected on the unreality, the evasiveness, of the life they had been leading for more than three years now. At his insistence they had continued to be tourists, living in a bubble, moving on haphazardly from place to place, paying little attention to the changes occurring in society at large. Until recently he had not given much thought to the depression that had soured commerce and industry around the world. Though vaguely aware of the social hardship it was bringing in many countries, he had been startled to learn that it was creating tension between different countries over markets and trade routes and access to materials. This struggle over the Mosquito Coast was just one symptom, he realised. The countries that he and Frances had been passing through as casual sightseers and samplers were now caught up in swirling crosscurrents – political, economic, social – that could well change the face and fate of nations before the century was out. Against that backdrop, their travelling seemed an idle pastime.

By the time they drew near to Bluefields, Frances had become feverish. Half-conscious, she began to confuse her words.

'Don't want to go to Blueskin Bay,' she murmured. 'Bad accident.'

'It's Bluefields,' he said, 'not Blueskin. What accident?'

She dozed off again. The sweat stood out on her brow and he fanned the air to keep her cool, waving his newspaper to and fro, but to little effect.

When they reached Bluefields, an ugly, muddy little town, William found temporary accommodation in a spare room at the back of a mine owner's cottage where Frances seemed to recover. Their timing was fortunate: three days after their arrival they arranged a passage on a freighter returning to Jamaica after delivering supplies and collecting mahogany for the furniture trade.

* * *

Since the children's deaths, Frances appeared to have turned her thoughts more solemnly to the consolations of religion. Most evenings now, she would ask William to read to her from Paul's epistles. Soon after they arrived in Kingston, she urged him to go with her to a worship service at Duke Street Christian Church. The minister there was Cedric Randall, an Englishman who, he mentioned proudly during his sermon, had been preaching the gospel to Jamaicans for thirty-five years, first with the Baptists and for the last decade with the Disciples' Board of Missions. Sitting in the pew, William felt remote from it all. The biblical phrases that were once laden with evocative meanings, even if he had never privately invested them with much credence, now sounded utterly empty.

Nevertheless he arranged with Randall that a deaconess would come to their hotel during the week and sit with Frances. Talking with another woman about her grief might give her some comfort. He himself felt too depleted and ineffectual to console her any further.

He made enquiries about onward travel to England. In the happier past they had often spoken expectantly of this destination – 'the land of Browning and Wordsworth', she called it. 'The place where so many lines run together.' But it would be more than a month before they could make the voyage in suitable comfort. Meanwhile her lassitude worried him. Reluctant to go out for a stroll with him even in the most pleasant weather, she would lie for hours at a time on the sofa in their hotel room, reading or resting. Several times he saw her hand press against her lower abdomen.

'Has that pain come back again?' he asked, wondering whether something other than pregnancy was the cause.

'Just a few pangs, now and then.' She waved the topic away.

Over the next few days she gradually lost her appetite. Then, as the fever began to grip her again, he spent a whole afternoon walking around the town in search of some place that might sell herbal medicine, but found nothing useful. When he returned he was shocked at the sight of her.

Frances lay curled on her side in bed, pallid and wan, her once beautiful hair streaked with sweat, her eyes fixed on her beloved Kutani bowl beside the bed. When he took her hand in his it was hot and moist and slack. The cramping pains in her belly that had come in spasms during the previous night continued to wrack her. He ran along the corridor towards the reception desk, crying out loudly for help. The manager emerged from an office, looking alarmed.

'Please fetch a doctor here at once,' William pleaded. 'For my wife. Urgently. She's very ill. Serious emergency.'

It was more than half an hour before the doctor came, and after examining Frances he seemed as uncertain as William about what to do. She was miscarrying, he said, and they would have to let nature take its course. Giving her some morphia, he left with a promise to return in the morning.

The night seemed endless. Early in the morning, as William sat with her, holding her hand, she gave a sudden cry and threw the sheet aside, twisting her torso and jerking back her head. Blood spilled out of her. In a mindless panic he reached for the Kutani bowl at her bedside and angled it between her drawn-up thighs. Clots emerged like pieces of dark red pulpy fruit, and then a small translucent shape.

But the ordeal had not ended. Something was still dreadfully amiss, and he had no idea what to do. She was convulsing now, screaming. He ran to the door to call for help, knocking over the bowl. It smashed on the floor.

* * *

There were just four of them at the dusty graveside: William, the deaconess, Cedric Randall, and the boxed body of Frances. The committal was brief. At William's request, Randall read from the dispirited last chapter of Ecclesiastes. After the coffin was clumsily lowered and a handful of dirt cast on its lid, Randall clasped William's hand and then left him alone with doleful scriptural phrases still hanging in the air. Broken bowl. All is vanity. Long home.

The long home: the burial pit, the final resting place, the home that everyone would come to in the end. There was also an earlier home, where each person's life journey had begun, left behind and irretrievable. Suspended between those two, between the memory of one and the prospect of the other, was a shimmering idea of finding some place perfectly congenial to one's spirit – home as a chosen location. He wondered whether Frances ever believed she had found it, even for a moment.

He told himself there were things he should be doing, practical things like sorting her personal effects. He could hardly bear to look at her clothing, her sketchbooks, her worn volume of Browning's poems; nor could he bear to dispose of them, not yet. Meanwhile he ought to write at once to her Dunedin relatives to let them know of her passing, but could not face the task. The gulf seemed far too wide. The years of wandering had isolated her from family and friends. Now she was utterly lost to them, adrift forever, and they would hold him responsible. No, he could not send them a letter. He would have to leave it to others to convey the sad tidings.

Ada's elliptical note haunted him: 'Very sad go home.' He had always thought that the journey mattered most, and the important thing was to keep moving on. 'The Earth is all before me...' But the simple, damning truth, he now saw, was that he belonged nowhere.

Forty-eight

In the weeks after her death, all the warmth that she and the children had brought into his life evaporated. In its stead, vengefulness returned, hard and cold, like the feeling that had filled him during his time at Dannemora. He would make the living pay for the lost. Punish survivors. Resume old roles. Return to what he had been.

For nearly three years he ranged up and down the east coast of North America, roaming from Florida to Maine, back to New Orleans, grasping any opportunity for profitable deception. Sardonically he pictured himself as like the mythical marauder in one of the strange Tlingit tales he had heard in Juneau – a man-eating giant with his heart in his heel, who could turn at will into a swarm of bloodsucking mosquitoes.

William no longer took much care to cover his tracks, sometimes becoming reckless. He was detained for a few days by the New Orleans police but managed to wriggle out of a prison sentence by producing such a convincing performance of contrition that the judge decided to be lenient.

He took the railroad towards Dallas, but by the time he reached the Texas border he was feeling ill at ease, and turned back at once towards the coast. Journeying eastwards again, it occurred to him that he had tended to become more and more tense whenever he was away from the sea for long. As the train chugged its way through Louisiana he reviewed the stages of his life. Thinking of his brief return to La Chute as a young man, he was seized by a remembered sensation of being shut in there, oppressively enclosed. Then there were those years in the inland prison: much more suffocating. Later, in places like Franklin Falls, the rush of water sluicing down between riverbanks was not enough to assuage his anxious awareness of being landlocked.

He saw a pattern. Increasingly he had been attracted to coastal locations – Juneau, for instance, and San Francisco. Even more to islands; whether large or small, an island always reassured him with its rim of coastlines. To be surrounded by sea, as he was in New Zealand, Malta, Hawaii, Japan, Vancouver, Jamaica, even in the huge island continent of Australia, was to be confident that when the time came he could get away quickly, leaving behind what he no longer wanted to do or be.

He thought of the breaking wave on the broken Kutani bowl. Frances, for reasons that differed from his, had shared with him a sense that one's life could find its direction most readily at the point where earth and water met.

But now he felt stranded. Her death had taken her away from him, far out into a shoreless sea, implacably black and silent.

* * *

On his first day at Woods Hole, the southernmost corner of Cape Cod, William wandered down a winding dirt path to the wharf and fell into conversation with a pair of wizened tobacco-chewing old-timers who deplored their home's rapid commercial and social decline since the Pacific Guano Company closed its doors.

'Used to be two hundred men labouring here, y'know,' the more talkative one told William. 'Mostly Irish, like us. Oftentimes you'd see a line of schooners anchored in the Great Harbour, waiting their turn to unload cargoes.'

'Guano. Phosphorus,' the other explained, and then turned away with a weary sigh as if the effort of so much speaking – or perhaps the memory of hard work – had utterly exhausted him.

'How long ago was this?' William asked the first man.

'Still seemed to be going strong ten years ago. Then suddenly the business got into trouble somehow. Don't know the ins and outs of it. They went bankrupt, y'know. Everything here came to a halt. People left. Many people. No work, y'see. Nothing to do except a bit of fishing, and not many fish to be caught any more, apart from scup and sea bass.' He spat out a jet of brown juice.

'But I've heard that things are looking up now,' said William. 'There's a group of scientists who work here in the summer months. Research on fish stocks, isn't it? And someone was telling me on the train from Boston that more and more vacationers are spending time and money around here these days.'

'It's not the same. They're all just visitors. Linger for a few weeks, then off again. In times gone by, this place was packed with working men all year round. Hardly a trace of the old life to be seen now. They went and knocked down our factory. Even dynamited the big chimney.' He shook his head.

'I miss the factory,' blurted his companion, moved by nostalgia to the verge of loquacity. 'I liked the stink of those big vats.'

* * *

Rain gusted across the harbour throughout the next day and the next. William sat for hours at a time beside the streaky window of his cramped boarding-house room, staring out sightlessly into the grey whistling weather. His clothes smelt sour, and he could not remember when he last washed a shirt. The beard that he used to keep carefully trimmed had become unkempt. Too much bother. He was unsure what had brought him to this place, what to do here, how long to stay. In the past it would have been clear: he would be looking for ways to exploit the credulity of the holiday crowd and pluck a feather or two before moving on quickly. But now he felt tired, lacking purpose and energy. This sombre mood had crouched over him for most of the time since Frances's death. Nothing, lately, had provided any relief from his isolation and melancholy.

The skin on his palm had begun to itch, reddening and flaking off in patches. He imagined layer after layer of skin disappearing until there was nothing left to touch with.

On his fourth day the wind dropped, the skies cleared, and he made his way down to the wharf once more. A sign at the rail terminus showed departure times for the steamer ferry to Nantucket and he decided on impulse to make the trip. As it would be more than an hour before the vessel arrived, he walked back along the streets of the village to fill in time, past the empty stone building still known as the candle factory, past the forlorn-looking little church and the small weather-worn houses, up and down aimlessly, and then back again towards the wharf, where the sidewheel steamer *Island Home* was just docking. Passengers from the train were making their way to the ferry's gangplank, and he joined them.

Island Home was narrow and long – fifty yards or more from bow to stern, perhaps sixty, by his reckoning. As its giant wheel began to turn and they moved out into the harbour, he had a good view of the Nobska Light with its red tower and wondered idly what kind of person could tolerate the confined life of a lighthouse keeper.

To live, for William had always meant to move on. Did the same incessant motility, unresting and uncircumscribed, still drive him now? He knew it did not. He knew, watching with a trance-like detachment their vessel's churning wake, that something deep within himself had changed, languished. He had gone through the motions of continuing to be an opportunistic vagrant but his heart was no longer in it. He had no liking for himself. 'Salt without savour,' he murmured. 'Wherewith shall it be salted?' The best part of his life, the part that Frances had brought to him, was gone irretrievably. He used to think it clever to be leaving no trace; now it seemed grievous.

He stood leaning at the rail, his mind vacant, and spoke to no-one. Only as they approached the Nantucket wharf did he lift his eyes from the water to the land: to the old town rising in irregular terraces, its churches and banks, shingled dwellings, custom-house, standpipe, post office, the windmill high on the slope. He disembarked with the others but there was nothing he wanted to do or see. For an hour or more he sat on a bench in front of the brick wall of the Coffin School, gazing at the scar across his peeling palm. The warmth of the sun began to oppress him, and he found it hard to steady his breathing.

He walked slowly along the street to a general store and, for the first time in his life, bought a bottle of whiskey. He put it in the pocket of his frayed coat and returned to the bench beside the dreary wall where he sat in a reverie, subdued, almost asleep. A procession of remembered people shuffled across the screen behind his eyes like figures in a magic lantern show. His loving parents, the young brothers who had looked up to him, and others from the early days in La Chute and Owen Sound: the teachers who had faith in his gifts, James Meikle and Father John Cushin; his bluff guardian, Jerome Davin; and men who had been in truth what he had only pretended to be, the steadfast preachers Frank Hall and Jonathan Harrison, the Juneau physician David Henderson. He imagined that they all turned together and looked at him with deep disappointment. Then the reproachful phantoms became more numerous: a silent drifting crowd of women he had wronged and men he had swindled. And following behind he saw his wife and children, the juice of life sucked out of them.

When *Island Home* pulled away from Nantucket on the return journey to Woods Hole, William took up a silent station at the rail, staring at the triangular track of foam behind the boat and beginning to swig from the whiskey bottle. In his veins there was a flush of alcohol and self-disgust.

Waves knocked and sucked at the sides of the steamer. His cheek, he noticed, was wet with spray – or was it with tears? The borders of selfhood were seeming to blur. He continued to gulp long draughts that seared his throat.

He rolled up his sleeves. Holding the empty bottle by its neck, he struck it hard against the rail. In its jagged end he glimpsed himself as a boy, standing in the small snow-coated cemetery of Owen Sound. What he had done then he did again now, but more savagely. He slashed and sawed at his wrists until crimson ribbons spurted from them, twirling down into the current and instantly disappearing without a trace.

Eyes closed as he slumped forward and began to topple overboard, he was conscious only of his fading pulse, 'feebler and feebler' (his teacher's voice echoed distantly, faintly, from the small cold classroom long ago) '...till all was tranquil as a dreamless sleep.'

Afterword

A married couple bearing the same names as the two main characters in this novel did actually travel to the places described here at exactly the times indicated, and had similar experiences. Some of the other people, events and circumstances in *The End of Longing* also correspond closely to the historical record.

Little can be discovered about the real-life Frances Phillips and even less about the man she married. The main sources of information are a few letters and newspaper reports. While drawing on these to provide a narrative framework, I have done so selectively and have taken a number of liberties. It has not been my purpose to adhere to all the known facts or even to follow the probabilities. *The End of Longing* is a work of fiction; most of it is freely invented, including almost everything about William Hammond's life.

Nevertheless I gladly acknowledge a substantial debt to a series of people who faithfully preserved the fragmentary story of Frances, especially to her sister-in-law Mary Phillips, Mary's daughter Rhoda Glover, Rhoda's daughter Nola Bartlett, and Nola's daughter Lorraine Jacobs. These are all part of my own family; Frances was the sister of my great-grandfather Frederick. Among other family members who have also contributed to my interest in what happened or could have happened all those years ago, I want to mention gratefully Ethel Roiall, Melva Versteeg and Yvonne Laing. As so often, women have been the faithful custodians of memory lines.

A writer of historical fiction needs to ensure that the imaginary carries a sense of authenticity. In trying to create a credible tale about what people like Frances and William might have experienced in various places at particular times in the distant past, I have used a wide range of documentary sources. Citing them all would be impossible; but in addition to numerous pamphlets, maps, photographs, websites, diaries, essays, articles, poems, hymns and other miscellaneous materials far too various to itemise, I can list the following books, some of which have not only provided many factual details but also generated ideas and episodes.

For scholarly information about particular topics in the late Victorian period, I have drawn on the research work of Judith Flanders, *The Victorian House*; Jan Morris, *Pax Britannica*; Matthew Sweet, *Inventing the Victorians*; Dario Melossi and Massimo Pavarini, *The Prison and the Factory*; James F. Neil, *The New Zealand Family Herb Doctor* (thanks to Jack Glover); A. B. Maston, *Jubilee History of the Churches of Christ in Australia and New Zealand* (thanks to Nola Bartlett); Pamela Wood, *Dirt: Filth and Decay in a New World Arcadia*; and Anne Maxwell, *Colonial Photography and Exhibitions*.

For historical, geographical and cultural insights into specific places where parts of the story are set, I have found much of value in Graeme Davison, *The Rise and Fall of Marvellous Melbourne*; Andrew Brown-May, *Melbourne Street Life*; Tim Flannery (ed.) *The Birth of Melbourne*; Elizabeth Willis, *The Royal Exhibition Building, Melbourne: A Guide*; Ian Morrison (ed.), *A New City: Photographs of Melbourne's Land Boom*; Tamsin Spargo, *Wanted Man: The Forgotten Story of an American Outlaw*; Alexander W. Pisciotta, *Benevolent Repression: Social Control and the American Reformatory-Prison Movement*;

Vera Mackie, *Feminism in Modern Japan*; Edwin C. Guillet, *The Pioneer Farmer and Backwoodsman*; and G. R. Rigby, *A History of La Chute*.

Among writings from the late nineteenth century, the following have been especially helpful for my purposes: T. D. W. Talmage, *The Abominations of Modern Society*; Joseph Cook, *Vital Orthodoxy: Boston Monday lectures*; Jonathan Baxter Harrison, *On Certain Dangerous Tendencies in American Life*; Rudyard Kipling, *Letters of Travel*; Lafcadio Hearn, *Glimpses of an Unfamiliar Japan*; Winwood Reade, *The Martyrdom of Man*; Robert Louis Stevenson, *Vailima Letters* and *Father Damien: An Open Letter to the Reverend Dr. Hyde of Honolulu*.

I also want to record my appreciation of the efficient professional assistance provided by the custodians of several special collections in museums and libraries: Elizabeth Willis, Senior Curator at Museum Victoria (Melbourne), for details about events held at the Exhibition Building; Ali Clarke, Assistant Archivist, Hocken Library (Dunedin), for access to the manuscript diaries of Sarah Marsden Smith and Catherine Fulton; Jill Haley, Archivist, Otago Settlers Museum (Dunedin), for help in locating various register transcriptions and elusive items; and both John Krueger, Director of the Kent-Delord House Museum (Plattsburgh), and his predecessor Jeffrey Kelley, for access to letters and diaries of Frank Bloodgood Hall held in the Feinberg Library, SUNY Plattsburgh and transcribed by Jeffrey Kelley.

UWA Publishing has been a congenial partner, and I particularly acknowledge Terri-ann White for her admirable expertise and Linda Martin for her skilful use of a fine-tooth comb.

I am profoundly grateful to Brenda Walker for her faith in this enterprise and her timely practical assistance. For their generous blend of encouragement and advice, I also give warm personal thanks to these critical friends who read part or all of the novel in draft form and provided thoughtful comments: Brenton Doecke, Duncan Mackay, Vera Mackie, Anne Maxwell, and especially (for all her insight, tact, patience and unwavering support throughout the writing process) Gale MacLachlan.